With many thanks to Dr Richard Rush, for letting me pick his brains on all matters medical!

CHAPTER 1

Hillary Greene tuned the morning radio programme away from the annoyingly cheerful Fox FM DJ to the more middle-of-the-road delights of Radio 2, trying not to wince as she did so.

She wasn't that old, was she? Not much over forty.

Still, when cool DJs began to grate, it surely couldn't be a good sign.

She sighed and turned off the kettle. Pouring herself a cup of instant decaf, she wished she had an egg or two to pop into a pan. And a bit of bacon. Some sausages maybe.

But, luckily for her, the minuscule fridge, like the minuscule cupboard, was all but bare. Which was as good a way to try and shed a few pounds as any other, she supposed glumly. Was it a subconscious slip, or simple mismanagement?

It was too damned early in the morning to wonder.

With a yawn, she pulled out the simple wooden stool from under the fold-down table and rested her elbows on top. From outside the condensation-smeared windows, a cheerful whistle had her looking up, and a moment later a soft thud landed on the roof.

Had to be the postman.

Abandoning her coffee, she duck-walked up the three steps to the front of the boat and opened up.

It was perishing outside. Hoar frost coated every dead-looking hawthorn and sorry-for-itself willow. The roofs of the moored narrowboats were furred with it too, and her own breath feathered around her head as she blinked in the bitter cold. Her cheeks began to tingle, and her nose twitched ominously.

* * *

Hastily scrabbling one hand along the narrowboat's icy roof, she reached for the stack of mail, helpfully held together by a rubber band, and shot back into the warm.

She carried her prize to the table and inspected it warily. One mobile phone bill, a *Reader's Digest* informing her she'd been selected to become a millionaire, an offer for a personal loan (ha!), and an ominous-looking, white, typed envelope from a firm of solicitors.

And not her own firm of solicitors either.

She looked at the unfamiliar logo and felt her stomach churn.

Most people, on receiving a mysterious letter from a solicitor, might immediately think of maiden aunts popping their clogs and leaving a favourite niece a hand-some little legacy.

Hillary merely sat and regarded the envelope as if it might contain something nasty.

She'd once been the recipient of a letter bomb. Back in her uniform days, at the station in Headington. Still green, she'd haphazardly opened it, only to find herself covered in undetonated fertilizer. Luckily for her, whoever had made the device (and they'd never found out precisely who it was who'd had such a downer on Oxford's constabulary) hadn't exactly been an Einstein. Or even a Heath Robinson, come to that.

2

Now, although she didn't suspect this particular letter of containing anything in the way of semtex (or even anthrax), she nevertheless swore her way through the exorbitant mobile phone bill and binned the other letter before opening it.

She read it through once, a feeling of almost hysterical disbelief washing over her.

This had to be a joke, right?

She started again, reading more slowly this time, noting the legalese phrases, the authentic-looking letter-head, the usual arrogant scrawl of a signature at the bottom.

If this was a gag, someone had gone to an awful lot of trouble.

'Oh shit!' she snarled, realisation finally dawning.

This was no joke.

She snatched her cooling coffee and took a gulp, halting her snarling just long enough to prevent herself from choking, before roundly cursing her dead husband once more.

Over a year dead, and still the bastard haunted her.

She glanced at her watch and realised that her car, an already ancient Volkswagen, wouldn't be all that keen to start from a frozen battery. So if she didn't want to be late for work she'd better get cracking. She shoved the letter into her briefcase (but not away from her thoughts) and chugged down the last of the decaf.

Could a charity really sue someone? Well, technically, of course, Hillary — as a detective inspector in the Thames Valley Police Force — knew only too well, *anybody* could sue *anybody* for *anything*, provided they did it in civil court and didn't mind wasting their time, frying their nerves, and keeping solicitors and court staff rolling in clover ad infinitum.

But surely the news contained in her morning's letter was chancing your arm to the nth degree?

She walked through the very narrow corridor towards the *Mollern*'s front door, shrugged into her padded parka, and thought yet more dire thoughts about Ronnie Greene.

Her husband of eight years had died in a car crash before she could divorce him, but although he was long and most definitely gone, he was certainly not forgotten.

He'd made sure of that.

Certain members of another police force, for instance, had been *very* interested in him, investigating allegations of corruption that had, only last month, been officially published and acknowledged.

Ronnie Greene had been on the take in the most spectacular way. In fact, he'd been an active member of an animal-parts smuggling operation that must have netted him mucho dinero. Current whereabouts of the ill-gotten gains: (officially) unknown.

Although this same report had also totally cleared Hillary of any complicity, as she'd known it eventually must, it was obvious now that the whole mess just wasn't going to go quietly away. Hence this letter on behalf of the Endangered Species Animal Army.

It sounded a bit iffy to her. A bit eco-warriorish? She'd look them up on the computer when she got in (strictly a no-no, but who the hell cared?) and see what she could find on them. But even if they were on the up and up, it didn't mean to say that she considered they had the right to her house!

For, unless she'd suddenly lost the ability to read lawyer-speak correctly, that was exactly what the ESAA were planning to do.

Take her house away.

According to their solicitor's letter, they were already petitioning the court to freeze any future sale of Ronnie's house until an agreement had been reached or the subsequently threatened court case had been settled.

Their argument, as far as Hillary could make out, was simple. Ronnie Greene had made his money illegally out of animal suffering. So it was only right that all his assets should be sold and given to an endangered species charity in order to try and right the wrongs he'd done.

All very commendable, she supposed, except for the fact that the bastards were trying to do her out of her house!

Although Ronnie had all but forced her to move out of the smart semi on Kidlington's main road a few months before he'd died in the car crash, and had been energetically playing silly buggers with lawyers on his own account in order to try and chop her off at the knees in any divorce settlement, that house was still hers! Not that she'd ever wanted to move back in again. Too many memories. But she'd been paying the mortgage on it jointly up until she'd finally left the toe-rag. And it was now, after probate, legally hers. All along, her dream had been to sell it and start afresh. Surely these Endangered Species Animal Army people were just trying scare tactics?

No court in the land would uphold their claim, of that she was almost certain. *She* hadn't been found guilty of illegally importing tiger penises, or rhino horns. Let alone bear bile.

Still, they could take her to court in an attempt to win their claim. Which meant hiring solicitors of her own to fight it. Expensive. Very expensive. Not to mention time-consuming.

She couldn't see her superior, Superintendent Marcus Donleavy, for instance, being very sympathetic to one of his DIs having time off to fight a civil law suit. Especially when it meant that all the publicity and furore that had surrounded Ronnie Greene was likely to be raked up all over again.

'Shit,' she muttered quietly, slamming the door behind her and ramming the padlock home.

She leapt off the boat on to the towpath and set off. Still too angry to watch where she was going, she stepped on to a frozen puddle. Instantly, her foot shot out from under her and propelled her forwards. Her heart leapt into her mouth, and her startled squawk as she tried to keep her footing sounded out across the still air like a jackdaw with croup.

She dropped her case and instinctively shot out her hand, breaking her fall and preventing her from doing an actual nose-dive into the gravel. Nevertheless, she winced as her knee hit the towpath with a jarring thud.

Conscious of her dignity, she hastily looked around, but the small village of Thrupp was doing its usual ghost-town impersonation.

But from the front of her neighbour's boat, a sleek, dark head was emerging, and she quickly shot upright, grabbed her bag, and wiped off the grit and frost particles from her dark blue skirt.

'See you tonight, then,' a woman's cheerful voice boomed from inside *Willowsands*. 'And bring a bottle of something.'

Nancy Walker's latest conquest, wearing a smart dark jacket and what looked like a Corpus Christi college tie, promised he would and paused to lean against the boat, looking a bit shell-shocked.

Hillary grinned.

He still hadn't seen her, and when he turned and walked very carefully down the towpath towards the village proper, Hillary didn't think it was the treacherous going that made him walk so carefully. He looked, ever so slightly, as if he were in pain.

'Hello, Hill. Bleeding brass monkey weather, innit?' The voice belonged to Nancy Walker, her nearest neighbour. She and *Willowsands* had been marooned at Thrupp for at least five years. Her engine seemed to be constantly snafu. Or so she claimed. But everyone knew she found the pickings just outside Oxford too good to pass up.

She could have been aged anywhere between forty and sixty, and never failed to look impressive but also, in some strange way, maternal. Her make-up, for instance, was perfect — even at this time of the morning — but as she watched the young student stagger off she looked like nothing so much as a benign tabby.

'Hell, Nancy. The poor sod looks knackered,' Hillary said as the boy, slightly canting over to the right, reached the car park of The Boat and opened up the door of a Mini. He slumped inside like a ton of nutty slack.

'Theology student,' Nancy said simply.

'Oh,' Hillary said.

That explained it.

Nancy ducked back inside out of the cold, and Hillary herself hurried on, trying to pretend that her toes hadn't gone numb.

She'd been living on the *Mollern*, her favourite uncle's boat, ever since she'd walked out on Ronnie. Both he and she were beginning to think the arrangement might just be permanent! Nancy was one of the few who, like herself, didn't up anchor and chug away after only a brief stop. Still, the constantly changing drift of neighbours was something she tended to find more reassuring than unsettling. After all, if one day you found yourself moored next door to the neighbours from hell, the chances were they'd be gone by next week.

Her car was, as she'd guessed, most reluctant to start, merely coughing at her with a you-must-be-joking expression in its voice as she fruitlessly turned the key.

She cursed some more, wondering if she could persuade any solicitor she knew to take on the Animal Army for free. Yeah, right.

Or on a no-win, no-pay basis.

Yeah. Equally right.

Perhaps she knew one with an arm that could be twisted? After nearly twenty years on the force, surely some sod, somewhere, owed her one.

She'd have to think about it. Seriously.

Of course, she was fairly sure in her own mind that the Animal Army mob were simply after a settlement — a nice bit of perfectly legal blackmail. *No court case, love, just bung us fifty though.* No doubt they thought the still-serving police wife of a bent copper would be an easy touch. That she'd be too anxious to avoid more aggro to take a stand. Just a poor wilting flower, ground down by life's cruel jests, and a nice easy mark for someone to take a bite out of.

Hillary grinned savagely as the car finally turned over.

Boy, were they ever going to be in for a surprise.

* * *

It had taken her nearly ten minutes with an ice scraper to clear even a small patch on her windscreen, so when she pulled into the police headquarters in Kidlington, and felt her rear wheels begin to slide out from under her, she had only a limited view of the parked Ford Mondeo she was gracefully sliding towards.

She touched the brakes lightly, turned into the skid left, and with a carefully timed use of the handbrake, missed DCI 'Mellow' Mallow's pride and joy by about an inch.

She felt the sweat pop out on her head as she reversed and positioned the Volkswagen a bit more conventionally. As she got out, she heard a ragged cheer go up from an emerging group of uniforms, who began giving marks out of ten for 'artistic merit.'

Cheeky sods, Hillary thought, grinning back.

Back in *her* day on the beat, humble constables went in fear and trembling of plain clothes.

She flipped them the finger as she walked towards the main lobby, smiling at some of the more unprintable comments she got in return.

The desk sergeant gave her his usual laconic greeting as she trudged up the steps to her floor and punched in the code number that gave her access to the big, open-plan office where she had an open-sided cubicle.

Bunny Palace, as she secretly thought of it.

The place looked depressingly bare now that the Christmas decorations had been taken down and the

Christmas tree chucked out for the bin men. Through the open blinds, the Oxford skyline looked a smudged dingy brown, the sky above an uninspiring grey.

Post-Christmas gloom.

And a nasty letter from a solicitor.

All in all, a lovely start to a cold Monday morning.

And because she was still stubbornly off men with a capital 'OFF,' she didn't even have the memories of a shell-shocked theology student to warm the cockles of her too-long celibate heart.

Surely her cup runneth over.

'Hill, got something for you,' her immediate superior, Detective Inspector Philip 'Mel' Mallow called from his office. Well, he called it his office, but in reality it was a prefab cubicle made with plywood doors and plastic that passed for glass.

Still, at least it stood out from the savannah of desks and chairs that passed for the main office.

She saw him duck back inside without waiting for an answer, leaving the door open. He was already jacketless, his sleeves rolled up to his elbows and his tie undone. Yet still managing to look like one of those men in a Brooks Brothers catalogue.

Hillary only had to undo the top button of her white blouse and put one wrinkle in her jacket and she looked like a walking disaster area. Or a tart on the razzle.

As she headed for her lord and master's domain, she passed a small knot of plain clothes clustered around a desk. The atmosphere was definitely dark.

'Sam, something up?' she asked curiously, spotting a sergeant she knew in the scrum.

'The guard finally snuffed it.' Sam Waterstone, a big, hefty lad who looked at home on a rugby pitch but nowhere else, looked up as he heard his name, his face speaking of too much overtime and not enough sleep.

For a second, Hillary looked blank, and then she remembered.

A week or so ago, there'd been a raid by an animal lib group on a laboratory out Long Hanborough way. No end of beagles and assorted furry and feathery friends had been liberated, but a night-watchman had also been savagely hit over the head.

He'd been lingering in hospital ever since, with the medicos wavering about his chances of recovery.

Now, it seemed, they wavered no more.

'So it's murder,' she said, unnecessarily.

But that couldn't be what Mel was calling her in about. The case already had a DI assigned to it.

She sighed heavily and moved on. Even before she'd received the letter from the ESAA, her sympathies — as had those of nearly every cop at the station — had been firmly with the guard, if not with the laboratory he worked for.

Nobody actually liked the thought of animal experimentation, but in her book it didn't justify an attack on a sixty-seven-year-old man who was merely trying to eke out his pension so that he and his seventy-year-old wife could enjoy a bit of beef once a week. Or a night out at the bingo.

Now his wife would be getting a widow's pension.

She was still muttering something very unpolitically correct about animal lovers when she walked into Mel Mallow's den.

'Hill, there's a dead student out at St Anselm's. Probably just an overdose, maybe a suicide. Sort it out, will you?' Mel said shortly.

He didn't even look up from the report he was reading.

Well, well. Looked like she wasn't the only one who got out of bed on the wrong side this morning.

Then she wondered exactly *whose* bed Mel might have got out of, and scowled.

'Sir,' she said, just as shortly. And left, very quietly closing the door behind her.

CHAPTER 2

Hillary headed for her desk, noticing that DC Tommy Lynch was just coming through the door. Good, she could use him. The young black detective constable had been working on her team for nearly six months now, and she was fairly sure he was made of the right stuff.

Still a bit green, but learning fast.

'Boss,' said Detective Sergeant Janine Tyler, already at her desk. She was early. This was not all that unusual, for Janine was ambitious as well as blonde and beautiful, and worked as hard as Hillary could ever wish. And yet Hillary couldn't help but wonder if Janine's early appearance had anything to do with Mel's sour mood.

Usually Mellow Mallow was just that. Mellow. Or at least, he was careful to always appear so. Many a villain, not to mention an unsuspecting junior (or even senior) officer, had been taken aback to learn just what ferocious jaws Mel's smiling face could actually be hiding.

But all men had weaknesses. And in Mel's case, it was women — as two divorces and his current merry-go-round with Janine Tyler could testify.

Scuttlebutt at the station had it that Mel and Janine were definitely 'at it.' But in a very on-off, hole-in-the-corner way.

Nobody was quite sure why they were playing it that way. Did they hope the brass wouldn't get to hear of it? Could it be that they just genuinely didn't know what the hell they were playing at? Or was Janine being canny and/or crafty? Was she hoping to get a promotion? Or was it Mel who was insisting they play 'hands off' whenever anyone was looking? And since nobody at HQ seemed to know, it made life very uncomfortable for the rest of them. Especially for DI Hillary Greene, who had to tread the tightrope between keeping her boss sweet, while still making sure that Sergeant Tyler never forgot that Hillary Greene was a DI — and therefore a superior.

This morning's conundrum was just one more example of a situation that was giving her a right headache. Had Janine been kicked out of Mel's bed, thus her early start, or had she herself stormed off, foregoing a morning quickie, thus giving Mel the hump? Or not the hump, as the case may be.

One thing was for sure, Hillary was too damned sick of the whole situation to care.

'Janine, glad you're in. We've just got a call. Dead student at St Anselm's,' she said shortly. She kept on going to her own desk, and noticed Tommy Lynch looking across at her with all the earnest hope of a spaniel. With big brown eyes, full of pathos, he could no doubt melt marble.

'You too, Tommy,' she said flatly, totally unmelted. She was almost certain the dead student would turn out to be either a suicide or an accidental overdose — maybe even natural causes — but young detective constables needed all the experience dead bodies could give them.

She'd detoured to her desk only to pick up messages. There were the usual updates, mostly relating to her

12

current top-priority case, the closing down of a chop shop out Witney way.

Not that it wasn't all but tied up anyway. Colin Raide was a seriously good motor mechanic who was too greedy to settle for a seriously good living. So he'd recruited a proper gang of desperadoes from the poorer districts of Oxford to steal cars and deliver them to his premises. Not hard, since most of them had been joy-riders from the age of ten upwards, and enjoyed the challenge set by the security devices used on high-performance motors. Once at Raide's garage, he and his brother-in-law, another fair mechanic, had done the actual butchering of the stolen cars for parts, and shipped them off to the continent.

She only needed to nail down the transport end of the team, alert customs, and bingo. Kudos all around.

On the surface, it all sounded rather glamorous — like one of those Nicolas Cage movies where good-looking guys in Armani suits stole gleaming Porsches and enjoyed car chases with bumbling cops through the mean streets of San Francisco.

But in point of fact, Colin Raide had only been caught when his wife, furious at having found him in bed with her younger sister, had turned him in.

Not so much mean streets of America as fed-up avenues of suburbia.

Well, no copper was going to turn her nose up at such a nice little collar. Even if it was handed over on a silver platter.

Still, dead bodies took precedence.

She noticed a handwritten note, jammed at the bottom of the spike, probably left there over the weekend.

It was from the pensions officer, asking to see her tomorrow.

Now what the hell could *he* want?

Although money had been stretched lately (hence her living on her uncle's boat for the last year), she hadn't opted out of paying into her pension scheme.

She shrugged and stuffed the note into the pocket of her coat. The mood Mel was in, he'd be likely to stick his head out of his office any minute and ask her why the hell she was still hanging around here.

She was heading for the door, Janine and a very happy Tommy Lynch in tow, when they met Frank Ross coming in.

He was late.

But then, nobody minded when Detective Sergeant Ross was late. Nobody minded, in fact, if he never rolled in at all.

'Guv,' he growled, daring her to challenge him. Technically she could, but what the hell was the point? Frank Ross, a close crony of her late husband, had always hated her guts and the feeling was more or less mutual.

'Frank,' she said, and sighed. 'Just in time.'

She'd have to take him with her. If she left him behind in the office, she'd be in *everybody's* dog-house.

* * *

Tommy Lynch drove. It was usual for a junior officer to take the wheel, but Janine preferred to drive her own Mini. Frank, naturally, had elected to go with her. The look on the pretty sergeant's face was still making Hillary secretly smile.

Well, Janine might — or might not — be currently boffing the boss, but nobody was safe from Frank Ross. It was probably a universal law or something.

'Any info on the DB, guv?' Tommy asked. He was a big man, with ebony skin and the lanky but hard-packed firmness of a runner. Wasn't he the regional hundred metres champion or something? Hillary didn't know for sure. Sports weren't her thing, and she never attended station events.

'Nothing,' Hillary said shortly. Mel hadn't been exactly forthcoming.

She frowned as they got caught in traffic at the Kidlington roundabout. Rush hour was a sod in any city, but Oxford seemed to have a special penchant for it. You'd think, she mused, with all those environmentally-conscious students and dons whizzing around on bikes, it would be less so.

Probably some other universal law was at work here but it was too early for philosophy.

She sighed and settled back against the seat. Tide and traffic moved for no one, that was for sure. Not for King Canute, and certainly not for policemen on their way to corpses.

They could, she supposed, have had uniform whip them up to the Woodstock Road's bus lane, blue lights a-blazing, but Hillary didn't think the principal of St Anselm's College would appreciate the advertisement.

This was Oxford, after all. And Gown, not Town.

As an arts graduate of Radcliffe College herself, Hillary had no doubts as to why Mel had cast this particular cherry into *her* lap.

It was generally acknowledged back at HQ that Hillary Greene, as an OEC (Oxford-Educated Cop), was a good senior investigating officer in cases such as this. And since being regarded as a specialist was usually good in the promotion stakes, she never demurred.

As Tommy fought the traffic, she tried to recall all she could about St Anselm's College. Which wasn't much, truth be told.

To non-Oxfordians, the University of Oxford was something of a mystery. For a start, there was no 'university' as such, something that was forever puzzling American tourists.

The number of times she'd been stopped in the city by bewildered Bostonians and puzzled Pennsylvanians asking where the university was didn't bear thinking about.

The fact was, Oxford University was comprised of over forty separate and distinct colleges, such as Balliol,

Christ Church, Trinity, et al, and assorted departments, such as the Oriental Institute annexed to the Ashmolean Museum, or the Science Building on Banbury Road.

As if that weren't bad enough, you then had the non-affiliated colleges — such as her own, Brookes University, and colleges like St Anselm's.

Snobs sniffed at these lesser vassals of learning, and tried to pretend they didn't exist. But the fact was, they varied from the more respectable and academically-minded institutes, like Ruskin, to the more venal, take-the-money-and-run establishments, set up merely so that the rich parents of the thick and disinterested could pay exorbitant fees in order to be able to legitimately claim that their son or daughter had been Oxford-educated.

As far as she could recall, St Anselm's sat somewhere in the middle of this particular minefield. It was, she was almost certain, basically an establishment for foreign students. Languages were its speciality, if she was remembering rightly. But it was almost something of a finishing school as well, in that it offered elocution lessons, deportment, art, music, and anything else that a well-bred young lady, in the third millennium, might still be expected to practise.

And now that she thought about it, hadn't she read somewhere that the current principal had worked in the oil industry all his life, and been given the post at the college in order to cement 'business interests,' acting as a liaison between bright young students and industries desperate for the right sort of executive?

It all sounded par for the course to her.

Of course, a real Oxford college probably wouldn't even know it existed. Which no doubt left St Anselm's with a bit of an inferiority complex. And now this dead body and, horror of horrors, the involvement of the police. Not something rich parents in Singapore wanted to hear about.

Hillary sighed heavily.

She could see she was going to have to tread very nimbly indeed if she was not to squash some sensitive toes.

So as they crawled towards the city of dreaming spires, she prayed for a natural cause of death. Or, at a pinch, suicide. Then everyone could be very discreet and sensitive, and nobody would have to write nasty letters to Superintendent Marcus Donleavy complaining about flat-footed police inspectors. Which would please him no end.

* * *

From the moment she looked down at the dead body of Eva Gerainte, aged nineteen, from Lille, France, she just knew she could kiss any hopes of a simple case goodbye.

Although it was not exactly obvious why.

St Anselm's occupied several lushly grassed and wooded acres in the north of Oxford, sandwiched snugly between the main Woodstock and Banbury Roads. It had as a near neighbour the hallowed grounds of St Hilda's (the real McCoy!)

There was a sports field, ornamental pond, well-tended gardens and a main, mellow Cotswold-stone building.

It looked all very Evelyn Waugh.

They parked round the back, where a small, newer wing housed the offices and admin staff. There they'd been met by the college secretary, Mrs Mencott, a composed, middle-aged woman, who'd handed them a college prospectus — complete with a very helpful map of the campus inside the front cover — and who proceeded to give them a brief, obviously well-rehearsed speech.

Eva Gerainte was on a one-year course to improve her English, they were told, had arrived last Michaelmas term, and lived in the main house. (The house, no doubt, had once belonged to some well-to-do Oxford family, but had long since been turned into student dens.)

She was well liked, apparently, had gotten consistently good grades from her teachers, and had been discovered dead in her room by one of her friends at roughly 8.30 a.m.

As she spoke, the college secretary led them from the rear gravelled park area to the front of the impressive stone house. It had a wide paved patio in front, with genuine stone balustrades, and a wide, elegantly fan-shaped set of steps leading off to the croquet lawn.

It looked as if it should have been inhabited by imperious peacocks and humble gardeners in smocks, not the muffled-up bodies of students scurrying to and fro.

At the bottom of the lawn was a red-brick building — maybe once stables, but now used, Hillary guessed, as the main teaching block. Various other outbuildings, of differing architectural delights, housed discreet signs outside like 'Music Room,' 'Conservatory/Botany Lab' and, more simply, 'Studio.'

She suspected it would look even more spectacularly beautiful in summer, with roses in bloom, the currently bare twigs of wisteria covering the mellow stone flushed with pale lavender flowers, and probably visiting ducks waddling around by the ornamental pond.

Even covered in hoar frost and wreathed in the last tendrils of an overnight fog, it looked ghostly and perfect.

The college secretary showed them into a vast main hall and headed for a long wooden staircase. It was highly carved and almost too ornate. Whoever had finally taken over this place and turned it into a college had been careful to preserve all its glories.

Janine looked around with a wry twist to her lips. She was a strictly comprehensive girl. Tommy, who was also a stranger to such hallowed portals of academe, looked around, but with real pleasure on his face. The oil paintings were nineteenth-century second-raters, but they were at least the real thing. A dirty chandelier, which was probably never used, hung from the high ceiling and caught his eye.

He began to feel nervous.

This was a far cry from drunken domestics, knifings in the local pub, and RTAs.

He was glad, very glad, that Hillary was SIO. None of this would be making *her* palms sweat. He looked at her out of the corner of his eyes. She looked, as she always looked to Tommy's tender eye, perfect.

True, her blue skirt had a slightly damp and smudged patch over her right knee, but her dark brown hair gleamed in the light coming through the somewhat dirty windows, and her figure, a real hour-glass concoction, was the kind men dreamed of.

Or at least, that Tommy Lynch dreamed of.

Silently, they'd followed the college secretary to the third floor. Here the corridors were bare of paintings, but the walls were painted a cheerful and crisp white. The carpet underneath was no longer patterned oriental, but it was still thick-pile and had been cleaned recently.

The third floor, undoubtedly, had once been the domain of servants, but St Anselm's had done its best to make students feel at home. Even here.

Hillary wondered if the second floor, with its no doubt bigger rooms and higher ceilings, housed the richer, more important students, while the also-rans were relegated to the attic. Or was St Anselm's a bit more cosmopolitan than that?

The trouble with any Oxford college was it could be hard to tell. You had raving communists (still) living cheek-to-jowl with gleeful libertines, who in turn rubbed shoulders with scholars of truly awesome brain power, who were given the task of teaching socialists the delights of John Donne's metaphysical poetry.

It was, Hillary had always thought, something of a madhouse. The trick was to find out what particular kind of a madhouse you were dealing with, and go from there.

She suspected St Anselm's was simply a money-maker, no more or less. Which would mean that Eva

Gerainte, the dead girl, would have well-off parents, but wouldn't be in the mega-rich bracket.

Interesting, and perhaps relevant.

On turning a sharp right angle, Hillary instantly spotted the uniformed constable standing outside a door. He straightened up a bit as she approached.

The college secretary muttered a discreet farewell and left.

Hillary sighed. So it was going to be like that. Sooner or later she'd get an 'invitation to tea' with the principal. The battle lines had firmly been drawn. Which was fine by her.

'Constable, report,' Hillary said quietly. The constable, a twenty-one-year-old, gave the details of the call-out in a flat, professional monotone. It began with the initial phone call from the principal's secretary, their arrival on the scene, how they'd set up the proper procedures to guard the possible crime scene from contamination, and so on and so on.

When he was finished, Hillary nodded. So far nobody had called in SOCO. Well, that was to be expected. Nobody yet knew what they had, and the decision would be hers.

Doc Partridge, she'd been informed, was already inside. When she walked in, she found him leant over a bed, studying a young woman.

The room was small but pleasant. A large sash window looked out over some copper beeches and a view towards the city centre. The walls were washed a delicate shade of apricot, and a beige carpet lined the uneven floorboards. The bed was slightly larger than a single, and had a padded headboard. The wardrobe, dresser and desk were all of light-coloured pine. An expensive-looking computer rested on the desk. A bookshelf, crammed full with books mostly on fashion, fabric and clothes design, added cheerful colour. As did the posters, of catwalk models wearing outrageous outfits, which were scattered across the walls.

Hillary thought back to her own cramped, damp and shared room back in the old, old days, and wondered why the young always seemed to have it so good.

Then Doc Partridge moved away, giving her a view of the dead girl, and Hillary remembered that, for one youngster at least, things hadn't been so good after all.

Doc Partridge was one of those men who looked thirty even though he was in his fifties. He always dressed well. He kept his hair perfectly dyed. He was a very good pathologist.

'Well, take a look,' he said, moving off to give Hillary room. She moved across and looked down at the dead girl.

And that was when she knew she was in trouble.

Not as much trouble as Eva Gerainte was in, true. If the dead could be said to have any troubles at all, that is.

And yet, as Hillary stared down at the dead girl, she couldn't have said exactly why her spirits sank in such a way.

She wasn't a big girl — 5'5", perhaps, not more than nine stone. She was dressed in a black pencil skirt and a bulky, expensive-looking sweater. Were these the clothes she'd been wearing last night, or had she donned them this morning? Until she had the ME's report on time of death, there was no telling. The bed was unmade, but that meant nothing.

She had raven-black hair, cut in one of those geometric bell shapes that looked utterly chic and was probably hell-on-wheels to maintain. Light make-up. The eyes were closed, the chin sharp and pointed, like her cheekbones. Red lipstick made her mouth look shockingly red. She looked asleep. Even dead, she looked more alive than almost anybody Hillary could think of.

And this was surprising in a corpse.

But none of this unexpected élan was the cause of her unease. It was something far more subtle.

'Heart attack?' she asked hopefully.

'Don't think so,' Doc Partridge said promptly. 'Notice how very pale she is? And see these slight dappled bruises on her hands and the backs of her legs? All indications of internal bleeding. Course, till I get her back on the slab . . .'

He didn't finish. He didn't need to.

Behind her, Janine was already slipping on the rubber gloves. She had picked up on Hillary's mood. Frank Ross lounged in the doorway, a fat, cherubic-faced slob, trying to get a look at the dead girl's legs.

'Noticed this,' Doc Partridge said blandly, and reached for the sleeve of the long, cream cashmere sweater the girl was wearing.

He pulled it up.

And there, in the bend of her arm, was a small red dot, surrounded by a faint blue smudge. The girl's skin was pale, almost translucent. Which made the sight of the recent needle-mark almost grotesque.

'Oh shit,' Hillary said softly.

CHAPTER 3

Although she'd yet to meet St Anselm's principal, Hillary could already hear his upcoming howl of anguish. For, staring down at the dead girl's arm, she had a fair idea of how much that single needle-mark was going to haunt the college's reputation for years to come.

Students dying because of oral overdoses was one thing.

Shooting up was quite another.

Drugs that you swallowed, popped or smoked belonged in one category.

Drugs requiring needles were always, to the public mind at least, another category. Not so to the police. Hillary sighed. To her a dead girl was a dead girl, whether she died of a fatal reaction to a single Ecstasy tablet, taken on impulse on a girls' night out, or as the result of years of hardened heroin addiction.

But to an establishment such as this one, she had no doubts at all that she was now looking at a full-scale disaster. Not that she could allow it to affect her behaviour. Her loyalties always lay with the dead.

She was aware of Doc Partridge watching her, and shrugged wordlessly. Like all pathologists, his job was to tell her, if possible, how and when.

Not who. Or why.

'Well, we'd better get SOCO here,' she said, more to buy herself time to think than anything.

Something about the scene was striking her as odd. No, perhaps odd was too strong a word. Incongruous, maybe.

For a second she couldn't think what it was, although she was fairly sure that Doc Partridge had already got it nailed. But then, he'd been here longer.

And then it hit her.

A *single* needle-mark.

Not a long-time user then. Or even a diabetic. Although natural causes might be fast fading from the list of possibilities, they couldn't be totally discounted. Not yet.

She frowned thoughtfully, bending closer to stare at the tender white skin on the girl's underarm. Definitely no trace of older, faded marks.

If this had been her first time shooting up, her being a total novice might explain things. She'd either misjudged the dose or suffered a fatal allergic reaction.

But if so, where was the needle? Or the dope itself?

'OK, glove up. I want the place given a preliminary, very preliminary search. Remember SOCO won't want too much disturbance.'

But if the girl had something nasty stashed some-where it shouldn't be too hard to find.

As the others began a methodical search, Hillary stayed by Eva Gerainte's body, staring down at her thoughtfully.

'She's definitely not an addict,' she murmured, almost to herself. Of course, not all drug addicts were shambling wrecks, blundering around in a miasma of their own body odour, twitching and sweating and looking like a living menace. Men and women could, and did, live perfectly normal and seemingly average lives, and still maintain a drug habit. And this girl was still young and undoubtedly beautiful, and might have kept her looks for a good few years yet, even if seriously hooked.

So why was she already so convinced this scene stank to high heaven? It was hardly unheard of for students to die as a result of experimentation with narcotics, after all.

'I agree, for what it's worth.' Doc Partridge must have caught her near-whisper. 'Not that I would be able to give a definite opinion till I've had some bloods done, and examined her in more detail,' he added, as ever careful to cover his own back. Hillary nodded, catching his eye. 'But you get a feel,' she added softly.

Doc Partridge, who'd always found Hillary Greene one of the best coppers to work with, smiled briefly in agreement.

So, Hillary thought, the first thing she'd have to do was try and find out who the girl's supplier was, even though, in her own mind at least, she almost certainly wouldn't have one.

A waste of bloody time and man hours, but one she couldn't reasonably avoid. Mel for one would have her guts for garters if she didn't follow it up, simply because her 'feminine intuition' (which would be called a gut instinct, or copper's nose on a male colleague) told her it was a waste of time.

On the other hand, this was just the start of the investigation, and she didn't want to waste DC Tommy Lynch or Janine on a dead end. Which meant . . .

She grinned widely.

'Frank!' she called.

She watched DS Ross, who was searching gleefully through a drawer of what looked like very expensive silk French underwear, look up guiltily. His eyes, set deep in the folds of flesh that hung from more or less every part of him, went flat and hard.

'You're the man who knows the sewers best,' Hillary said, not at all sure that she wasn't, in some obscure way, actually complimenting him. 'Find out who her supplier was.'

Frank grunted. On the one hand, he was loath to leave his perusal of the underwear. The real thing wasn't something he got to handle often. On the other hand, the SIO was being forced to admit that, of all the people she had here, he was the only good, old-fashioned copper who would be able to do the job. He could have told them that there would always be times when a university degree and computer fancy-pants technology meant nothing.

And while he hated to actually take orders from Hillary Greene — Ronnie's old lady, for Pete's sake — he couldn't help but smirk in satisfaction.

He pulled off his gloves, gave the constable a triumphant grin, and swaggered off.

He could have saved himself the performance. Tommy, although the newest member of the team, knew enough to realise that Frank had no reason to preen.

Hillary was back to staring at the corpse. Janine, after calling in SOCO, hadn't interrupted her search.

Shrugging, Tommy returned to his own efforts. The girl had an awful lot of stuff — expensive French perfume, sheer silk stockings, shoes that looked, even to his inexperienced eyes, as if they might cost the earth. But no signs of a stash.

Hillary sighed softly, trying to get a feel for the victim. The girl's eyes were closed and she wondered sadly what colour they were. Dark brown, to match her nearly black hair? Or startling blue? Whatever, they would never be opening again, viewing the world with youthful optimism, or French *sang froid.*

What happened to you, sweetheart?

Had a friend persuaded her to try a hit? And then, when he or she had realised that the French girl was dead, taken the needle, dope and any evidence of their presence and legged it?

If so, someone, somewhere, was fighting back the panic right now. Wondering.

* * *

Janine paused in her perusal of the dead girl's wardrobe, trying to pretend she didn't envy the sheer volume and quality of the clothes on offer, and wondered what had set Hillary Greene's detector going. For the young sergeant was fairly sure now that something had.

Janine was only too aware that Hillary's reputation was good. Solid gold, in fact, in spite of her husband's fall from grace. She had one of the best arrest records going, and her conviction rate was even higher. Everyone knew that Superintendent Donleavy rated her, as a detective, if not as a player.

No doubt that was why she was still only a DI at forty plus.

So Janine (who had ambitions to be a superintendent at least) was wise enough to watch and learn. But try as she might, she could find nothing about the scene that struck her as out of the ordinary. Their victim was a student — young, footloose and fancy-free — and had either got hold of some dodgy stuff or had had a bad reaction. It happened more often than people liked to suppose. Bad, yes. But nothing to get riled up about.

And yet she would have bet a tenner that DI Greene was cooking on juice. She might not have the DI's years of experience or detective's nose, but she had a good brain. And knew how to use it.

The fact that Hillary Greene, who loathed Frank Ross as much as the rest of them did, had given him what looked like a plum assignment, for instance, augured *something* in the wind.

It was almost as if she had done it just to get Frank out of the way. (Not that they weren't all grateful to her for that!) But it was as if she expected Frank to fail. Or maybe she didn't think anything would come of it. And yet the girl had a track-mark in her arm. It was a drug-related death, as plain as the nose on your face.

But, as the doc and her DI murmured together, she felt the hackles rise pleasantly on the nape of her neck.

Perhaps this case wouldn't be so boringly predictable after all?

* * *

SOCO arrived, and they all trooped out. Even taking it for granted that the scientists needed space to work, nobody was in a hurry to get the black powder they used for fingerprints all over their clothes. That stuff had a habit of working its way into every nook and cranny — not to mention orifice — the human body could harbour.

It was a lesson DC Lynch had learned the hard way. As had they all.

Leaving the technicians to it, they began to walk slowly down the corridor.

'Anything?' Hillary asked unnecessarily. If they'd found anything, they'd have called her over. 'No suicide note?'

'Nothing guv,' Tommy said promptly.

'No, boss.' Janine, who hated to call anyone 'guv,' 'ma'am' or 'sir,' had found her own title for her immediate superior.

Hillary didn't seem to mind. To be fair — and Janine was always fair — the DI was all right to work for. She didn't play favourites, was willing to teach, was more or less even-tempered, and definitely together. It was just that Janine didn't like working with another woman. Not out of jealousy, but because of the way her male colleagues tended to regard them as a sort of female double act.

'So, if she didn't have a ready supply of drugs on hand . . .' Hillary mused out loud, prompting the others to join in with questioningly raised eyebrows.

Not surprisingly, it was Tommy Lynch who jumped in first. 'You reckon it belonged to someone else?' the DC said excitedly. 'A boyfriend?'

'Maybe,' Hillary said cautiously, trying to slow him down some. She could remember — just — the dim and distant days when she'd been eager, too.

'It looked like there was only the one track-mark on her arm, boss,' Janine said, wishing she'd been able to get a better look at the body herself.

'There was,' Hillary confirmed. 'What do you make of it?' She wasn't, and never had been, one of those officers who liked to hog all the goodies to themselves.

Janine nodded. She was beginning to see where her DI was going with this.

'First-time hit?'

Tommy Lynch shook his head. 'How unlucky can you get?' he asked softly.

And Hillary wondered.

What if it wasn't just bad luck?

The trouble was, until she had the full results of the autopsy, she couldn't be sure what she was dealing with here.

The needle-mark might not even be related to the cause of death. Yeah, a long shot. But stranger things had happened to her in her career at Thames Valley.

* * *

Hillary sent Tommy off to get a list of the girl's closest friends, and posted Janine outside the room, in case SOCO needed any direction or something turned up.

The order hadn't gone down well with the pretty blonde, Hillary noticed, and wondered, just a touch uneasily, if she'd complain to Mel about it later. That was the trouble with this whole Janine-and-Mel thing. It left stumbling blocks all over the place, and she knew it was only a matter of time before she took a pratfall over one of them.

Sighing, she made her way back to the college secretary's office, where, as she'd expected, the principal had arranged to see her, over coffee and biscuits, in his private study.

The principal's office-study was on the top floor with a view across the gardens. No surprise there. The walls were panelled in oak up to halfway, and heavy armchairs, in deep maroon-coloured leather, sat either side of what looked like an original Adam fireplace. Oil paintings of dignitaries lined the dark ochre walls. Full-length curtains in rich velvet and matching maroon fell to the floor on either side of big sash windows. A large leather-topped desk, with an antique silver ink set, sat squarely in the middle of the room.

It looked like the drawing room of a country squire, circa 1920, and was all very much as Hillary had expected.

The only incongruous note was a modern computer and laser printer that occupied one side of the desk.

The man rising from behind this twenty-first century interloper looked like a banker. He was dressed in a navy-blue, pin-striped suit, wore a tie of some minor public school, and had the silver brushed-back hair of a matinée idol.

'Ah, Wendy. This must be the police?' His secretary, a surprisingly young, jean-clad woman, had shown her in. She smiled now by way of acknowledgement, and left to get the coffee.

Hillary was almost willing to bet her month's salary that the coffee would come in its own pot, and that there would be some trendy accompaniment, like amoretti biscuits, to go with it.

'I'm Dr Havering.' The principal held out a well-manicured hand, and Hillary shook it. 'Detective Inspector Greene, sir,' she said formally.

She accepted one of the chairs — scaled-down versions of the armchairs over by the lit fire — that were placed at strategic angles to the desk, and glanced outside the window.

From up here she had a good view of the Oxford skyline — and could even pick out the unmistakable ridged dome of the Radcliffe Camera.

'Lovely view, isn't it?' Dr Havering remarked, sitting back down behind his desk. Only the way his fingers couldn't find a place to rest betrayed his inner nerves.

'Have you been principal here long?' she asked, interested in getting some background as well as a measure of the man. Something told her she'd be spending some time at St Anselm's before all this was over. And there was no point in alienating the big chief.

'Oh, just two years. My predecessor was a church man. The college board decided it wanted to get someone in with a more business-orientated view of the world.' His smile was just self-deprecating enough to be endearing. Hillary nodded and smiled back.

'So, what can you tell me about Eva Gerainte, Dr Havering?' she asked quietly, getting down to business.

'Ah yes. Eva,' he said sadly. It made her wonder if Dr Havering actually knew the French girl well enough to use her first name in that avuncular way, or whether it was just for show.

He pulled a slender, buff-coloured folder towards him and opened it up.

'I'd like a copy of her file, if you don't mind, sir,' Hillary said at once, before he could speak. 'Perhaps your secretary could take a photocopy and get it to one of my officers?'

'Eh? Oh, er yes . . . yes, of course,' he said brightly. But he clearly wasn't happy about it.

Hillary didn't attach much importance to his reluctance. Most businessmen, in her experience, had a healthy respect for knowledge, and didn't like sharing it, simply as a matter of principle.

'Er, let's see. Oh, Wendy, thanks,' he said. Hillary had heard the door open behind her, and waited now, patiently, as the secretary deposited the coffee tray on the table. The aroma of freshly ground coffee made her taste buds water. The lovely dark liquid was separated into two glass jugs. On the tray was a silver jug of real cream, a bowl of brown sugar, and a plate of ginger snaps, stuffed with something creamy and smelling faintly of liqueur.

Oh well. Close enough.

She let the good doctor pour, and accepted her cup with a smile. She tried not to look at the ginger snaps. Already her breasts and hips were too big. It was only a matter of time before her waist and thighs began to go the same way.

'Now, let's see. Eva. Ah yes — simple and straight-forward application form,' Dr Havering began, in a muttering-to-yourself sort of tone.

Was he really as laidback as he was trying to appear? Perhaps it was only a defence mechanism.

Whatever. She was beginning to get vibes off Dr Havering.

'Both parents living, her father the owner of a pharmacy, one brother. Good grades from a secondary modern school, yes. Nineteen years of age on entry. Ah, a scholar.'

Hillary's interest was piqued. 'An intellectual?' Funny how appearances could deceive. The dead girl had hardly been her image of a bluestocking.

'Oh no. I mean, she might well have been, but I was referring to the fact that she was one of . . . er . . . several here who came on a full scholarship.'

Ah. Hillary understood everything at once — including his hesitation.

St Anselm's almost certainly gave out embarrassingly few scholarships to poorer students — maybe even only one or two. Hence Havering's rather pained use of the world 'several.' And any scholarships they had handed out were very likely sheer window-dressing. No doubt it looked good in the college prospectus to point out these 'scholarships' to the deserving poor as a way of flaunting St Anselm's liberal credentials, and soothing the feathers of those well-heeled patrons who had consciences about such matters.

But in reality, they were bound to be a sinecure. Still, somebody had to be awarded them, and in this case, it was the dead girl.

Interesting. Very interesting. And maybe relevant?

And she was right after all about the lesser students being relegated to the attics.

So, their dead girl wasn't a *rich* dead girl.

The more that fact sank in, the more it struck Hillary as being significant. Although she couldn't have said exactly why. Drugs affected the rich and poor indiscriminately, and the drugs culture crossed all financial as well as social barriers.

'There've been no problems with Mademoiselle Gerainte?' Hillary asked next, and could see she'd surprised the principal with her proper use of the French sobriquet.

'Er, problems?'

'No complaints have been lodged against her? She hasn't been failing on assignments lately, or things of that nature? Coming in drunk at all hours, giving cause for concern?'

'Oh no. No, I'm sure not.' Dr Havering hastily scrambled through the few scraps of paper. 'There's no mention of anything like that.'

Hillary nodded. Well, she hadn't expected there to be anything. If the girl had problems, she'd probably be careful to keep them well away from the college's notice. Being here on a scholarship (on sufferance?) must have driven home to the French girl the vast differences between herself and those of her peers from far more high-flying backgrounds.

Reading between the lines of her application form, this was a girl from a strictly provincial background. No doubt her father's shop had been handed down, generation to generation, earning the immediate family a good enough living, but hardly affording them the lifestyle that most of St Anselm's students were used to.

She'd attended a state school and been encouraged by those good grades to try for a scholarship to Oxford, and good for her. But what kind of culture shock had awaited her here? Had she been lonely? No, surely not — not a girl as beautiful as that. And she had one good friend at least — the girl who'd found her.

So what had led her to that single needle-mark in her arm, and death at a mere nineteen years of age?

'Have you, er, established the cause of death yet, Inspector?' The principal's voice broke off her train of thought.

33

'No, sir, not yet,' she said firmly. She had no intention of explaining the circumstances now. There'd be time enough for that later.

'By the way, have you contacted her parents yet?' she asked.

'No. No, I thought it best if it came from you.'

Hillary nodded. She didn't blame him for not volunteering for the task. She herself was going to pass it on to the French authorities in Lille.

'I was hoping to interview her closest friends, perhaps some of her teachers,' Hillary said crisply. 'I take it they'll be made available?'

It was a rhetorical question and they both knew it.

'Oh, of course.'

Hillary nodded, then jumped as her mobile phone rang. She kept it in one of the voluminous pockets of her jacket. With a murmured apology, she reached for it.

'Janine, boss. SOCO have finished, and Doc Partridge wants to remove the body. But he wants a quick word first.'

'OK, I'll be right there.'

She folded the phone away, chugged back the coffee — it was too rare a treat to leave proper coffee undrunk — and gave the ginger snaps another reluctant miss.

'Perhaps I can have a word again a bit later in the day, sir,' she said, getting to her feet and again shaking the hand the principal thrust forward.

'Of course, any time. Just let my secretary know if you need anything.'

Hillary smiled and wondered how long that offer was going to stand. Probably until the first mention of the word 'drugs.'

Then it would be all hatches battened down.

* * *

Back in Eva Gerainte's room, Hillary paused as the police photographer took the last of his close-ups of the body, then joined the pathologist.

'She's all bagged up, ready to go,' he said unnecessarily, but reached down to pull up one of her sleeves again. For a second, Hillary couldn't think what he was doing. She hardly needed to see the track-mark again.

'I noticed these,' Partridge said, pulling up the arm of the baggy cashmere sweater even further. 'There are matching marks on her other arm. See them? They're rather faint, but unmistakable.'

Hillary did. Pale lilac-blue smudges. Four of them. She knew, without having to ask, that there'd be another, single mark on the back of the arm.

They were bruises caused by someone having held on to the tops of her arms. Tight.

She straightened up, her face grim.

What was the betting that, once he'd got her stripped and on his slab, he'd find other bruising, in the middle of her back, perhaps? Where someone had rested a knee?

The doctor gave her a helpless shrug. 'I'll try to get to her tomorrow,' he said, by way of sympathy. They both knew this case was getting darker by the minute.

Hillary nodded. 'Thanks, Doc,' she said softly.

Of course, someone might have had any number of reasons to catch Eva Gerainte by the upper arms. Perhaps she'd been about to fall, and some Good Samaritan had made a dive and caught her, bruising her where he grabbed. It had been slippery underfoot for the last week, what with all the frost and rain.

The marks might even have been caused by energetic dancing or love-making.

Then again, they could have been caused by someone holding her down and forcing a needle into her arm.

She was going to have to call Mel.

She could only hope that the DCI wouldn't take the case away from her now that it looked as if it might be murder.

35

CHAPTER 4

Hillary found Janine and Tommy conferring outside, and all three watched silently as the body was removed. One of them would have to be present at the autopsy. Hillary had done her fair share in the past, and could now at least rely upon her stomach not to let her down.

A good strong salve applied under the nose always helped with the smell.

Other things weren't so easy to combat and, she'd often thought, shouldn't even be attempted. The pity she always felt while watching a pathologist unemotionally set about exploring a human body devoid of life, for instance, wasn't something she wanted to go away. Once a copper lost compassion for the dead, they were useless on a murder inquiry. Or they were as far as she was concerned.

Then there was the fear. She often felt afraid when watching a person being sliced and dissected. And perhaps that, too, was necessary.

Death should always be frightening.

But Janine and Tommy hadn't attended nearly as many autopsies as she had, and since they were a necessary evil that every officer needed to tackle, she felt no guilt in delegating the task. It was all part of the learning curve.

'Tommy, you can attend the PM,' she said, seeing Janine breathe out a crafty sigh of relief.

'Yes, guv,' Tommy said glumly.

Briefly, she brought them up to date on Doc Partridge's discoveries.

'So you think she was held down, boss?' Janine asked calmly enough, but her eyes gleamed eagerly. Murder inquiries were always good career boosters.

'Maybe. We'll have to wait and see if the doc finds any more evidence,' Hillary said, far more cautiously. 'In the meantime, we stick to the good old tried and true. Janine, I need a schedule set up for interviewing all her friends, classmates and teachers. You might have to get some uniforms in to help with the also-rans. Tommy, check out her financial situation — according to the principal, she was here on a full grant, so you'll probably find she was more likely to be in debt than anything else. And there's nothing in her background to indicate money. Then—'

'Hang on, boss,' Janine said.

'That doesn't gel with—' Tommy began at exactly the same instant and broke off quickly. Interrupting a sergeant wasn't a very clever thing for a lowly DC to do.

Hillary looked from one to the other with interest. She turned to Janine. 'What?'

'Her clothes, boss,' Janine said, remembering that gorgeous wardrobe. 'It was packed with good stuff. Real suede, leather, satins, silks — you name it. Designer gear. The real thing, not knock-offs.'

'Same with her perfume, guv,' Tommy said, when Janine had finished. He was nearly engaged to his girlfriend Jean, and thus spoke with some confidence. 'I noticed it was all good stuff — Miss Dior, YSL, even some Chanel No. 5. It didn't look like knock-off market-counterfeit neither.'

He didn't admit he'd even sniffed one pretty decanter made to look like a pink seashell. Purely for the purpose of trying to figure out whether or not Jean would like a bottle for Valentine's Day, of course.

Hillary nodded thoughtfully.

'So she had money somewhere, boss,' Janine said.

Hillary shrugged. 'Or had a very generous boyfriend. Or more than one.' It was not uncommon for pretty girls to be well maintained.

Of course, when you came across signs of unexpected wealth in a victim, one word always leapt straight to mind.

Blackmail.

But who was a French student, only in the country one year, likely to be blackmailing? Someone at the college, maybe? It was the environment she knew best, after all. And there were plenty of rich students — not to mention faculty members — who might make targets. Of course, this might have been a long-term thing, and not even started in Oxford at all. After calling the French police in Lille to break the news to the girl's family, she'd have to ask them to look around for any signs that Eva might have had her hooks into someone over there.

Perhaps her killer had followed her over from the continent? If so, they were in a whole world of hurt. Since the advent of the EU, tracking movements from country to country was a nightmare.

'Right, Tommy, make that financial check number one priority. She must have a bank account, but don't stop there.' The dead girl was beginning to take on a distinct personality, and a certain acumen with money wouldn't be surprising. 'See if she's got a portfolio — stocks, shares, that kind of thing. Or even a hidden stash of cash. I want her room gone over with a fine toothcomb. And don't forget to check her personal computer.'

'Guv,' Tommy said, then hesitated, wondering which she wanted done first. He was desperate to do well, and promotion wasn't at the forefront of his mind. Of course, he knew it was mad to even hope that Hillary Greene might look at him and see the man, not the constable. But maybe one day . . .

He decided on tackling the room first. After all, the computer would always be there — as would bank managers.

'Janine, round up the girl who found the body. And find out from her if Eva had another close friend, or a group she hung around with,' Hillary carried on, blissfully unaware of the flutterings she was causing in Tommy's tender heart.

'Right, boss. I think the girl's in her room with the college matron.' Hillary nodded glumly, hoping the nurse hadn't already doped her up to the eyeballs on sedatives.

* * *

They didn't have far to go to find out. In fact, the girl who'd found the body was literally next door.

Which made sense, Hillary mused, when you thought about it. Who else would a girl, who presumably knew no one in England, become friendly with, but her immediate neighbour? They'd probably moved in on the same day, just before term started, and gotten to know each other right away. After that, of course, the dead girl would have gradually extended her range of friends, from the people she shared certain classes with to those she shared interests with. And Eva Gerainte was bound to have joined some club or other. (Unless colleges had changed drastically since her day, St Anselm's would almost certainly have clubs that catered for everyone from philatelists to shoe-fetishists.)

The girl's name was Jenny Smith-Jones. An unlikely-sounding name, Janine thought, on reading the name tag slotted into the metal envelope on the front of the door. If you had two such boring names as Smith and Jones, why the hell use both?

The room was a carbon copy of next door's, with just a slightly different colour scheme. The posters here were all to do with theatres and films, not fashion. Presumably drama was Jenny's main choice of study.

She was young, and looked incredibly pale, but she was, thankfully, fully compos mentis. She was dressed in jeans and a chunky, hand-knitted sweater that dwarfed her stick-like frame. Long blonde hair, looking limp and washed-out, hung to stooped shoulders. Big grey eyes watched their approach thoughtfully.

What a contrast they must have been, Hillary immediately thought. The petite chic French girl, with her daring make-up and fashion élan, and this tall, awkward English stripling.

She wondered, vaguely, if Jenny Smith-Jones was a good actress. Sometimes it was the plain-looking ones who could dazzle.

Sitting beside the girl was a middle-aged woman who couldn't have looked more like the epitome of a school matron if she'd been picked out of a Hollywood studio's central casting office. She was rounded without being obese, and had well-padded rosy cheeks and kindly twinkling brown eyes.

Hillary couldn't help but wonder if this paragon of common sense and comfortable-looking competence had been hired as the result of her nursing qualifications or simply because she looked as she did.

What anxious mama or papa wouldn't be reassured to leave their darling girl or boy here, knowing someone like Matron was there to monitor their every sniff or cough?

'You must be the police,' the woman said, casting a swift glance at the young girl. 'Do you have to interview Jenny now?'

'I don't mind, really,' Jenny Smith-Jones said at once, if a little shakily.

Hillary smiled at her gratefully. 'It won't take long, Miss Smith-Jones, and I won't ask you anything about this morning. I understand you've already given one of the constables a full report.'

She noticed Janine look at her in surprise, and could understand why. Any SIO would rather get witness statements first-hand. But Hillary wasn't too concerned about the nuts and bolts. Sometimes murder inquiries turned on forensic evidence, and the minutiae of evidence, but she didn't think this was going to be one of those cases.

So why antagonise the good matron and upset her witnesses when she could win brownie points by going down the softly-softly route? Already she could see that the matron was looking a lot less tense.

And she simply couldn't go on thinking of her as Matron. It was making her feel like a 'Carry On' character.

'Perhaps, Mrs . . . ?' She turned to the older woman, who smiled politely.

'Beamish. Miss Beamish.'

'Perhaps Miss Beamish wouldn't mind waiting outside for a few minutes?'

Janine watched the older woman struggle with that, and had to admire her boss's technique. Hillary hadn't sounded impolite. She hadn't even sounded unduly pointed. And yet she'd managed to convey that it would be very gauche of Miss Beamish to object. This was police business, after all, and well-brought-up women knew when to beat a discreet and tactical retreat.

Hillary Greene held the older woman's eye for just a second longer. 'Sergeant Tyler will see you out. We won't be long, and then you can get back to your patient.'

And somehow the matron, who was used to having her orders followed punctiliously, found herself on her feet and thence out into the corridor.

When Janine closed the door firmly behind her, she found Jenny Smith-Jones staring at Hillary with distinct admiration.

'That was neatly done,' Jenny said, as Hillary took a seat. 'I've been wishing she'd go for ages, but couldn't think of a way of making her.'

Hillary nodded. 'You wanted to be alone. Yes, it gets you like that sometimes. When something totally unexpected happens, something that's never happened to you before, it knocks you off your orbit. Then you feel lost.'

Jenny blinked. She hadn't expected the police to be like this. She'd expected a man, to be honest. And moreover, one who'd be all spit and polish, demanding times, dates and numbers.

She began to relax.

'So, what can you tell me about Eva?' Hillary said, keeping her opening question deliberately vague.

Jenny wiped her cheek with one hand, and sniffed loudly. 'What do you mean?'

'Did you like her?'

'Yes. Of course.'

'Why?'

Jenny shifted uncomfortably on her chair. 'What do you mean?' she heard herself repeating, and blushed. This woman — what had she called herself? DI Greene? — must think she was a moron. She looked so together herself. Cool and competent, just like her mother. She wanted to please her, but she was feeling wrong-footed and dim.

'Why did you like Eva? Was she kind to you? Was she generous? Did she loan you stuff? Did she make you laugh?'

'Oh. Oh, I see. No. Well, none of that. I mean, she wasn't particularly kind,' Jenny said. 'Sometimes she could be quite sharp — but in a French kind of way. You know, sardonic. Witty. Not that she was ever deliberately unkind, but I think she found people amusing. As if they were entertainment. But she'd loan me stuff, if I asked for it.'

Hillary nodded. 'Did she speak good English?'

'Oh yes. Well, better than I could speak French,' Jenny added, with assiduous fairness. 'And sometimes I thought she emphasized her French accent, especially around boys, you know. She could act all little-girl-helpless, orphan Annie abroad, that kind of thing. But that was just something she put on. She liked fooling boys. She was good at it,' Jenny added matter-of-factly.

Hillary wasn't sure whether it was something the other girl admired or not. Perhaps Jenny herself wasn't quite sure.

'So she was an extrovert?' Hillary said.

'Oh yes, totally. But then, that was Eva. She was really creative, you know — she was going to be a fashion designer. She had all these plans to be as famous as Armani, or Gucci, or one of those. She was good, too. She was always doing these fabulous drawings of gowns and lounging pyjamas, shirts, skirts, even scarves. You name it. And of course, she could wear anything herself and look gorgeous. She used to design stuff just for me. Tell me that if I got them made up, I'd knock spots off all the girls around here.' Jenny sighed. 'I think, you know, that I'll do that now. Get Mummy's dressmaker to run them off. Oh — you don't want her drawings back, do you?'

Hillary assured her they wouldn't. Though she might take a quick look at them at some point.

Janine's lips twitched. *Mummy's dressmaker?* Hell, these girls really did live a different life.

'And you have no doubt that they'll suit you,' Hillary said, but it wasn't a question. She herself had no doubts.

'Oh no,' Jenny said. 'You could always trust Eva about things like *that*.'

Yes. But what *couldn't* you trust Eva with, Hillary wondered. Well, not with your boyfriend, certainly. And probably not with your money. And yet Hillary could see why this painfully thin, not particularly attractive girl would have been drawn to someone like Eva Gerainte.

'Did she party a lot?' Hillary moved on.

'Oh yes. All the time. And she never seemed to get tired.' Jenny sounded a little wistful now. 'Unlike me. I always need to sleep till tea-time after being up all night. But Eva would be up first thing, all full of beans.'

'Ah, she did drugs,' Hillary said, super-casually. 'Uppers, by the sound of it,' she added, careful not to sound even remotely condemning or surprised.

43

'Oh no!' Jenny said at once, making Hillary pause and look at her sharply. That hadn't sounded in the least bit defensive. There was nothing of a best friend guarding the reputation of her dead pal about it. In fact, Jenny Smith-Jones had sounded almost contemptuous.

'Eva would never take drugs,' Jenny said hotly. 'She despised them — and the people who got hooked on the things. She said they were all weak, stupid people. They lined the pockets of drug dealers, and ruined their own bodies and looks.'

Jenny paused for breath. Then frowned thoughtfully. 'You know, Eva never even got drunk, not for all the parties she went to. And she didn't smoke. She always said to me the thing to do was to order the best drink on offer — it didn't matter what it was. The best or oldest brandy, the best-label wine, or the fanciest cocktail, and then drink it very slowly and savour every mouthful. But not to drink more than two, and never to get drunk. It dehydrated you, Eva said, which was bad for the skin. And it made you lose control. She was always in control,' Jenny explained. 'You just don't understand,' she finished lamely.

But there she was wrong.

'I think I do, Jenny,' Hillary said quietly. 'Your friend was very strong, wasn't she? She knew exactly what she wanted, and meant to get it. She had a goal, she was clever, and she had the guts to go for it.'

Jenny sniffed again at the thought of all that energy gone for ever, but her big grey eyes were once more regarding Hillary with surprise.

'Yes, that's right. You've described her well.'

Hillary nodded. She glanced at Janine, wondering what she was making of all this, but she was busy scribbling in her notebook, as all good sergeants did.

Hillary nodded. So, Eva scorned the use of drugs and drug users. And she was fairly sure that wasn't just a crock, either. She'd met people of Eva's ilk before. Ambitious. Unscrupulous, even. Hard-headed and maybe hard-hearted. Not the type you might particularly admire, but the last sort of person to let herself get caught up in the drugs trap. Those types were too self-aware, and cared too much about their own skins, to flirt with something so dangerous.

No, Hillary was getting to grips with Eva Gerainte now. And she agreed with Jenny Smith-Jones.

'What else did Eva like doing?' she asked curiously. 'Did she join any clubs, for instance?'

'She joined my drama group,' Jenny said at once. 'But only the wardrobe department. She didn't want to act. And she used to go to the music room a lot. But I don't think she actually played an instrument. If she did, she never played it next door. I'd have heard her practising. And she sometimes hung out in the computer room but I think she liked to play games and mess about with graphics — you know, for her designs — rather than because she was a computer nerd or anything.' Jenny shrugged helplessly. 'I can't think of anything else.' She looked, in that moment, impossibly young.

Was I *ever* that young? Hillary thought helplessly.

'What about her boyfriend?' she asked bluntly.

Jenny looked startled for a moment. 'I don't think she had one. I mean—' She blushed as both Janine and Hillary looked obviously surprised '—she had lots of men and boys hanging around her. You know, they'd always be hovering around her in the JCR, and that—'

'JCR?' It was Janine who spoke.

'Junior Common Room.' It was Hillary who answered. 'It's like a student bar-lounge area,' she added a little impatiently. She wanted to get back to this boyfriend issue. Surely someone like Eva must have had a sex life?

'But you're saying that she wasn't going out with anyone in particular?' she asked again.

'No. No, I don't think so. She never talked about anyone special.'

Jenny began to frown again, as if it was starting to strike her as odd, too.

'You know Eva was here on a scholarship,' Hillary probed, trying another tack.

'Oh yes. Her father owned a huge pharmacy company,' Jenny said blithely, 'but Eva wanted to be independent. So she applied for a scholarship. And, of course, she was so clever that she got it.'

Hillary nodded. So Eva had exaggerated about her background. Well, no surprises there, surely. Who wouldn't, in a place like this? Even Jenny, shy, approachable and friendly Jenny, probably went home during the vacations to a mansion in the country, or a Kensington flat. How could Eva tell someone who obviously hero-worshipped her that her father owned a lowly chemist shop in Lille? Jenny must have seen Eva as the original woman-of-the-world, the gay Parisienne. And Eva would have revelled in that image.

Which was why this lack of any noticeable lover was troubling her so much. Either Eva Gerainte was a closet virgin, or she had a man she wanted to keep secret. The first was so unlikely it wasn't even worth seriously considering. Which left her with a murder victim who had a secret lover.

Why keep him a secret? From what she'd heard, Eva would have been only too ready to parade her sexual conquests for Jenny's delight and admiration — so this apparent reticence worried her.

Again, the thought of blackmail raised its ugly head.

They talked some more, but nothing else useful came up. At last Hillary thanked her and left.

* * *

In the room next door, Tommy was on his hands and knees inspecting the wooden floor. If the dead girl had made herself a nice little niche under the floorboards, he'd find it.

'How's it going, Tommy?' Hillary asked, and he leaned back on his heels and wiped his forehead with the back of his hand. The room's radiator was pouring out heat, and he hoped he wasn't getting BO.

'No luck on any money yet, guv,' he said, 'but I did find two interesting things.'

He got up and dusted off his hands. 'I found this sellotaped up behind that picture,' he said, nodding to the only formal piece of artwork — an uninspiring print of a country landscape that no doubt came with the furnishings of the room. It had a heavy ornate frame and was glass-fronted.

Hillary looked at the slim diary, now bagged up, that Tommy indicated on the dresser top. 'I was careful not to handle it too much, guv, but it fell open when I took off the sellotape, and I noticed it was all in French.'

Hillary nodded. 'We'll have to get it translated after SOCO have had a look at it.'

Not that she expected it to hold any forensic clues — although it might be interesting if they found a strange set of prints on it. It would prove someone other than Eva Gerainte had taken an interest in her private thoughts and jottings.

'Shouldn't be hard, boss,' Janine said wryly, and Hillary grinned back.

'No,' she agreed shortly. They were in Oxford, after all. If the dead girl had written her diary in ancient Egyptian hieroglyphics interspersed with a now-dead language and the odd sentence or two in an obscure Hebrew dialect, they'd find half a dozen or so scholars who could tackle it. Simple modern-day French shouldn't pose any problems.

'There's a modern languages teacher here,' Tommy said brightly. 'I was talking to him earlier. He could do it.'

'No,' Hillary said sharply. 'I don't want anyone from this college even knowing we've found a diary,' she said flatly.

Tommy's face fell. He could have kicked himself. Of course not. Why the hell had he said something so daft?

Janine grinned at his gaffe, but without malice. She herself had made her fair share of howlers.

'You said there were two things.' Hillary, aware of the young DC's mortification, briskly changed the subject before his self-confidence could take too much of a hammering.

'Yes, guv. Her keys. There are two that don't fit. I mean, don't fit the front door of the hall, or this room. I thought it odd. If you look—' He reached for a bagged set of keys '—all four look like room keys. Not like a locker key, or the key to a suitcase or padlock or something.'

Hillary nodded. 'You're right. Well done, Tommy.' And she wasn't merely being tactful.

As she stared down at the keys, she felt a small tingle shoot up her arm. This could indeed be significant.

Because why would a girl who lived in college with all her living expenses pre-paid have a strange set of house keys? Answer: she wouldn't. Unless these keys belonged to the mysterious, non-existent boyfriend?

If so, things must have been pretty serious between them.

And, what's more, it put other boys at the college out of the running. Which didn't surprise her. Eva wasn't the sort to go for callow youths, mere students like herself, when she could hunt for bigger game. Older men, richer men, well-established men who could give her career a boost — those would have been her targets.

Yes, Hillary would be very interested indeed in finding the door that matched these particular keys.

'Boss,' Janine said, a sharp note of triumph in her voice. 'The waste-paper basket. There's an envelope here addressed to the victim.'

Hillary took the envelope by the edges and glanced down. And immediately saw what it was that had made Janine's day.

For although the letter was addressed to Ms Eva Gerainte, the street address was not that of St Anselm's, but of a flat somewhere in Botley.

CHAPTER 5

Oxford is a beautiful city — but only in places. Mention London to a foreigner, and they think of the Tower of London, London Bridge, Buckingham Palace. They don't think of Tower Hamlets or Fulham football ground, or the dirty end of the docks.

Hillary supposed the same could be said of any city. Paris, for instance. Why, what else was Paris except the Eiffel Tower, the Champs-Élysées and Notre Dame?

But Oxford seemed to suffer from this syndrome more than most cities. Yes, as well as all those famous dreaming spires it had ancient colleges in abundance, endless acres of quads composed of mellow Cotswold stone and centuries-old lawns like velvet, and yes, too, the Isis (note the romantic name for the common-or-garden River Thames) overflowing with weeping willows and punting students and marauding swans.

But it also had its unlovely commercial centre and bland suburbs, just like any other city. And Botley fell firmly into the 'any other' category. It was clean enough, pleasant enough, but if you were blindfolded, set down on its streets and asked to guess where you were, you wouldn't say Oxford.

Janine, who was driving, idled almost to a standstill to consult the street map while simultaneously giving the finger to someone honking their horn angrily behind them. She then confidently turned off into a narrow cul-de-sac and parked. Illegally.

Hillary got out and looked up at the unimpressive ring of houses. Built between the wars, she would have guessed. Once solid middle-class residences, now almost all of them chopped and diced into bedsits for Oxford's needy students.

Not the sort of place where she imagined the rich and probably married lover of Eva Gerainte would choose to live. Already she could feel one theory going down the drain.

She frowned as they picked out the house number they were looking for. Once at the doorstep, sure enough, as expected, there were the usual four doorbells and little rectangles lettered with different names.

Ms E. Gerainte had Flat 4. Hillary gazed at the name, frowning, wondering why she had expected an alias. Janine pressed all the bells for the others. A faint buzz sounded and the door clicked open.

'Great security,' Janine muttered, disgusted, as always, by the great British public's inability to look after itself.

Hillary wasn't listening. She was wondering why a student on a full scholarship, who had room and board readily provided for her, should also have a small flat in bedsit-land. It didn't make much sense. Why waste money paying rent when she already had a (probably) much better room and a (definitely) better view back at St Anselm's?

Inside, the tiny hallway was a bright green concoction with lime-coloured linoleum and apple-green walls. Even the threadbare carpet on the stairs looked as though it had once been more or less green. Now it was a sludgy mint colour, courtesy of constantly tramping feet.

Upstairs, the landing had two doors leading off it — one belonging to a Mark McCormick, the other devoid of any name tag at all. Janine took the keys from the evidence bag and glanced questioningly at Hillary before inserting the Yale into the lock of the unmarked door.

It turned as smoothly as silk.

Slowly Janine pushed open the door and walked inside, Hillary right behind her.

There, they stopped dead and gawked.

Over in one corner was a small sink and an even smaller stove in white enamel. Both were pristine clean. A large black-wood dresser stood against one wall, and a matching dressing table occupied the other.

But it was the huge four-poster bed taking up almost the entire middle space that caught the eye. That and the decor.

The room was a stunning display of pale lilac, sky blue and cream. It looked as if a team of interior designers had just been and gone. The four-poster bed had swathes of sky-blue curtains, while the linen was pale lilac. The cream carpet looked as if it had just been cleaned. Bouquets of cream roses in cut-crystal vases adorned the dresser and a small, bow-legged coffee table.

This was clearly not how the room had been rented out. There were no bookcases, no desk, nothing that a hard-working student would need. No tins of beans or jars of coffee lined the small work surface by the sink. The whole room had the air of a mirage: it was as unlikely as finding a diamond in a slice of pork pie.

There was even the scent of lavender in the air, and Hillary noticed one of those plug-in room fresheners steadily pumping out fragrance near the light switch.

It screamed style. Elegance. It screamed, of course, Eva Gerainte.

Without a word, Hillary walked to the wardrobe — and found it awash with baby doll nighties, peignoirs, Grecian-style nightdresses of silk so pure they were transparent. They rubbed shoulders, incongruously, with leather-and-chain bikers' outfits, tight-fitting jumpsuits, and uniforms. Lots of uniforms. Schoolgirl uniform, nurse's uniform, sub fusc, and what looked like an authentic WPC's kit.

Janine went to the dresser and, after donning gloves, began calling out the contents of the drawers.

'Handcuffs, ointment, surgical jelly, dildos, more condoms than a vending machine in the local gents . . . You name it, it's here,' she said cheerfully.

Hillary nodded, still gazing at the contents of the wardrobe.

'Well, that solves the mystery of where she got her money,' she said flatly.

She was hooking.

But she was no street walker. If she knew Eva — and Hillary felt like she was beginning to — this was a strictly private enterprise. There'd certainly be no pimp. She simply could not picture Eva Gerainte knuckling under to anybody, taking crap or watching her hard-won earnings go to some bully-boy with a fist. Perhaps she had pissed off the local pimp? No, surely if that was so, he'd have roughed her up first, tried to make her see the error of her free-enterprise ways.

Besides, this was hardly your average hooking set-up. Here the clientele would be strictly select. And nobody who liked the rough stuff (nothing and nobody would be allowed to mar that perfect body of hers), even for a price. And precautions would be taken — hence the condoms. No AIDS-defying unprotected sex took place on Eva's watch.

Even so, all of them would pay for the privilege of her attentions. And pay well.

She sighed and closed the door. 'Better get SOCO over here too, Janine,' she said.

Before, she'd been chancing her arm a bit, calling in SOCO and using up hard-pressed resources on what might still turn out to be a natural death, suicide or death by misadventure.

But this changed things.

Prostitutes were more likely to be murdered than any other class of people in society. Those and derelicts. It was a fact of life. And of death.

Yes, with this new discovery, everything had changed. She sighed, reached for the phone and dialled home.

Detective Chief Inspector Mel Mallow listened without interrupting as she gave a full litany of her morning's activities. It was now getting on for late afternoon, and already the daylight was fading.

Hillary hated winter, not because of the cold, but because of the quality of the dull, grey, energy-denying light.

'So, no doubts she was on the game, then?' Mel said, when she'd finished.

'High end of the market,' Hillary reiterated. 'But no, sir. She had to be on the game all right.' Some women, she supposed, kept sex toys to spice up their love lives. Some men liked it. But this was way over the top for a gal and a single lad out to have a bit of fun. This was all business.

'Sir, I think we should call in Vice,' Hillary said at last, managing to sound reluctant. Even so, Janine gave her a long, slow look, but there was nothing overt to be read in her eyes.

No cop liked calling in another division, but there were times when protocol had to be followed. And this was surely one of those times.

'Regis?' Mel said, making Hillary jump. For a second, she wondered if her boss had been able to read her mind. Or was it just her guilty conscience at work?

On her last murder case, DI Mike Regis had been called in, once they'd proven the obvious drugs connection, and the dour, confident DI had left an indelible impression on her mind. It was not that he was handsome — because he wasn't — but it had become apparent that they thought the same way, were of the same generation, and the same kind of mind-set.

He had made her toenails curl.

They'd had nothing more than a friendly drink together after the end of the case, but Hillary had found Mike Regis lingering on in her mind for a long time. Now, here she was, suggesting Vice be called in, trying to pretend that Mike Regis had nothing to do with her sudden spirit of inter-police agency co-operation.

'Sir,' she said non-committally. No way was she going to put her oar in on this one. It had to be seen to be Mel's call.

'I'll have a word,' Mel said ambiguously, and Hillary let her breath out in a long, careful exhale.

'Sir,' she said again, and waited to see if any axe would fall.

But she didn't seriously think he was going to take her off the case now. For a start, he had no tangible reason for doing so. She was no longer under investigation by her own kind, and she was still the best person for the job. And they both knew it.

'Right, keep me posted,' Mel said, sounding terse and grumpy. Whatever crisis he and the pretty blonde sergeant were going through was still bubbling along nicely, it seemed.

She watched Janine out of the corner of her eye, but the DS was silently whistling through her teeth as she went through stacks of slit-crotch panties and peek-a-boo bras. She seemed cheerful enough.

Perhaps she was just house-training him.

Hillary switched off the phone and wondered if Mike Regis would be in the office tomorrow. He usually worked with a silent, seemingly all-knowing DS called . . . what was the man's name now? Colin Tanner. That was it. A lanky individual who had a calming influence on almost every-one and everything. A human mind-reader, as rumour had it, who'd worked seamlessly with Regis for nearly ten years, and was generally acknowledged to be a very handy Robin to Regis's Batman.

And who did Detective Inspector Hillary Greene get stuck with? The likes of Frank Ross, and a blonde bombshell currently porking her boss.

Surely somebody somewhere had to be taking the piss?

* * *

Whether or not Regis called in at HQ the next day, Hillary wasn't sure, for she went straight from the boat to St Anselm's.

The alarm clock hadn't worked because it was electric, and the boat's battery had run low. She left the battery recharging before battling her way once more through the traffic to the college. She hadn't even had time for a warming cup of coffee, let alone breakfast, and the weather, if anything, had got even colder. Plus, she had some sort of oil stain on her second-best skirt after her battle with the bloody generator.

And to cap it all, her car heater was playing up.

She sat in the traffic jam, swearing and muttering under her breath and blowing on her numb fingers. She hated that bloody boat. The sooner she got out of it and back into her house the better.

Although her part of England rarely saw snow nowadays, she wouldn't be surprised to see some falling later on.

She inched the car forward another foot and sat staring at the rear end of a city bus. Why the hell wasn't it in the bus lane?

She let her mind wander to her Animal Army problem. Last night she'd gone through her mental filing system and recalled one or two solicitors who might be willing to take on the charity chancers for a rock-bottom price. Now she reached forward to switch on the phone attached to the dashboard, ready to make an appointment with the best of them. She didn't make the mistake of thinking the threat of legal action would simply go away.

Not without them getting a broadside from an opposing solicitor first, that is.

As she went through her appointment options with the solicitor's secretary and made a note of her choice in her Filofax (yes, she still had one, yuppie retro or not), the traffic line moved forward and a nippy Mazda overtook and snaffled the space.

Hillary swore, then had to apologise to the startled legal secretary still on the other end of the phone. She felt guilty to be illegally using the phone, but she was stuck in traffic. Still, it would serve her right (and be just her luck) if one of her colleagues in traffic caught her out and gave her a right rollicking. She inched her car forward and tried not to fantasize about wrecking her ancient and rusting Volkswagen by smashing into the back end of the Mazda. The idiot even had personalized number plates. He deserved it.

(Nobody, but nobody, did mental road rage better than Hillary Greene.)

* * *

Janine and Tommy were already at St Anselm's when she arrived. In fact, the DC had already started the preliminary interviews, having organised an itinerary of ten-minute time slots with anyone who even remotely knew the dead girl. It would take up the whole of his day, and probably yield nothing, but you just never knew. And that just about summed up the job in a nutshell, as far as Tommy could tell. It had the same kind of allure as gambling, he supposed now that he thought about it. Most of the time you lost, but just once in a blue moon, your number came up and you felt like you'd won a million quid.

Or fishing. Waiting for a nibble, with the float doing nothing but bob around all day, and then suddenly — wham. Some unseen fish took the bait and the float disappeared.

He sighed and looked up as the next student walked in. He smiled and asked for a name, wondering if he was going to get writer's cramp.

Janine had managed to commandeer a small cubby-hole for a makeshift incident room (as distinct from the larger empty classroom where Tommy was currently getting writer's cramp). It looked as if the cleaner should keep his mop and bucket there, but it had electrical sockets, room for a table and chairs, and even a solitary window.

She was sitting at the desk going over forensic reports when Hillary, who'd had the way pointed out to her by the college secretary, walked in. Her eyes went straight to the room's most vital piece of equipment — the coffee maker. She poured a cup as Janine filled her in. It was the usual depressing stuff. There were no fingerprints found in Eva Gerainte's college room that couldn't be accounted for. Namely, the dead girl's own, the scout's (what Oxford colleges like to call the cleaning staff), and prints from various other college friends, prominently those of Jenny Smith-Jones.

The flat in Botley, of course, was teeming with unidentified prints.

'Punters,' Janine added, sipping her own cup of coffee, and looking as if she'd never overslept a day in her life. Or even knew what an oil stain was. 'Not one of them has form.'

Hillary could have told her that. Bankers, stockbrokers, execs and other high-flyers only need apply for Eva's services. She wondered, idly, how much the French student had been making. Eva, she was sure, would have seen her business as nothing more or less than that. A business. She certainly wouldn't have seen it as anything shameful. Or even criminal. She probably wouldn't see it as even remotely naughty.

Hillary tried to remember back to when she'd been nineteen. She'd not long lost her virginity — to Tony

Brewer, the son of one of her father's best friends — if she remembered rightly. She'd been going to college too, but the vast difference between her own mind-set, and that of this murdered girl, nearly twenty years later, couldn't have been wider if they'd been species from different planets.

'I suppose we'd better tackle his nibs, the principal, again,' Hillary said, having done her quota of philosophical thinking for the day. Nice to get it over and done with.

'What, give him a heads up?' Janine asked curiously, wondering if her boss was getting soft in her old age.

'See if he knew about it,' Hillary snorted, wondering if she had time for a second cup of coffee. Probably not. 'Perhaps Eva wasn't a one-off,' she added, although she was not sure if she was being entirely serious.

'What, you think this might be a knocking shop with the best cover, like, ever?' Janine laughed.

They were still laughing together as they climbed the stairs, past the disapproving gaze of a vaguely well-known eighteenth-century rubber plantation owner.

Hillary didn't know why the portrait of a slave-owning rubber baron should be hanging in the main hall of the now ultra-politically-correct St Anselm's College. But if she asked, no doubt someone would be able to tell her.

This was Oxford, after all.

* * *

Gerald Havering tried his best to look pleased to see them. He rose with a smile, sent the secretary out for coffee and biscuits (yes!), and invited them to sit down. He was very careful not to look at Janine's legs.

He had no problems, however, with looking at her face. Janine was most certainly beautiful, as opposed to merely good-looking, or pretty. Most people didn't mind looking at Janine's face. Perhaps that was what was eating at Mel Mallow's bowl of cornflakes.

'This is DS Tyler, Dr Havering,' Hillary introduced them briskly. 'We have uncovered something rather unexpected, concerning the murder of your student, Eva Gerainte,' she said, coming straight to the point.

Instantly a wariness flashed across the blue eyes and was just as quickly concealed. But was that just a general reaction to what was obviously not going to be good news, or did the principal have a fair idea of what was coming next?

'It seems Ms Gerainte had another residence,' Hillary began.

Whatever he'd expected her to say, it certainly hadn't been that, Janine thought at once. Interesting. What *had* he been expecting? Had college rumour already begun to whisper that ghastly word? *Drugs*.

If so, this must be coming as a distinct relief. *But not for long, chummy*, she thought, hiding a smile. Not for much longer.

'Oh, er, really?' he said, and behind the bland exterior, both policewomen could almost hear the frantic activity going on between his ears. 'Well, there's no law against it. I meant, college rules,' he corrected hastily, suddenly remembering that these two women did, in fact, represent the actual law. 'But I don't see how that's relevant to her death?'

Hillary smiled. 'Flats are expensive to rent in this area,' she pointed out. 'You don't seem surprised that one of your scholarship students should be able to afford a second residence.'

Havering flushed. It came up from his neck in a tide of ugly brick-red, which did nothing for his distinguished silver hair or Stewart Granger good looks.

And then Hillary suddenly twigged that it was embarrassment causing it, not guilt. He'd been caught out being very slow on the old uptake, and *that* was what was making him sweat in his boxers.

'No. Well, that is surprising. Yes, indeed,' he muttered unhappily.

'And we're almost sure that Ms Gerainte got her funds from the proceeds of prostitution, Dr Havering,' Hillary said, abruptly putting him out of his misery.

Or, to be more accurate, changing the root cause of his misery. Because dismay was certainly flooding his face now, this time in the form of *receding* colour. He looked suddenly pale, and ever so slightly sick.

He blinked.

'I don't know what to say,' he said at last.

And that's probably the first honest thing he's said all week, Hillary thought uncharitably, if accurately.

The DI was now fairly sure that the principal had had no previous knowledge of this. If he had, he could give Al Pacino and Robert De Niro a run for their money in the old Oscar stakes.

'You, er . . . that is, you don't intend to release this information, do you? To the press, I mean?' the principal asked, swallowing hard. And no doubt visualising himself up before the college board, furiously running through a damage limitation agenda.

'It's not our policy to run our murder investigations in tandem with the press, Dr Havering,' Hillary said, and waited.

And waited.

And still no comment came from the principal about that all-important word, 'murder,' which she'd just slipped into the conversation for a second time.

She could just see Janine rolling her eyes.

Yes, Hillary thought, poor old Dr Havering really wasn't on the ball today. Or was he just being incredibly canny?

'Well, sir, we'll be sure to keep you informed,' she lied brightly. She finished her cup of coffee and was just reaching for one of the Garibaldi biscuits when she managed to stop herself.

Missing breakfast was only good if you didn't make up for it with elevenses.

Or so she told herself, all the way out of the door.

* * *

At lunchtime Tommy took a break, as did his diminishing line of interviewees. He reported back glumly to Hillary that nobody seemed to know anything.

'But we've got her last known movements more or less accounted for,' he added. It had been one of the first things Hillary had asked for.

'Apparently, she didn't go out that night. After dinner in Hall—' He read from his notes through bites of the sandwiches which 'Chef' had thoughtfully brought to them from the kitchens — 'she went straight to the JCR with two friends, where they drank some alcopops, shot a few frames of pool, argued over the relative merits of Sartre versus . . . er . . .' He squinted at his short hand as if in agony. 'Er, some other French writer or other, then she left, saying she was going straight to her room.' He paused to take a much-needed breath. 'No one's seen her since then. The porter at the lodge says all students have their own keys, and come and go as they please, though the main gates are locked at eleven. He says he didn't see Eva Gerainte leave the college grounds, but that means nothing.'

'And nobody's come forward who's seen her since leaving the JCR?' Hillary pressed.

'Not so far, guv, but I've got a score more to see this afternoon.'

'The bed was unmade,' Janine put in, inspecting her sandwich critically, and looking surprised to find fresh prawns, rocket and what looked and tasted suspiciously like homemade mayonnaise.

'Means nothing,' Hillary said dismissively. But the French girl's outfit had looked like something a fashion-conscious student would wear for an evening in. Good, but not fancy.

Doc Partridge had put the time of death at between 10 p.m. and 4 a.m. So it was very unlikely that she'd gone out, died, and then been taken back to her room.

'So someone came visiting her in her room,' Tommy said, through a mouthful of gloriously tangy cheese and raw onion, 'with a hit.'

'Or she shot up herself,' Janine put in.

'Then threw away the needle and stuff?' Tommy guffawed.

'I don't suppose the porter noticed anyone coming in?' Hillary said, then sighed. What a useless question that was!

'Saw plenty, guv, but no one suspicious-looking. Dons and students, staff, and anonymous late teens to early twenty-somethings.'

Hillary nodded. Right. A modern college was an open invitation to anyone. So long as you didn't frighten the horses or walk on the grass, who would notice?

'If she let him into her room, it must have been someone she knew, guv,' Tommy pointed out. 'I mean, there were other people living all around her. Even at half ten at night, there would have been someone to hear her if she'd screamed and kicked up a fuss.'

And nobody had.

'That doesn't necessarily follow,' Hillary pointed out. 'Say Chummy walks up to the door, knocks, and the moment she opens the door, whams a hand over her mouth, pushes her in, and closes the door . . . She was small, remember. Any male of reasonable size and fitness would have no trouble manhandling her.'

Tommy nodded glumly.

'Still no word from the ME about cause of death?' Hillary looked at Janine, but without much hope.

'The autopsy's scheduled for first thing tomorrow, guv.' It was Tommy who spoke. He didn't need any reminding. He wasn't looking forward to attending.

One thing was for sure, he wasn't telling his mother or Jean about it. Both of them would screw their faces up in disgust. Thinking of Jean, his steady girlfriend of two years or more, he felt the usual sense of guilt. But it wasn't as if he was actually cheating on her. Hell, Hillary didn't have the faintest idea that he pined for her, and nothing would come of it even if she did. He was enough of a pragmatist to know *that*. And what Jean didn't know, couldn't hurt her. Besides, it was not as if she had anything to worry about, really. When he thought of the future at all, it was still Jean's face he saw.

At the moment, though, he was still living with his mother, what with the price of houses in the area being so high, and a humble DC's wages being so low. It was a plight many of his fellow workers shared, but that didn't help much. Of course, if he and Jean one day got married and pooled their incomes, they might be able to afford a two-up two-down out Headington way, perhaps.

Hastily, he shied away from that thought.

'Janine, get back to the Botley flat. SOCO must have finished. And see if Vice have turned up. You never know, they might have Eva Gerainte on their books already.'

Yeah, and pigs might fly, Janine thought sourly. But hers was not to reason why.

'And you, boss?' she said, shrugging into her coat and staring outside. 'Bugger me, it's snowing,' she said blankly.

For a second, all three police officers stared, like fascinated and delighted children, at the white flakes falling outside.

Then Hillary grimaced. She hoped her battery was still recharging all right. Otherwise, she'd be spending the night freezing under a duvet.

'I'm off to see the music teacher,' she said at last. 'See what musical instrument our Eva found so fascinating.'

Well, it beat going back to HQ and seeing what sort of mood Mel Mallow was in today.

CHAPTER 6

Molly Fairbanks had once been a concert pianist. Not a very famous one, or a particularly popular one, but she'd done the circuit, and was every inch the professional. Hence her plum appointment to an Oxford college when middle age and a touch of rheumatism had put paid to even minor public appearances.

Hillary was not aware of the music teacher's history. But what she did know, from the moment she walked into the music room and had her ears assaulted by the efforts of a struggling, solitary flautist, was that she was in the presence of a distinct personality.

And the nineteen-year-old male student, unhappy in both his breathing and his bridging of two discordant notes, wasn't even in the running.

'Stop, for the love of anybody you care to mention!' The voice was like cut glass, the tones strictly reserved for 'polite society' and yet devastatingly honest.

The male student flushed, and stopped.

'Have you practised even an hour since our last lesson, Mr Answara?' the hectoring voice demanded.

The youth, who might have been Turkish, (might have been anything that added jet black hair, a straight nose and coal-black eyes to the human gene pool), looked distinctly guilty. He mumbled something like a humble sheep.

'Thought not,' the voice shot back, but this time laced with wry fatalism. 'Go away and practise. Then come back. My ears can only take so much.' But the words, though harsh, didn't sound angry. In fact, in an odd way, it was as if the tutor had granted some kind of absolution. It was a master stroke of psychology, and Hillary, no mean shakes in that department herself, felt like applauding.

The young man flushed and slunk away, but with a small, slightly sad smile. It said much of the woman tutoring him that his wasn't the slouch of chagrin, hurt pride or even resentment, but the genuine guilt which came when you knew you'd let down both yourself and somebody you respected.

He went past her with a small sigh. Hillary moved further into the room and was instantly speared by a pair of probing, dark brown eyes. Dr Molly Fairbanks — for such was the name tag on the music-room door — was in her mid-fifties, Hillary gauged, with iron-grey hair swept back in what she guessed would always be an untidy chignon, and a long, sensitive, horse-like face bare of make-up.

'And you are?' she asked abruptly, in a tone that would have made even the most unruly of frisky dogs come to heel without so much as a snarl. A whimper, maybe, but not a snarl.

'Police, Dr Fairbanks,' Hillary shot back, her own voice less antagonistic, but nonetheless, one that any dog-handler would equally have recognised and approved.

She thought she saw the older woman give a ghost of a smile in acknowledgement.

'Oh. This is about Eva, I imagine?' she asked. It didn't surprise Hillary that this woman would come straight to the point, with no messing about. But she thought she caught something in the voice that touched on pain.

'Yes. You knew her well?'

Molly Fairbanks began gathering up the flautist's musical score and shuffled it into a folder. Then she opened a small wooden chest and dropped it inside. Then she folded away the music stand on which they'd rested and let it lean against one wall.

When she'd done all that, and Hillary still hadn't moved, or said another word, she nodded her head once.

'Yes, I knew her fairly well.'

'What instrument did she play?'

Molly Fairbanks blinked.

'The oboe,' she said quickly. Too quickly.

In that moment, Hillary knew that she was lying. And she knew because of a combination of two things: copper's nose, and her own growing sense of Eva Gerainte. Her copper's nose she treated warily — instinct was nothing you could go on in court, and it could sometimes lead you astray. But Eva Gerainte, she was sure, would never have chosen the oboe. It was too dull for the likes of the French Miss from Lille. No, she would have chosen something far more daring and sexy to play. The tenor sax, perhaps. Or a rock star's electric violin. Or she may have gone strictly for class. Maybe cello or double bass. Something that screamed élan.

But not the oboe.

So why had the music teacher lied to her?

'She didn't strike me as the oboe-playing type, I have to say,' she said mildly, and had the satisfaction of seeing the older woman glance at her quickly, eyes narrowing.

Then she looked slightly angry, and Hillary understood that too. Molly Fairbanks didn't like lying. It probably didn't go with her self-image.

She could also sense that moment when the older woman became slightly afraid of her.

Now that was interesting.

OK, the public were generally wary when talking to the police — for the vast majority, it wasn't something they did often — but it was always tinged with a touch of interest, a bit of excitement, a certain amount of bravado.

This woman's fear was far more concentrated than that. It had a target. And that interested the DI greatly.

Time to make her even more afraid.

'You used to be a concert pianist, didn't you?' Hillary asked. It was a reasonable guess to make, under the circumstances. She knew how Oxford colleges, even those not officially linked to the university, liked to hire the best. It was a simple bit of logic, but to a suspect already rattled, it would sound far more menacing than it actually was.

Molly Fairbanks laughed. She laughed like a horse. And she didn't sound particularly menaced. She was obviously the sort to recover quickly.

'Well, I never played the Albert Hall,' she said succinctly, summing up her life with admirable honesty.

Hillary nodded. 'You were good enough to know you weren't quite good enough. It must have stung,' she said softly.

The brown eyes turned back to her, like lasers. Oh yes, the fear was gone now. Defiance was firmly in control. 'Bit of a shrink, are you? I suppose most police officers nowadays like to play Freud.'

'Oh, Jung, please,' Hillary said, pained, and without thinking. 'Or Nietzsche, at a pinch.'

And suddenly, both of them were laughing.

'Want a cup of coffee? I keep a private jar of instant and a kettle,' Molly offered. 'Strictly against college regs, of course, but none of the students would dare shop me to the bursar.'

This, Hillary could well believe, and gratefully accepted yet another cup of coffee.

You could never have too much Java.

'So, tell me about Eva,' she said, and perched on a tall stool, watching as the swollen-knuckled fingers spooned out the instant and the sugar. Since the older woman had her back to her, she had a good view of the stiffening spine and tensing up of shoulder blades.

So she'd hit a nerve. Obviously, Molly Fairbanks had had some sort of a relationship with the dead girl. She was not just another anonymous student, that was for sure.

But supposing Eva Gerainte hadn't come here for musical tuition, exactly what *had* she come for?

Was it possible Molly was gay? Did Eva swing both ways — at least with paying clients?

Somehow, Hillary didn't see it. Not that she was hard-pressed to imagine cosmopolitan Eva being willing to give it a go. But she *was* fairly sure that this woman, if gay, would have more — yes, all right — *horse* sense and sheer good breeding than to foul her own doorstep. 'I imagine you've been building up a picture of her ever since you got the call out,' Molly dodged effectively. 'There are rumours going about that she died of a drugs overdose. That's bollocks, of course.'

Hillary nodded. 'Yes, all her friends have told us she was very anti-drugs. Of course, that might have been mere camouflage.'

'Bollocks,' Molly repeated firmly.

She was dressed in black slacks and a loose-necked black silk jersey. She had a single strand of what looked like very real pearls around her neck.

Yet Hillary could picture her in wellies, cocker spaniels at her heels, walking across the countryside ready to do battle with both the Women's Institute and any vandal writing graffiti on a bus-shelter wall. She was easily recognisable as a middle-England, salt-of-the-earth, dying-breed phenomenon.

Her father could have been anything from a retired colonel to a magistrate to 'something in the city.' She'd have gone to a good local primary school, then a girls' boarding school, then Roedean, or Cheltenham Ladies College.

She might not have quite enough money to live on, would scrupulously pay her taxes, and wouldn't suffer fools gladly. And she could say 'bollocks' with total élan.

And yet here she was, lying through her teeth to the police. Which didn't fit. Didn't fit at all.

'You were going to tell me what you thought of Eva,' Hillary said, with an edge to her voice. Just enough to let the musician know that she wasn't going to be allowed to wriggle out from under.

Molly Fairbanks turned with two mugs of coffee and thrust one out.

'I was? Well, let's see. She was typically French — and by that I mean she could dress in burlap and look good. She was smart, without being particularly academically clever. She thought the world was hers to do with as she liked, naturally. She knew what she wanted, and was prepared to work hard to get it. Those last two are very rare in the young, you know.' Hillary did know. She was a cop. Who knew better? Many young people did not know what they wanted, and even if they did, had no particular inclination to work hard for it.

'She wanted to be a fashion designer, perhaps own a range of boutiques, yes?' Hillary said. No harm in confirming her data.

'That's right. She'd have done it too. I expect she had a heart defect, or maybe suffered a stroke or an aneurysm?' Molly probed. 'It's something you see sometimes. The brightest and the best of the bunch get winked out, just like that. People forget that tragedies — normal, straightforward tragedies, I mean — happen all the time.'

Hillary smiled wryly. 'You're talking to a Detective Inspector of the Thames Valley Police Force, Dr Fairbanks,' she said quietly.

Molly snorted. Like a horse. 'Quite right. I shouldn't try teaching my old granny to suck eggs, should I? Anything else I can do for you?'

She sounded hearty enough. Blunt and a little uncaring. And yet it was a sham. Hillary was sure that the girl's death meant far more to her than she was allowing to show. So what now? On the one hand, she was tempted to show Dr Fairbanks that she hadn't fallen for all the lies and evasions — see if she could rattle her some. Get back some of that interesting fear. On the other hand, it might be better to let her stew and come back later.

Besides, she was fairly sure that Molly Fairbanks was intelligent enough to already be well aware that this particular policewoman wasn't satisfied with the interview. The knowledge was there in the way she held Hillary's eyes in such a direct, level gaze. People only looked that steadfast when they were hiding fear, guilt or shame.

And she rather thought Molly was feeling ashamed of herself.

Good.

Hillary smiled. 'No, nothing at the moment,' she said, and handed back the half-drunk mug of coffee.

* * *

Molly Fairbanks watched her go, and felt curiously mollified. Which was ridiculous, under the circumstances.

Even so, it was nice to know that the police were still recruiting people of calibre and competence. It made her proud.

Then she thought about what a pain in the neck DI Hillary Greene was going to be, and swore roundly.

And 'bollocks' was amongst the mildest of the words that she came up with.

* * *

'Tommy, just the man I wanted to see,' Hillary said, tracking down her DC to his hidey-hole, and unknowingly making his heart leap like a gazelle in his chest.

'Guv?' he managed to mumble around a mouth gone suddenly dry.

'The music teacher, Dr Molly Fairbanks. I want a full financial check run on her, and get me some background detail.'

'Guv.'

It would be interesting to find out what was making the upright and highly individual Molly Fairbanks so twitchy.

'Anything from the last set of interviews?' she asked, walking to the window and staring out. Tommy had a first-class view of the pond here, she noticed. Then she froze as she spotted a heron — the real flesh, blood and feathered thing, nonchalantly stalking the college goldfish.

She blinked.

'No, guv. But we've got the diary back. Someone in the path lab has a French wife. She did it for us.'

Hillary frowned, her eyes still glued to the elegant water bird. She hoped the interpreter would be discreet. But then those married to people in police work had to either learn to be discreet or be quickly side-lined. You didn't talk to strangers, or friends, because you never knew if the stranger was a reporter on the make, or the friend might know a reporter on the make. You never knew what crook might be in the supermarket line beside you as you chatted on your mobile phone. Silence on all things work-related became a way of life.

The heron slowly lifted one long-toed leg and replaced it half a foot further in, without causing so much as a ripple. The snake-like black and white feathered neck elongated, seemingly in slow motion. The whole grey body seemed to turn so still it could have been made from granite.

What was a shy country bird doing in the middle of the sodding city? She rarely saw the bird after which her boat was named, even on the canal at Thrupp. To see it in the middle of Oxford struck her as something of a slap in the face.

Why should St Anselm's be so privileged? Wasn't it privileged enough already? Privileged, in fact, right up to its collegiate eyeballs?

'There's no soul-searching involved, guv, but a lot of notes about meetings, and coded memos to self.'

Tommy wondered what she found so fascinating outside. He hoped it wasn't a good-looking student. On the other hand, if it was, it meant she was into younger men . . .

'I haven't read it all the way through, but it looks like her John book,' he added.

But even that little bit of bait didn't get her attention.

Hillary nodded. 'Right,' she said vaguely, and jumped. Outside, the heron had just shot its spear-like head forward, as fast as a bolt from a crossbow, and was now raising it up again, something gold and wriggling already slipping down its long, pale beak.

She shook her head and turned back to the room, catching Tommy staring at her.

He looked quickly away, hoping she hadn't noticed. It was embarrassing enough being moonstruck over a superior officer, moreover a white superior officer, and moreover still, a superior officer very nearly twice his age. But having said superior officer aware of it was one camel-breaking straw too many.

For her part, Hillary hoped her DC didn't think she was going off her trolley. Staring at herons in the middle of what was almost certainly a murder inquiry wasn't the kind of thing that inspired confidence.

And that was another thing. 'I'll be glad to get some solid evidence about cause of death to go on,' she said grumpily. 'Or even official confirmation that this is a suspicious death. As it is, it's like treading on eggshells.'

What Molly Fairbanks had said about heart attacks and embolisms or whatever, had not passed her by.

She'd feel a right fool if, after all this, the needle-mark on Eva Gerainte's body had nothing to do with the price of butter. For all she knew, it might be evidence of nothing more sinister than the fact that Eva Gerainte had had a blood test taken by a nurse!

She picked up the diary, slumped into one of the surprisingly comfortable chairs grouped around Tommy's desk, and leafed through it. Inside, written on ruled paper, was the corresponding translation into English.

Tommy was right. This was no soul-searching, angst-ridden written record of a troubled teen. But along with notes about library opening times, fashion ideas, and comments about the college food (atrocious, apparently) and the peculiar smell you always got inside English buses, lay scattered far more pertinent details.

Some dates were marked with asterisks, and were almost certainly there to indicate nights when she was 'working.' Each of these star-marked nights had a name to go with them; but not, unfortunately, a proper name like Geoff Shanks or Michael Dale, something a cop could work with.

Hillary gritted her teeth. Oh no. She had to use pet names.

On 18 December, for instance, there was a star and the name Liberace.

Liberace? For her, that conjured up the camp, long-dead, besequinned piano player and nothing more. Perhaps the American entertainer had been something of an icon for the dead girl. But could the nickname mean something else? Was she saying he was gay, for instance? Hillary groaned to herself.

Come on, Hill, a gay John made no sense! She grinned, then told herself off. First herons, now flippancy.

She turned the next page: 22 December, Red Rum.

Red Rum? A man who looked like a race horse, perhaps. What was it with horses all of a sudden? First Molly Fairbanks, now Red Rum.

Her mind fled to a certain Dick Francis book back on her boat, Ronnie's final ironic legacy, and she instantly pushed the thought aside.

No. She wouldn't think of that now.

Red Rum? What had that meant to Eva? Was the John a fast ejaculator? Always first past the winning post? It wouldn't surprise her. She could imagine the French girl had a wicked sense of humour.

She fast-forwarded to the last asterisk before the girl died. 5 January. 5 January. For some reason that rang a bell.

She frowned, turning it over and over in her mind, but it wouldn't come. Oh well, if she forgot about it, experience had told her that her subconscious would carry on working on the problem and come up with the solution sooner or later.

'Frankie A,' she read out loud. A real name at last. Or was it? None of the others had real names. So the unknown 'Frankie A' probably wasn't called Frank, Francis, Fred or any other such name.

Frankie A.

Unlike the other pet names, this conjured up nothing at all.

She went back. There was a Stripes, a Clark Kent and a Lambkin. She could think up reasons for all of them. Clark Kent was probably a journo. Or did he just think he was Superman? Or was he actually a superman, going at it all night?

Lambkin was anybody's guess, but just the name made her smile.

But Frankie A just didn't conjure up a single image at all. Hillary shrugged. So, their victim had an even half-dozen regulars. She had the pad. She had her money, she had her dreams, she had something — as yet unknown — going on with the music teacher.

What else?

How did any of this add up to Eva Gerainte being forcibly injected with something that killed her? A jealous wife? A bit far-fetched, that. A rival hooker, perhaps, mad at having some good Johns snaffled out from under her nose. It was possible.

Maybe the French police would come up with some prime suspect over there.

Who did you piss off, Eva? A pimp, who didn't want to take no for an answer? Or maybe one of your Johns thought he was an exclusive, and didn't like it when he found out differently? She sighed and went back to the diary.

Some of the asterisks were marked as 'all-nighters.' The French interpreter had carefully written out the translations in biro but beside this particular notation had pencilled in a 'lucky girl' comment of her own.

It made Hillary smile. But she'd have to rub it out before presenting it to the brass.

Also, beside some of the asterisks, Eva had put in a half-moon sign. Now what did that mean? Half-moon. Perhaps it meant something to someone from France. A cultural reference, perhaps? If so, the interpreter hadn't had any particular thoughts on this, and she'd been French as well.

The last date, 5 January. That was a half-moon night. What did it mean? And why was that date still bugging her? It was only six days ago. Surely she should remember.

It wasn't until she got to the back of the diary, and found the six neat lines of telephone numbers, that she began grinning.

Tommy looked up. 'I got the addresses to go with the phone numbers, guv,' he said modestly.

'Tommy, I could kiss you,' Hillary said, then looked up as Janine walked in.

'Thought I might find you here,' her sergeant said cheerfully. 'DI Regis and DS Tanner have called in at HQ. They're with Mel now.'

75

Hillary nodded. 'Well, at least we've got something to show them,' she said, and waved the diary in the air. 'And six punters for us to interview. Janine, I need prelims on them all. Tommy, you take three as well.'

'You don't want to sit in on any, boss?' Janine asked, surprised. Although it was standard for sergeants and constables to do most of the interviewing, everyone knew DI Greene liked fieldwork. Not even Mel was able to keep her behind her desk where she belonged.

'No, I have to head back to the station,' Hillary said nonchalantly.

And, when she thought Janine gave her a knowing look, added defensively, 'I didn't call in this morning — had a late start. I need to check for messages, if nothing else.'

She went out in a bit of a snit, wondering why the hell she'd felt the need to justify herself. And to Janine, of all people.

Going back to HQ had nothing to do with the fact that she knew Mike Regis was there.

Nothing at all.

'Well, well,' Janine said, as the door closed behind her DI. 'Looks like spring is in the air early this year.'

CHAPTER 7

Hillary had just locked the door of her car in the HQ parking lot when she remembered her appointment with the pensions officer.

Angling away to a side door, she checked her watch and hoped it wouldn't take long. It was almost certainly something to do with Ronnie, given the length of time paperwork took when it came to dealing with the dead.

The pensions officer, if she was remembering correctly, was a sergeant nearing retirement age.

Like a lot of others, Hillary didn't truly think of press liaison officers, counselling supervisors, those who represented police officers themselves accused of crimes and all the others who worked in the ancillary services, as proper cops. They didn't get call-outs in the middle of the night, weren't obliged to put life and limb in jeopardy, didn't have to pitch in when public riots or football hooliganism spilled over into the streets.

They weren't 'them' but they weren't quite 'us' either.

The pension officer had once been in CID, she knew, and rumour had it that he'd transferred to a desk-bound job when his wife had been diagnosed with cancer.

As she knocked on his door and entered at his cheerful 'come in,' she wished she could remember whether or not his wife was still alive.

'DI Greene, come in. Please have a seat.' He was a tall, thin, bespectacled man, and looked more like a chemistry teacher than a policeman. But she wasn't about to let appearances fool her. He was part of the mighty admin, and as such, had power.

'DS Lorrimer, isn't it?' she said, taking a seat beside a sadly wilting spider plant. The room was small, and the equally small windows didn't let in much light. She automatically pitied the plant, but didn't try to move it.

'Right. I won't keep you, DI Greene. I know you've got a big case on.'

Did he? Hillary wondered. How?

'I'm afraid it's about your late husband's pension.' The older man came straight to the point, pulling out a folder and opening it to one of the middle pages. Hillary was almost certain that he needn't have bothered. He was obviously the kind of man who had almost total recall. She envied such people, and wondered uneasily just why he felt in need of a prop.

Perhaps it was a way of showing that he was only the messenger, not the instigator. A way of saying, *Look, it's what it says in here, in the mighty dossier, and it's really nothing to do with me.*

Slowly but surely, Hillary began to get a very definite sinking sensation in the pit of her stomach.

'As you know, there are several standard pension packages available to police officers, and your husband, DI Greene, chose one whereby, on his death, three-quarters of his pension should normally have gone to his main dependant — in this case, yourself, of course.'

Hillary nodded cautiously. She hadn't missed the significance of that 'should normally have gone' remark.

It hadn't sounded good. Not good at all.

She glanced once more at the spider plant, but it didn't look in any position to help.

'And, again, in normal circumstances, this condition would have been met. There were no suspicious circumstances surrounding your husband's car accident, and in any case, whether or not he'd died while on duty is immaterial to the pay-out of the pension.'

Hillary nodded. She knew all this. She'd adopted the same pension plan herself, at the same time as Ronnie. She wondered if she should change it. After all, now that Ronnie was dead, who'd get her three-quarter pension if she kicked the bucket tomorrow?

She had no idea. Her mother, maybe?

'However, things are a little more complicated in the case of your husband. Since the internal investigation into his, er, illegal activities have been proven, I'm afraid the matter of his pension had to be referred to a higher panel. They have adjudicated that your husband's criminal behaviour has, well, to all intents and purposes, nullified his pension. You see, since he was . . .'

Here the DS seemed to stall, like a car suddenly running out of petrol.

'Bent,' Hillary said hard and flatly, and with a grim smile. 'It's all right to say it.'

I won't crack.

DS Lorrimer flushed a little, but smiled back just as grimly. 'As you say. Since your husband used his rank to amass moneys, and since none of those moneys have been found, but his criminal guilt has been established . . .'

Once again, he seemed to flounder and Hillary sighed heavily. She didn't see why she should make things easier for him, but on the other hand, time was a-wasting, and she had a murder to investigate.

Besides which, none of it was this poor sod's fault.

'What they're saying is,' she began drearily, 'that the money taken from his salary which went towards his pension was almost certainly tainted money, money he'd accrued illegally due to his position as an officer of the law, and the brass don't see why they should pay legitimate money back to his widow now.'

The pensions officer spread his hands in a helpless gesture. 'You can, of course, take this up with the beagles, but I wouldn't recommend it, DI Greene.'

'Beagles' was cop speak for legal eagles, those whose job it was to defend cops who found themselves in need of defending, whether it be against criminal charges, inter-house accusations, alleged cases of sexual harassment . . .

Or, in her case, being screwed by the system.

'You don't think I have a case?' Hillary said, and saw the other man hesitate.

He was obviously one of those scrupulously honest sorts of men who sometimes found themselves in a cleft stick.

She waited curiously, wondering what was coming next.

'I'm not a legal expert, of course,' he began cautiously, 'but I've been in this job some years now and one picks things up. Legally I would say you have a fairly good case for appeal. After all, the inquiry totally cleared *you* of any wrongdoing. And you were legitimately married to the man, who legitimately died and had been paying — perhaps not so legitimately to a pension scheme. However . . .'

He hesitated, looking at her with a silent appeal to let him off the hook without actually having to say the words out loud.

Hillary nodded glumly.

'However,' she repeated heavily, 'any officer making waves can't expect to be looked upon favourably when promotional opportunities come knocking.'

The older man looked relieved. It was always easier to deal with somebody who had no more illusions left. The young and the innocent were the ones who broke your heart.

Hillary didn't need telling this either. And, yes, she knew how things worked all right. Legally, morally and socially, she had the right to appeal against a slightly dodgy decision that was giving her a good old hefty boot up the backside. Nobody would challenge her, and probably very few would even blame her. Well, not the rank and file, anyway.

But the brass were another matter. They didn't like it when waves were made. And they always remembered. Like bloody elephants.

And if rumours were true, and Superintendent Donleavy was in line for promotion any day now, that meant Mel would probably be booted up to replace him, which meant a Chief Inspectorship would be in the offing.

She had seniority and experience and was popular enough not to be out of the running.

Unless . . .

Did the 'higher panel' who'd been asked to assess Ronnie's pension rights know about this? Call her paranoid, but she somehow thought they might. Some helpful little birdie would have dropped a word in the right ear.

Hillary, like nearly every other member of the human race, hated being shafted. She especially hated being shafted by big, anonymous corporations. To them, Ronnie's measly pension represented a mere drop in the bucket. So it was especially galling when their 'pocket change' was more than enough money to get her off the boat and back into a decent house.

And yet, if she fought for it, she'd be stuck as a DI for ever. Come to think of it, that wouldn't be too bad. The higher one climbed, the less hands-on you got and the more paperwork you handled. And she enjoyed the actual investigation of crime.

So being stuck as a DI wasn't such a bad thing.

But, if she went ahead and made a nuisance of herself, she might get edged out of CID — if they felt vindictive enough to do it. And who wanted to be a controller of traffic at fifty?

OK, maybe that was being paranoid. But just because she was paranoid didn't mean they weren't out to get her, did it?

Hillary almost laughed out loud.

What was this? First the barmy army of animal righters were trying to take her house, now her own police force was trying to do her out of a pension.

OK, not *her own* pension, it was true, but still.

Before today, she'd barely given Ronnie's pension a single thought. And if she had thought about it, it would have brought an instant sour taste to her mouth. She wanted nothing to do with her late, nearly ex, and totally unlamented husband. Not his money, not his tainted reputation, not anything.

And yet here she was, feeling as aggrieved as a virgin after her first unsatisfactory encounter, just because she was being granted her wish to be given nothing of Ronnie's.

But it was one thing to decide for herself to take the moral high-ground, and it was something else entirely to be poked into it by a long official bargepole.

'I see,' she said at last, and saw the older man look away, obviously shame-faced. It didn't help to know that she had the pension officer's unspoken sympathy. And it wouldn't help, she suspected, to have the sympathy of the entire station, once scuttlebutt about it got around.

Damn it, she could have *done* with that money. And she'd earned it. She'd put up with marriage to Ronnie bloody Greene for over ten years, so hell, yes, she'd earned it. She could have afforded to rent a flat with that extra dosh. She could have kissed the *Mollern* goodbye once and for all, with its battery that needed recharging, and its water tanks that needed constant replenishing, and its low roofs and claustrophobic walls and narrow beds, narrow corridors, narrow everything.

To live once more on floors that didn't move, cook on stoves that didn't gently bob about . . . to open full-sized windows and look down on the world from a second-storey floor . . .

She got up abruptly and marched to the door, before she started howling.

* * *

Upstairs, she detoured into the ladies' room and scowled at her reflection in the mirror.

What was to stop her from taking Ronnie's dirty money and swanning off to the Bahamas?

Well, practically, nothing. There was the little matter of breaking the law, of becoming an accessory after the fact to her husband's foul trade in endangered animal parts. Just the little circumstance of becoming a criminal.

But she had the nous to pull it off and not get caught. She knew enough to make herself safe.

It had been at the end of her last murder case that she'd accidentally stumbled on what the internal investigation team had been searching for so diligently for months. And it had been Gary, her stepson of all people, who'd been the catalyst.

Called to his father's old police station in Bicester, he'd cleared out Ronnie's locker and found a Dick Francis book, supposedly inscribed by herself, and had returned it to her. It was only later that she'd realised she'd never given Ronnie the book, and the writing inside was only a very poor forgery of her own writing. On closer inspection, she'd then noticed that some of the words on various pages had been underlined. Words like 'too,' 'for,' 'sex' and 'heaven.' Obvious numbers.

Numbers for the anonymous bank account that Ronnie had joked to his son Gary that he'd set up in the Caymans. The phoney inscription probably held the key to the bank account's password.

That had been last summer. So far she'd done nothing about it. She'd made no attempt to find the bank or access the account to see how much Ronnie had amassed. Nor had she reported her suspicions to the police.

She'd just sat on it. Waiting to move back into her old home, once probate and all the legal wrangles had been sorted out. Waiting to get on with her life and pick herself up.

Now, all at once, it felt as if the whole world was out to get her. What was she supposed to do? Just take it, and live on her uncle's boat indefinitely? Let some animal lib group con or legally cheat her out of her house? Let her own employers screw her out of yet more of her hard-won dues?

On the other hand, the thought of taking Ronnie's dirty money and running was repugnant.

Yeah, so she could retire to a beach in the Caribbean and sip piña coladas for the rest of her life. It was probably overrated. They probably had mosquitoes the size of sparrows over there.

Yeah, but money could buy an awful lot of insect repellent.

Gigolos probably patrolled the beaches, just looking for middle-aged women with more money than sense.

Yeah, and fighting them off would be a real hardship, right?

She met her dark brown eyes in the mirror and wondered who she was kidding. She loved catching villains far too much to give it up.

So why not just hand the money in and get it over with? It would clear any last cloud hanging over her name, that was for sure, and remove any lingering temptation.

She sighed and washed her hands and face. Then she pushed open the door, used her key card to gain access to the main office and made her way to the desk.

Where Frank Ross waited, like a poisonous Buddha. His round, cherubic face looked sickeningly self-satisfied and he was obviously nearly drunk.

Wonderful. Just the man you wanted around you when you'd just been dealt a kick in the goolies. Or whatever the female equivalent was.

'Frank,' she said on an exhaled breath that seemed to generate from somewhere in her toes. 'Whassup?'

'Found the local drugs dealer, guv.' Frank, who was eating a soggy-looking cheese and pickle sandwich, didn't bother to straighten up in his chair or wipe the pickle stain from his tie. But then it went so fetchingly with the dried-egg stain already there, she couldn't really blame him.

A sense of aesthetics. That's what she liked to see on her team.

'There's several dirtbags who deal to students, but everyone reckons Bingo Baines is the chap.' Frank munched hungrily. 'He denies everything, natch. He's down below,' he added, angling his thumb down, indicating they had a suspect in the interview room.

Bingo Baines? There was a drug dealer called Bingo Baines?

Hillary shook her head. Sometimes, she felt as if her life was actually a painting by Salvador Dali. (Usually, when she felt like this, she told herself to cut back on the vodka.)

'Right.' She turned as she felt a presence bearing down on her from behind, and found not only Mel but Mike Regis and Colin Tanner headed her way.

She felt her stomach do a little flip, and told it to pack it in.

DI Mike Regis was probably a few years older than Hillary, roughly her height, and had receding dark hair and unusual, dark green eyes. He was not remotely attractive, unlike Ronnie Greene, whom nearly every woman he met agreed was very attractive indeed. Especially blondes.

'Hillary, glad you're back,' Mel said. 'Frank here tells me he's pulled in the local pusher. You want to interview him?'

Hillary didn't. 'Since Frank found him, why don't we let him and DS Tanner do that?' Having called in Vice, they might as well make themselves useful. And besides, the aggressive and nasty-minded Frank Ross should make an amusing contrast with the quiet, all-seeing, all-knowing DS Tanner. Together they should keep good old Bingo Baines amused all afternoon. Never let it be said that Thames Valley didn't take care of its low lives.

Mel was surprised to hear her give Frank Ross a plum job, and wondered what she was hiding.

Frank Ross looked absolutely stunned, then delighted. He'd been sourly confident that, having found the prime suspect, he'd be snaffled by the queen bitch. He looked, also, just a little bemused.

Mike Regis's lips twitched as he met the eyes of his sergeant, and Hillary wondered what silent communication was passing between them. And wondered, too, if she'd ever be able to forge a bond like that with one of her own team. Not with Janine, certainly. The pretty blonde sergeant resented her too much for that. No, perhaps resent was too strong a word.

But with Tommy Lynch, who knew? They got on well, and it was early days yet.

She followed Mike into Mel's office then gave her boss and the Vice man a quick-run down on what they had so far.

As she talked, Regis began to see why she hadn't minded Frank Ross doing the interview with the pusher. It was obvious that she didn't think the dead girl, or the dead girl's possible killer, would be known to the local dealer.

'So you're more inclined to think she was killed, if she was killed, by one of her Johns?' Mel summed up when she'd finished.

He seemed to be in a better mood today, Hillary noticed absently, and only hoped her own depression wasn't obvious.

'Sir,' she said, then frowned.

Regis shifted in his chair. 'You're not so sure?' he asked quietly, those dark green eyes of his fixed on her face.

'No, I'm not,' Hillary admitted bluntly. 'You know as well as I do, killings of Toms by their Johns tend not to be unpremeditated. They're violent, often by manual strangulation, and purely sexually motivated. This girl, if she was murdered, wasn't molested. It wasn't unduly violent, even. It was more . . . execution-style. No, perhaps not that. More . . . oh, I don't know — matter of fact.'

Regis was already nodding. 'Nothing personal.' Yes, he could see why she was having doubts.

Mel frowned. 'We still don't know if it's murder we're looking at?'

Hillary shrugged and spread her hands. The doc had promised to do the autopsy fast, but she'd never taken that as gospel. He'd no doubt have a good reason for not getting to Eva sooner.

'But I agree, the doc's on-site findings look as if she was held down and forcibly injected with something,' Mel continued. 'Probably crack cocaine or heroin, but it might just as easily have been something far more prosaic. Insulin, injected in a large enough quantity, can kill you.'

Hillary nodded. 'Until the blood results come through, we're having to go on assumptions.'

And no copper liked doing that. On the other hand, they couldn't afford to wait and let the grass grow under their feet.

'Janine and Tommy are doing the preliminary interviews of her Johns now. I expect most of them will be at work. If they can't track down their places of employment, they'll have to wait till tonight.'

Mel sighed. 'And the girl's diary didn't indicate if any of her regulars were violent? Liked it kinky?'

'No. But I can't see Eva putting up with violence. Kinky wouldn't bother her, I don't think.'

Regis nodded quietly to himself. He had no trouble understanding how Hillary could be so confident about the dead girl's personality. It happened to him, too, sometimes. The way you could connect with a dead victim — pick up clues about their life and get an almost eerie sense of them, without ever having spoken a word to them.

Obviously, this girl, this Eva Gerainte, had made a definite impression on Hillary Greene. But he was also sure that Hillary was experienced enough not to rely on that alone. He couldn't fault her actions, logic or reasoning so far, and he doubted he'd find reason to do so.

When his own super had told him Mel Mallow had requested Vice co-operation, and he'd learned that DI Greene was SIO, he'd jumped at the chance.

He told himself it was because he liked to work with professionals who saw the job as he did. That it would be good for him to get a taste of homicide. That it was all strictly business.

He wasn't so sure that he was succeeding.

She was looking really good today. Her nut-brown hair, cut in a bell-shaped bob that suited her strong, intelligent face, was the perfect foil for the stone-coloured two-piece she was wearing. And unlike the younger generation of female cops, she didn't have that pared-to-the-bone, lean fitness of the dedicated jogger or gym-goer. She had breasts, and hips, like a real woman.

He told himself not to look at her legs, and didn't. But he remembered from last time that they were just the shape he liked.

'I've had a look through our database,' he said. 'Eva Gerainte isn't on it. Not surprisingly. It sounds like a very private arrangement she had going. Unlikely to attract the attentions of our lot.'

'When Janine and Tommy get back, you'll have more info on her Johns,' said Hillary. 'But like you say, I doubt they'll have caught your attention any more than Eva did. Middle-aged to old high-flyers, unless I miss my guess. The kind who'd find a French mistress a bit of a kick.'

Mel grunted. Who wouldn't?

He wondered when Janine would be back. And if she'd be coming over tonight. She seemed to have got over her snit of a few nights before. Perhaps she'd had the good sense to realise that it was too soon to be thinking of moving in together.

He sighed, and wondered, not for the first time, if getting involved with a pretty blonde detective sergeant on his own team had been such a good idea.

But then, when had good ideas had anything to do with sex?

* * *

When Tommy and Janine came by at six that evening, they came bearing gifts.

'We've managed to interview the lot, guv,' Tommy said, slumping down wearily on his seat, and spotting, with some dismay, DI Mike Regis lounging around at Hillary's desk.

'Liberace isn't gay,' Janine said next, making Mike do a double take, before Hillary explained Eva's pet-name system.

'He just looks like the guy, and has the mincing voice. But he can't play the piano. I asked him,' Janine added with a grin. 'I know, I know—' She held out her hands — 'but I just couldn't resist. His name's Philip Cox. No puns, please. Fifty-two, married, three kids all at uni, runs a haulage firm out of Abingdon. Met Eva at a jazz club, he says. Something about that didn't quite ring true to me, but I let it slide. He didn't know about the others — again, or so he says. Has an alibi, but only of the at-home-with-the-wife kind. Haven't seen her yet.'

'Lambkin is woolly and white-haired all right,' Tommy said, not to be outdone. 'An old bloke in his seventies — Marcus Gagingwell. Widowed. One of those vague academic types of private means. Knew all about the others, and was highly embarrassed about it all. Has no alibi — he lives alone, with a housekeeper who lives out but comes in for a few hours every day to cook his dinner, that sort of thing. But I can't see him having the strength needed to hold down a fit, struggling girl, guv. He's got the shakes too — a touch of Parkinson's Disease, I wouldn't wonder.'

'Red Rum is a red-haired dentist from Woodstock,' Janine took over. 'An upmarket dentist, mind. Likes to see to the local celebs. Couldn't stop telling me about that local newsreader bird. Bad wisdom teeth she's got, apparently. His name is Jamie Prospect, unmarried, and fancies himself something rotten. Was at home alone, he claims, on the night of her death. My feeling is he had a married lady in, but if so, he's not about to give her up just yet.'

'Frankie A is a Mr Michael Bolder, interior decorator. Forty-one, unmarried, a bit of a looker,' Tommy took over once more. 'Elegant. You can see why he and Eva hit it off — both arty types. He too was home alone — says he was working on designs for a famous footballer's holiday home in Cornwall. I believed him — about working for a footballer, I mean, not necessarily that he was home alone. Said a neighbour popped in for a drink mid-evening. The neighbour brought with him a posh bottle of plonk. Haven't checked it out yet but I should be surprised if it turns out to be a lie,' he finished, and they all looked automatically to Janine again.

It was a bit like being at a tennis match, Hillary thought with a wry smile.

'Clark Kent's a freelance reporter, as you'd expect,' Janine obliged. 'Ryan Culver, thirty-eight. A bit of a star, apparently. Went to Bosnia, the Gulf, that sort of thing. Earned a prize for some sort of investigation of an old people's home. Considers himself a crusader, a proper professional, not the usual run-of-the-mill scumbag working for the *Daily Sleazoid*. A bit of an amateur photographer too.'

'Possible nudie shots?' Regis put in, even as Hillary was opening her mouth to wonder aloud the same thing.

'Could be,' she said, nodding.

'Would your girl be up for nude posing?' he asked.

Hillary nodded. 'Oh yes. Eva would have considered it art. Unless he'd tried to sell them or make money from them without cutting her in. Then she'd have hit the roof, I reckon.'

Regis nodded. 'I'll ask around. See if he's got a rep for amateur porno. Sounds unlikely, though.'

But it was a sniff of a possible motive at last.

Of course, all Eva's Johns would be gone over with a fine toothcomb, but that would take time.

'Anyone else?'

'Stripes, guv,' Tommy said. And grinned.

'Gonna let us in on the joke, son?' Regis said, and wiped the smile right off Tommy's face with surprising suddenness.

'Sir,' Tommy said, almost coming to attention. He didn't like Regis. Or rather, he didn't like the way Regis got on so well with Hillary.

'I reckon he gets his nickname from his clothes. He answered the door wearing a pair of wide-striped pyjamas. This was at—' He checked his notebook '—4:55 p.m. He was half-sozzled, in my opinion. Claims to be a composer. Of music. For the movies — Hollywood, that kind of thing. Says he's not in the country often. When I asked him what he was doing the night Eva died, he said he had the boys over. The boys turned out to be a guitar player, and a chap with an all-purpose synthesizer that can, apparently, sound like anything from a sixty-strong orchestra to a man playing the spoons. They were trying out the score for an advert for kitty litter. This last I only got from him after a good bit of perseverance,' Tommy said, deadpan. 'His name is Lewis Fenn. He said he was thirty-four. More like fifty-four in my opinion. I haven't yet checked in with "the boys" though.'

Hillary nodded. As she'd suspected. All successful(ish) and well heeled — a fairly eclectic lot.

And possibly one of them was their killer.

Suddenly, the loss of Ronnie's pension, the angst about his hidden dosh, even the threat of the barmy Animal Army, all faded away.

This was what life was all about.

Well, her life, anyway.

CHAPTER 8

The next day, Hillary was in early. The sharp frosts were still persisting, but the weather forecasters were predicting rain and milder weather by the weekend. She was not sure that would be much of an improvement: rain pounding on the roof of a narrowboat could sound like a full timpani band gone berserk.

Frank was the first of her team to put in an appearance after her, an event so surprising that she wondered if the reprobate had simply gotten drunk in the local and then persuaded some poor sap to let him spend the night in one of the cells.

She had an idea it wouldn't be the first time.

'Guv, Bingo Baines is as pure as the driven. Or at least he sticks to it he never even heard of our vic,' her salubrious sergeant said, by way of greeting. He was dressed in yesterday's artistic tie, and he hadn't shaved. With his podgy figure, podgy face and piggy eyes, he looked even more than ever like a rumpled Winnie the Pooh.

She'd often noticed how his outward appearance fooled people.

But never for long.

'Well, find out who his rivals are, and see if they're any more forthcoming. Tommy should be at the PM about now—' She checked her watch '—and with any luck Doc Partridge might have felt guilty enough to take some blood samples and send them off to analysis, when he realised he'd had to put off the full cut.'

Frank idly scratched his armpit and then inspected his nails.

Hillary was immediately reminded of a day out at the zoo when she'd been a child. The gorilla house. Or was it the chimps?

'The Vice man thinks it's a waste of time, going after pushers,' Frank said sourly, hardly leaping into action like a speeding bullet. (Or even merely reaching for the telephone like a disgruntled sloth, if it came to that.)

He obviously didn't think much of her orders, but then when did he ever? But in this instance, Hillary could sympathise with his predicament. Sort of.

On the one hand, sheer bloody-mindedness would make him want to disagree with someone from Vice, especially someone with an equal rank to his own. But on the other hand, he also liked to adopt a policy of rear-guard insubordination when it came to taking her, Hillary's, orders.

He defied her, she suspected, as a matter of principle. Or whatever it was that passed for a principle in Frank's mind.

Being married to Ronnie, Frank's best mate and longtime crony, placed her in a unique position when it came to being the recipient of Frank's hostility.

He couldn't, to this day, understand why Ronnie had married her.

And since she couldn't, to this day, understand why she had married Ronnie either, they seemed linked by a strange and definitely twisted umbilical cord.

A shrink would have a field day with them, she thought, just a shade uneasily.

She sighed and dumped her handbag on the desk. 'Well, when Sergeant Tanner is in charge of this investigation, Sergeant Tanner can call the shots. Until then—' She hooked her thumb in the general direction of the innocently half-awake village of Kidlington lying outside the double-glazed windows '—you can hit those dirty streets you profess to know so well, and bring in another dealer.'

It would keep him out of her hair for another day, and it was still a legitimate avenue that had to be followed up.

Frank sneered (Winnie the Pooh on acid) and slouched out.

As he trundled down the main staircase, he wondered what assignment Tanner would be given. He hoped it stank, big time. Still, all in all, he wasn't all that pissed. He liked being out of the nick, and out from under the gorgon's eye. It left him free to do as he liked.

If he could only find out where Ronnie had stashed his money, he would be long gone. Then he could send Hillary bloody Greene a postcard from Acapulco, with a drawing of a single raised finger. And perhaps the words 'up yours' written underneath, just in case the thick cow didn't get it.

Such cheerful thoughts were what kept him sane. He began to whistle as he passed the desk and headed for the doors, giving the desk sergeant a severe case of the heebie-jeebies.

A cheerful Sergeant Frank Ross wasn't something a man should have to face first thing in the morning.

* * *

Upstairs, Hillary settled down in her chair and found the dossier left for her on the desk, written in the big, pleasingly legible handwriting of Detective Constable Tommy Lynch.

She opened it up, wondering vaguely why Frank hadn't given her more grief about his assignment, and when Mike Regis would be in.

She read without taking in the information, turned a page, caught herself out, swore softly under her breath, and turned back to the beginning, forcing herself to concentrate.

It was Tommy's financial report on the music teacher. It wasn't very edifying. But her guess about Molly Fairbanks' background, she was gratified to note, had been more or less spot-on. Her mother had been an Hon., her father something big in the wine business (imports and exports.) She'd grown up on a country manor in Hampshire, attended a high-flying boarding school in Scotland, and come into a small but very handy amount on her father's death.

She earned a packet as tutor at St Anselm's, and lived well within her means. But there were no intriguing and mysterious donations of money into her bank account, either on a regular basis or in odd lump sums.

Well, she hadn't really seen the ineffable Dr Molly Fairbanks as a madam. Not in any true sense of the word, at least. But there was still something quirky about the music teacher. Something in her manner had definitely been a bit off.

She shrugged and mentally shifted Dr Havering on to a back burner, with cast-aside hopes of being granted a search warrant for her rooms. (Still, it would have been fascinating to have had a ferret around in Dr Havering's drawers.)

She sighed and went through her mail and in-tray like a ferret on speed, dealing with about two hours' worth of administration in half an hour. She only looked up when Janine came in, about ten minutes late.

Hillary didn't even comment. Cops worked such long hours of unpaid overtime, carping on about time-keeping was a nonstarter.

Janine, as usual, looked good in a pair of dark blue slacks, a pale blue jersey that looked suspiciously like real cashmere, and a matching pale blue scrunchie which pulled back her long blonde hair into a fetching pony-tail.

Normally, discovering one of her habitually low-paid officers wearing cashmere would have set the old alarm bells going, but everyone and their granny could have surmised that the jersey had been a present from Mel. Especially since they'd obviously made up some quarrel recently.

And nobody worried about *Mel's* expensive tastes. His second marriage had been to a surprisingly wealthy woman, and everyone knew that in the divorce, it was, for once, the man who'd come out of it the better off for alimony. Not only had Julia not wanted to continue living in their very desirable detached house in the Moors area of Kidlington, she'd let Mel keep the house as part of the divorce settlement in exchange for him agreeing to let their son live with her in London. She had a million-plus pad in Belgravia. Or was it Mayfair?

Hillary often wondered if Mel regretted that decision. She sometimes felt sure that he missed his son, now aged around eleven, far more than he supposed he would have. Cops worked long hours, everyone knew that, and their home lives inevitably suffered. Perhaps he was only used to seeing the family briefly at breakfast and at odd times on the weekends. But now he didn't even have that. Now he went home to a very expensive, very chic house — and emptiness.

Even though she herself went home to emptiness, at least the *Mollern* was small and cosy. She didn't rattle around in it like a pea in a sardine can. More like an elephant in a suitcase, in fact.

Janine was humming softly under her breath, and as she sat down at her desk and began to type up her notes from yesterday, she looked generally pleased with life.

Hillary wondered if the cashmere jersey had anything to do with it, then told herself not to be a cat.

Just because nobody gave *her* cashmere . . .

Of course, she could probably buy herself a whole wardrobe of cashmere outfits if she wanted to.

With Ronnie's money.

She shook her head. She was going to have to stop thinking about Ronnie's money. It was driving her crackers.

She opened the last of her letters — and found a formal letter from the pensions officer. With it was a form asking her to formally agree to the withdrawal of Ronnie's pension.

'The bastards don't waste much time, do they?' she muttered grimly.

'Boss?' Janine said, and Hillary quickly shook her head and shoved the papers away in the back of a drawer. She'd sign the damned forms in her own good time. Make the sods sweat a little.

'Nothing,' she growled, then reached for the phone as it rang, quickly grabbing a pen and notebook as Doc Partridge's mellifluous voice came over the wire.

'Just finished with your French girl. Your constable didn't faint, by the way. But I think he might have turned a little green. With his complexion, it's hard to tell.'

Hillary smiled. There were no racist overtones with Doc Partridge — just a sense of humour that liked to be politically incorrect wherever it could.

'Do you want the full monty?' he asked cheerfully.

'Nope,' she said at once. 'Just the highlights.' Going over the medicalese of the autopsy would be something she could give to Frank when he got back from his wanderings. He hated reading them.

The thought cheered her up no end. She might even ask him for a précis.

'OK. Well, it's interesting,' the pathologist began. 'There was bruising on her back, by the way, as we surmised, fully consistent with a knee being held down against her lower spine.'

So it was murder. At last, official confirmation.

'And the drug of choice was crack cocaine. However, it had another nasty little ingredient.'

Hillary wrote rapidly on the notebook, aware that Janine had come by and was reading over her shoulder.

'You're familiar with Warfarin?' Doc Partridge said, and Hillary paused, nodding, then writing.

'That's rat poison, right? Doctors prescribe it for people with heart problems, or thrombosis and stuff?'

'Well done, DI Greene. Yes, basically it thins the blood. Thus making clotting less likely, hence lowering the risk of one of those clots stopping the heart or going to the lungs, or doing other nasty things.'

Hillary sighed. The doc was in an expansive mood today. 'So you're saying . . . what, exactly? Is it hard to get, this Warfarin?'

'Oh no. Well, not particularly. It's been around for absolutely ages, you know. Thirty-odd years or maybe even more. Most drugs in that time would have been improved upon and long since made obsolete. But some doctors still prefer to prescribe aspirin. The fact that it's been around so long, and is still so popular, is highly unusual, in the field of medicine, I mean. Pharmaceutical companies make millions improving on drugs, as you know.'

Hillary could feel a headache coming on. She could do with some aspirin herself. She wished he'd get on with it, but knew from past experience that trying to hurry him on would only make him dig his heels in harder. 'So anyone could get hold of it,' she chivvied gently.

'Well, that's what's so interesting,' Doc Partridge said, a definite note of excitement in his voice now. 'People couldn't get hold of this particular stuff. Not very easily, anyway. You see, it's not just Warfarin. There's something else mixed with it as well. Do you want me to go into exact chemical formulae?'

'Hell, no!' Hillary yelped, making Janine jump. 'I don't want exact chemical formulae, thanks, Doc, just a general analysis,' she said, by way of explaining to her sergeant her sudden heartfelt reaction.

Janine grinned. 'Doc in a talkative mood, is he?' she whispered, and Hillary rolled her eyes.

'OK. Well, if I had my guess, I'd say this stuff wasn't for use as a medical tool at all. That is, I doubt whether any hospital or doctor would ever prescribe this particular Warfarin for a patient. It strikes me — and the spectro-analyst who ran the tests too, if it interests you at all — that this stuff is strictly experimental.'

Hillary frowned. 'Experimental?'

'Hmm. A chemist, perhaps, buggering about. Or some medical student with a bit of a hard-on when it comes to watching the process of red corpuscles breaking down. Which is what this stuff does, by the way. Your poor French student more or less drowned in her own blood.'

Hillary blanched, and swallowed hard.

No wonder Tommy had turned green.

'I see.'

'Narrows the field down for you, I would have thought, though?' Doc said cheerfully, and Hillary snorted.

'If she'd died in any other city in the UK, maybe. But this is Oxford, Doc,' she pointed out sourly.

Hillary didn't have any idea how many scientific laboratories there were in Oxford. But it had to be a lot.

'Is this super-Warfarin sophisticated stuff?' she asked hopefully. 'I mean, would it require expensive equipment at all? Or could some geek knock some up in a back garage?'

If their experimental druggist had made his own, they might get a line on him through specialist equipment he might have ordered.

The line was silent for a while. Then, 'Hmmm, see what you mean. Yes. Well, technically, whoever manufactured this drug would need basic lab equipment, but nothing off the wall. Nothing exotic. He'd have to know what he was doing, mind — chemistry-wise, he'd have to have either got his degree or maybe be a third year facing finals.'

Hillary groaned. So there'd have been no unusual purchases on the internet, then.

And just how many students with the necessary knowledge could there be in Oxford, right at this moment? Hundreds, probably.

'Time of death is about when we expected,' the doc continued blithely. 'She wasn't pregnant, and had no other health problems otherwise. It'll all be in the report,' he said and, giving further commiserations, hung up.

Hillary leaned back and sighed. Janine, who'd caught most of it, was anxious to talk.

That was one of the good things about Hillary, Janine acknowledged to herself. She didn't mind you batting ideas around. In fact, now that she thought about it, Janine had to admit that she'd learned more about good coppering from Hillary than from any of her previous superiors.

'So Eva had a seventh John, boss? Someone she didn't mention in the book? A chemistry or maybe medical student or graduate?'

Hillary shrugged. 'Could be. But why keep him a secret?'

Janine, still fresh from a sleep over at Mel's, smiled gently. 'Perhaps it wasn't business with this one, boss. Perhaps this was love.'

Hillary frowned thoughtfully as she considered this.

Had love killed Eva Gerainte?

It was possible. Maybe this man was younger, someone who wasn't a business proposition. He might even have come from a titled background. Would a French girl from the provinces consider an English nobleman in a romantic light? Someone to be protected? Someone who could still be hurt by scandal? Thus the need for total secrecy.

Possibly.

And Oxford wasn't short of members of the aristocracy, that was for damned sure.

But even so . . .

'It doesn't strike me as a crime committed for the sake of love,' she said, and caught Janine watching her oddly. She grinned. 'I mean, I've had men in here who've killed their wives by taking a wood chopper to them. They usually put it down to nagging, or something "just snapping". You know, the usual excuses. But they all invariably blubber, and tell me how much they really loved their wives. And probably did.

'I had one woman, once, who killed her husband by hitting him repeatedly over the head with a frying pan, because he said she'd burned his bacon. She said she really loved him too.

'Then you get your young lovers who usually throttle or strangle. Rarer still, you get the gentle Casanovas — those who dose their beloved with something then sit them in the car with the exhaust going and the old hosepipe through the window.

'Some take their wives — and kids too — out for a picnic and drown them one by one, as if they were kittens.'

Janine screwed up her nose, but was listening intently. Had Hillary really had that many murder cases? Well, not where she was SIO, obviously not. But she'd come up through the ranks. She'd been in the force nearly twenty years.

So she knew the ropes.

'Doesn't sound very romantic to me,' she said. 'Not the chopper or the frying pan, anyway.'

'Right. But the thing is, I can't remember a case where someone held down the person they loved, with a knee in the back, and injected tainted coke into their bloodstream.'

Janine shivered. Then said quietly, 'I see what you mean.' There was something very romantic about murdering someone who'd driven you mad with jealousy. Shades of *Othello*, and all that. (Janine had liked English lit. at school.) But the way this Eva girl had died . . .

'It was sort of brutal,' she said out loud.

Hillary, who'd actually once been posted at the scene of a crime where a teenage boy had beaten his mother to death with a sledgehammer, shook her head.

'No, this wasn't brutal,' she said firmly. She knew what brutal was. 'It was . . . cold. Necessary. Somebody wanted this girl dead. And went and killed her. It was . . . emotionless. Yes, that's what keeps striking me. I don't think this killer either loved or hated this girl. She was just a hindrance in some way that had to be removed.'

'Which could still be a secret lover, boss,' Janine pointed out. 'Cold fish still like to get their rocks off. Perhaps our vic tried a bit of blackmail?'

Hillary sighed. 'Could be.'

She glanced around as Tommy Lynch walked in. He didn't look remotely green now.

'Doc Partridge phoned in with the highlights,' she said, before he could speak. 'So no need to go through it again. See if you can raise Frank on the radio — tell him we're looking for someone going after crack. And tell him to concentrate on male buyers this time. Young men — students, or graduates.'

Tommy nodded.

'Mel's late,' Hillary said, but Janine wasn't rising to the bait.

'You'll be wanting to sit in on the second interviews of the Johns, boss?' she said instead.

Hillary nodded. 'Yeah, I think so.'

But none of the Johns seemed to have any connection with the worlds of medicine or chemistry. Surely Warfarin wasn't something freelance journalists, interior decorators or dentists ran across very often? But she supposed a dentist could be described as a sort of medical man. And the old fella, Lambkin, wasn't he something of an academic? She wondered what his subject was. Knowing her luck, it would turn out to be something like the significance of the Celtic cross on Lindisfarne. Or the symbolism of the Cheshire Cat in Lewis Carroll's life and works.

She was just reaching for her coat when Mel finally came in.

Janine watched him head for his office with that little thrill of pride that denotes ownership.

For an older guy he looked really good, she thought smugly. He dressed well, and with real style. He was definitely someone she wouldn't be ashamed to take home to her mother. (Not that she'd ever taken any of her lovers home to her mother.)

Still. At twenty-eight, Janine felt ready for a so-called 'grown-up' relationship. A full-on, commitment-type thing. She didn't want kids yet. Perhaps when she was thirty-one. Or thirty-two. Years off yet. But though she didn't particularly want to get married, something was telling her that it was time to move out of a converted house with three flatmates, and on to something more sophisticated. To a man you thought of in terms of years, not weeks or months. A real, honest-to-goodness, long-term male companion.

And why not Mel? If he got to take over from Superintendent Donleavy, which most people seemed to think he was in line for, he was obviously a man on the way up. It couldn't hurt her own career to be semi-attached to him, so to speak.

And if, after a few years, she found it was time to move on, well, there was such a thing as palimony. Or it might move on in the other direction — marriage and kids.

And that house in the Moors was something else. Like one of those illustrations in a glossy magazine. Come hell or high water, and no matter what kind of a fuss he kicked up, Janine was determined to find herself living there one of these fine days.

* * *

Blissfully oblivious of DS Janine Tyler's long-term plans, Mel looked up as Hillary tapped on his door, and listened without comment as she updated him on the Eva Gerainte case.

'OK, concentrate on the French girl,' he said, when she'd finished, 'but don't let your other cases slide.'

Hillary nodded. She wondered if Mel knew about the pension fiasco. She somehow thought he might, but she was damned if she was going to be the first one to mention it.

She was just heading back to her desk when DI Mike Regis and his silent sidekick put their heads around the door.

'Hey, Hillary,' Mike called, a bright, green-eyed smile lighting up his face. 'I come bearing gifts. Wanna come with us to the interview room?'

Well, what girl could refuse an offer like that? It was better than wine and roses, and Belgian chocolate.

OK. Perhaps not better than the chocolates.

* * *

Downstairs, in interview room twelve, Mike's gift turned out to be a vicious and notorious pimp by the name of Mungo Johns.

CHAPTER 9

Mungo Johns already had his solicitor present. This surprised no one. The Mungo Johns of the world always had a solicitor present. They probably lived with miniature solicitors kept permanently in their back pockets, to be brought out into the daylight as and when needed.

Hillary wondered if miniature solicitors came flat-packed, or if you needed a pump or a battery to operate them . . .

This particular solicitor was female and slightly older than Hillary, with a head of intensely thick, black hair. With it went a long, thin, quivering nose and a broad Scottish accent.

She had all the charm of a rabid mole.

She peered up at them suspiciously through thick-lensed glasses and immediately began the spiel.

Police harassment. Intrusive questioning. The fact that the police had no right to bring her client in. That her client might well exercise his right to silence. And so on and so on.

At least her almost impenetrable accent had the appeal of novelty.

Hillary took her seat, and wondered wearily, and not for the first time, why everybody and their pet toy poodle had rights, but not the police.

The police, according to solicitors like this one, had no rights at all. A maniac comes at you with a knife. You're not supposed to fight back, oh no. You might hurt the poor mentally defective yob with the flick-knife. Facing a riotous mob with Molotov cocktails? Well, what were you doing out on the streets in the first place? Didn't you know pigs belonged in a sty?

Hillary wondered what kind of mind allowed itself to defend poison like Mungo Johns. She herself could never understand such people.

They took their seats and let her wind down. Mike, without fuss, set about introducing them to the tape, scrupulously listing the time, and all those present. He went through everything so fastidiously that by the time he'd finished, even Mungo Johns was looking bored.

The solicitor, Ms Burns, even yawned. The way she elongated every 'r' consonant reminded Hillary of an ancient lawn-mower she used to own. What had happened to it?

'We'd like to ask your client some questions concerning the death of a student of St Anselm's. Her body was found on the morning of the twelfth.' Mike at last got down to the nitty-gritty.

'Has cause of death been established?' the rabid mole asked at once.

Mike demurred. They were still waiting for medical tests to be completed.

In which case, the rabid mole maintained, this interview was precipitously early. She got up to rise. Mungo got up to rise.

Hillary waited. She was used to this dance. She looked up and found the pimp watching her curiously. He was a tall, lean man, with a long, bony face, pale blonde hair and peculiarly colourless eyes. He was young, and looked younger still.

Only his reputation warned how violent and dangerous he could be.

His father had been killed in prison in an argument over a *Sun* pin-up picture with a GBH prisoner named Gruffyd. You'd have thought he'd have known better. The spider tattoo on his opponent's bald head should at least have given Mr Johns, Snr, a broad hint that this wasn't somebody you messed with.

His mother, now dead of cancer, had been a prostitute all her working life. It was she who'd turned her son away from his father's way of thinking, and on to her own. She had used him as protection on the streets since the age of thirteen. He hadn't been particularly big for his age, but he'd been, even then, vicious. He'd served time in juvie for cutting off the tongue of one of his mother's punters.

Now he obligingly took a seat as the rabid mole sighed and rolled her eyes.

The simple truth was, they wanted to know what the cops were after every bit as much as Hillary wanted to know what Mike had up his sleeve.

It was all standard play-acting so far.

'This girl, Eva Gerainte.' Mike pushed a picture of a smiling, happy Eva across the table. They'd got it from a friend of the French girl at college. 'Ever seen her?'

Mungo turned his colourless eyes on to the photograph. It had been taken at a sports event. Eva was wrapped in an oversized football scarf and a bulky winter coat. But not even the British winter could defeat her looks or almost palpable sense of vitality.

Mungo whistled silently. 'Nice. I could have done with her. You know, on a date.'

'You mean in your stable,' Mike corrected, and immediately set off the rabid mole.

There was no evidence that her client had ever been involved in prostitution. This was outrageous slander. They could sue.

Mike batted back a 'living off immoral earnings' beef that had netted Mungo a six-month stretch two years ago.

And so it went on.

Hillary still hadn't spoken. Mungo leaned back in his uncomfortable chair, crossed his arms across his scrawny chest and, from time to time, glanced down at the picture of Eva.

'She's lovely, isn't she?' Hillary said, very quietly, hoping that the rabid mole would be too taken up with sparring with Mike to notice. 'Not your usual run-of-the-mill Tom.'

'I can see,' he said laconically.

'She's French. Or rather was,' Hillary continued softly. 'You can always tell the ones with style. I'll bet she earned more for one bonk than all your girls earn in a single night. Must have made you mad.'

'You saying she was a pro?' Mungo asked, his voice raised in a scandalized squeak.

The rabid mole was on to her in a moment.

'DI Greene, is it? I'd appreciate it if you'd address your remarks to me.'

Hillary looked at the woman. She was in her early fifties, she'd guessed, and was a lot heavier than her well-tailored power dressing dark blue suit implied. Her eyes, behind the lenses, looked enormous and dark. And hostile.

'It's not you I wish to interview, Ms Burns,' Hillary said mildly.

'We have it on good authority that you haven't been happy for some time, Mr Johns,' Mike said, taking the lead once more. 'In fact, we understand that you believe somebody has been undercutting your business.' He tapped the picture of Eva again. 'This girl, and others like her, perhaps?'

That launched the rabid mole into orbit. When enraged, they could only understand about one word in every ten, but the gist was recognisable enough. And one of the things Ms Burns told Mike Regis to do was, surely, a physical impossibility. Even for the double-jointed. She was obviously not the sort to be polite in a police cell.

Mungo Johns smiled at Mike through the tirade, while Hillary wondered how much Mike was guessing, and how much he knew.

If the pimp had known about Eva Gerainte's free-lancing, he wouldn't have liked it. He wouldn't have liked it at all. As far as Mungo was concerned, Oxford was *his* turf. Women who got paid for bonking also paid Mungo. There was no other middleman. Other pimps tended to end up at the John Radcliffe Hospital. Or in the canal. There was certainly no such thing as an independent prostitute.

'That must have really burned you,' Hillary mused. 'An intelligent, attractive foreigner, moving in and setting herself up as the queen of the courtesans. Women like that, women getting ideas above their station — you let it pass and who knows what ideas the other girls in your stable might get?'

Hillary was almost whispering, and beside her, she heard Mike raise his voice a little as he did battle with the rabid mole, trying to give her cover.

No doubt about it, Hillary realised with a real thrill, they worked well together.

'None of my women ever forget who the boss is,' Mungo whispered back.

And Hillary could well believe it.

He let his eyes sweep over her. 'You've got good tits. Big, and the real thing too, I can tell. Course, you're a bit old, but if you want to lay up some extra dosh for yourself, I'll always take you on, darling.'

The rabid mole flushed crimson as she caught this last salacious comment. But not, Hillary was sure, because she felt obliged to feel empathy with her about the insult.

'Mr Johns, I really must advise you against letting yourself be angered by the police,' the solicitor said, and Hillary almost grinned.

Bingo.

Mungo grinned right back. 'Do I look angry?' he asked innocently.

Hillary was on to that in an instant. It wasn't often a copper got fed such good lines.

'But Eva Gerainte made you angry though, didn't she? We've got her diary. She was making over twenty grand a month,' she lied outrageously, and had the pleasure of watching his eyes narrow. 'Money like that . . .' She blew out her lips in a soundless whistle.

'Bollocks,' Mungo said flatly.

Hillary shrugged. 'If you say so,' she said mildly.

'Of course, the earnings of a prostitute are of no interest to my client,' the rabid mole said primly.

At that, Mike Regis laughed uproariously. Even Mungo Johns smiled.

'I never saw the girl before,' Mungo said flatly, and ignored the warning look his solicitor shot him. 'So if this is all you have . . .' He put his hands flat on the desk, and Hillary noticed the criss-cross white scars on the back of his knuckles.

Had someone slashed him with razor blades? The wounds looked old.

'What were you doing on the night of the eleventh, Mr Johns?' Mike said grimly, the menace in his voice making even Hillary's hackles rise.

She saw the muscle in the side of the pimp's jaw clench in reaction. Because he had such a bony face, it had been impossible to miss, but then, instantly, all expression was wiped from his face.

She felt Mike quiver, like a hunting dog spotting a falling pheasant, and knew just how he felt. She, too, was tingling all over.

That question had definitely shaken the pimp.

'The eleventh?' he drawled. 'Who knows? Who cares? This interview is over.'

'If you have nothing to hide . . .' Mike said, getting up too. The rabid mole was gathering her stuff together.

'You heard my client, DI Regis.' The thick Scottish voice dripped satisfaction.

'Why not just tell us where you were? It was only three nights ago, Mungo. Surely your memory can stretch—'

'DI Regis! I said this interview is terrrrrrrminated. For the record I'd like to register . . .'

Hillary tuned out as the rabid mole registered a whole battery of complaints. Mungo Johns said not another word.

Regis watched the door close behind them, then sat down. He calmly dealt with the tape and switched it off.

In the electric silence, Hillary slowly rubbed the side of her face.

'Our number one suspect?' Mike asked curiously.

Hillary sighed. 'Depends. Do you have any real reason to suppose he knew about Eva Gerainte?'

Mike spread his hands helplessly. 'Yes and no. We've got an undercover officer close to Mungo's operation. He told us something was definitely going down. We know Johns is up to something. But our agent isn't nearly trusted enough yet to be let in on it.'

Hillary sighed. 'Would just one independent be worth all this hassle, though? If Johns knew about Eva, why not just take her aside, rough her up and bring her into line.'

Mike nodded. 'Perhaps he'd already tried and she wasn't having any. Or maybe Eva isn't the only independent involved.'

Hillary snorted. 'I can't see her running her own stable, Mike,' she said. Then paused.

No, Eva might not have wanted to bother. She had far more different, more glamorous plans of her own. But what about someone else?

Pretty, clever but financially strapped female students made ideal high-class call girls. They gave discerning punters a class product, and students nowadays were always short of cash.

'You're thinking that some enterprising entrepreneur might be putting their studies of economics to a more practical use, you mean?' Hillary mused cautiously.

'It might not necessarily be a student,' Mike pointed out.

Hillary smiled. 'You're thinking some dusty don has a side-line in bordellos?' She laughed. 'I can't see it, somehow.'

So why did a picture of Molly Fairbanks immediately leap into her mind?

No, Tommy had run a financial check on her. She wasn't running a string of call girls.

And yet, now that she came to think about, someone like Molly Fairbanks would be in an ideal situation to become a madam. She'd know which girls were poor enough to be needy. And which girls, like Eva, would be sophisticated and cosmopolitan enough to regard the whole thing either as a good rag or as a purely business-like way of earning easy money. And she'd know the other end too — how many bored, lonely, middle-aged, wealthy men would a woman like Molly know?

Enough.

Yes. Molly Fairbanks would make an ideal madam.

'If Mungo *was* aware of a high-end invasion into his market, he wouldn't be a happy bunny,' Mike pointed out. 'There's good money to be had from expensive Toms.'

Hillary sighed. 'Getting a bit ahead of ourselves, aren't we? We've got one dead student, who happened to be making some money hooking.'

'And one pimp who's very antsy about what he was doing on the night of her death, and who we've reason to believe is up to something,' Mike pointed out reasonably.

Hillary nodded. 'Well, that's your day sorted out,' she said cheerfully. 'You take Mungo, and I'll concentrate on Eva's other Johns.'

Mike nodded and caught her gaze. Slowly he smiled. 'Sounds fair to me,' he said softly.

Hillary nodded, her mouth suddenly dry.

Had he been flirting with her just then? Or was she going off her trolley?

* * *

Back in her office, she had a load of faxes waiting for her from the French police at Lille. They contained lots of background details, but nothing helpful. Eva's parents had landed in London yesterday, and one of the uniforms had met them and set them up in a B&B in Summertown.

So far, they hadn't asked to meet the detective in charge, although they had been to the college.

She hadn't envied Dr Havering *that* interview.

Soon, she knew, it would be her turn to speak to them — when grief turned to anger and a demand for action and results.

But, according to the papers in front of her, it seemed unlikely that Eva had made any enemies in France, let alone an enemy determined enough to follow her to Oxford and kill her. Apart from her aggressive ambition and a slight tendency to teenage arrogance that had got up some people's noses, Eva Gerainte was a model citizen.

Not that Hillary had expected anything different. She sighed and pushed the results aside.

'I want you and Tommy to try and track down this experimental Warfarin angle,' she said, and pretended not to hear Janine groan. 'Start with the pharmaceutical companies. Then try individual labs. This is Oxford — if somebody is experimenting with rat poison, somebody else will know about it, of that you can be sure. You know academics.'

Janine did. Julius Caesar might have been said to suffer from the old knives-in-the-back routine, but that was nothing compared to the way academics spied and gossiped on their own leading lights. And eagerly sold them down the river.

'But first, let me have the address of Lambkin. I'll start with him. I'll be out interviewing the Johns all day if you need me.'

Her sergeant handed over the list of addresses, along with her and Tommy's own reports of the interviews.

Janine watched her go, wondering why she'd chosen Lambkin first. She'd worked with the DI long enough to know that Hillary never did anything without a good reason.

Frowning, she mentally went over their conversation about all six of Eva Gerainte's Johns.

What had DI Greene heard in Tommy's summation that she'd missed?

* * *

Hillary turned up the heater of her old Volkswagen, with little result, before pulling out of the car park and heading north.

She was glad to be getting out of the office, even if a grey drizzle had settled gloomily over the landscape. She flicked on the windscreen wipers and watched the skeletal trees go past her windows.

Just the sense of movement was comforting.

Marcus Gagingwell, aka Lambkin, lived in a small hamlet called Caulcott, not too far from Bicester. As she drove, and shivered, and turned up the heater yet again, she wondered how long it would be before the first spring lambs put in an appearance. Or the first snowdrop? The first crocus or daffodil?

At the moment, winter seemed set to last for ever.

She braked for a grey squirrel, which shot across the mud-caked road in front of her and scarpered under a gatepost. She doubted if the farmer, whose tractor had left all that mud on the road, would have bothered to do the same. Out in the sticks, grey squirrels were vermin.

Hillary, more used to the friendly squirrels of Worcester College — where she sometimes spent the odd few hours or lunch break, proximity allowing — changed down a gear and proceeded more slowly. She'd turned off down a narrow track after leaving the village of Kirtlington behind in her rear-view mirror, and suddenly realised she was on the site of an old Roman road.

She'd read about this particular stretch of road many years ago now. Locals still dug up the odd Roman coin in their compost heaps, even to this day.

But the small stretch of straight road soon gave way to the smell and sounds of a pig farm, and then a sharp right-hand bend. Small, old, renovated cottages straggled out on either side of her, and a ditch (or, if you wanted to be picturesque, a roadside stream) looked in imminent danger of flooding off to her left.

Marcus Gagingwell's cottage, 'Merewater,' was on the left, by an old weeping willow. She parked on a tiny strip of grass verge and hoped no tractors would be passing by. The village road was as narrow as her old granny's mind.

She pushed through a white-painted gate and up a small, flagged path. The cottage garden looked as if it would be spectacular in the summer. Even now, its rose bushes had been harshly pruned, leaf mould had been widely spread, evergreens were neatly clipped and bare bushes promised frothy coloured blooms later on. A keen gardener had been at work here.

At least the problem of keeping up a garden was something she didn't have to worry about, living on the *Mollern*.

She rang the doorbell and was answered almost immediately.

The man in the doorway could only be Lambkin. Fluffy white hair haloed a head that looked as silly as that

116

of any sheep. Watery, greeny-blue eyes (thankfully without a sheep's vertically slitted pupil) looked her over. He could have been any age from an old-before-his-time fifty-five to a well-preserved eighty-five.

He was dressed in baggy grey trousers and a baggy grey cardigan. Pink gums were revealed when he gave her a winsome smile. (Pity about the missing back teeth.)

The old geezer seemed to like what he saw, and Hillary fought back a smile. Being complimented by a vicious pimp and a randy old man, all in a matter of a few hours, could turn a girl's head.

'Mr Gagingwell?' She showed him her identification.

'A detective inspector? Well, well, a marked improvement on a mere constable. Come in, come in. Would you like some homemade cowslip wine?'

Hillary wouldn't. Hillary definitely wouldn't. She'd been had like that before. Some fifteen years ago, a fluffy-voiced sub-postmistress had offered her some damson wine.

It had very nearly taken off the top of her head. She could still remember the morning after, even now.

She followed the old man into a library-cum-study where a real fire glowed winningly in a hearth. She let him make her a cup of tea instead, and settled herself in front of the fire. A cat, asleep on the opposite chair, raised its big ginger head, stared at her for a second, then went back to sleep. Outside, some sparrows argued noisily in a winter-flowering jasmine bush.

It was like a different world.

She inspected the books with some interest. They were all on insects.

She sighed heavily. So much for Lambkin being a medical or chemistry buff. She supposed it had been too much to hope for.

Lambkin came back with a genuine nineteenth-century Worcester cup-and-saucer tea service.

The tea was the kind that came in a bag.

Ah well.

'You've come about Eva, I suppose. Lovely girl. She shouldn't be dead.'

Hillary nodded. It wasn't much of an epitaph, she thought, and then wondered. Perhaps it would be more of an epitaph than she'd ever get herself?

'You seem interested in insects, Mr Gagingwell,' she said, surprising the old man, who'd been expecting to be grilled about his peccadilloes. Who'd maybe been looking *forward* to being grilled about his peccadilloes?

If she were an old widower, living in this idyllic rural retirement, she might like the chance to play the old roué too.

'Oh yes. Dragonflies, especially. They were around before the dinosaurs, you know. Ancient things. I've made a study of them for over fifty years. I have three books published on the subject.' He got up and retrieved them. They looked to be as dry as dust, with small print and not even the odd photograph of a jewel-like subject to enliven the text. The latest one, she'd noticed, had been published way back in 1972.

Hillary nodded and looked around. 'You don't happen to have a laboratory, do you, Mr Gagingwell? For your more scientific studies of their anatomy?'

'Oh no. No, I didn't go in for that end of it much. The scientific side of it, I mean. I was more into habitat and behaviour. My survey of dragonfly numbers on one particular lake in West Dorset was one of the first early warnings we had about the perils of DDT, you know.'

He sounded so proud. Hillary wondered if Eva had complimented him on his past glories. She hoped she had.

'You did the chemistry analysis of those flies your-self?' she asked sharply, but already the old man was shaking his head.

'Oh no. Some fellows from the Ministry of Agriculture, Food and Fisheries did all that.'

Hillary sighed. Then scowled. DDT? Wasn't all that a big issue in the sixties and seventies?

She looked around at what was obviously a small, cosy retirement cottage, and knew that Lambkin's days as any kind of serious academic were long gone.

And even then, he'd obviously been one of those dying breed of 'gentlemen' entomologists, who were no doubt very dedicated and meticulous, but strictly in the 'amateur' league.

Just to cheer him up, she let him tell her all about his time with Eva, and play the shame-faced degenerate old man to the hilt. He used to drive to Oxford once a month, he assured her, where they spent an hour or so at Eva's Botley flat, trying out various positions from the *Kama Sutra*.

She guessed that, more often than not, he'd simply watched the girl striptease, then helped her eat the chocolates, or drink the wine he brought, or like as not play chess.

She sensed a genuine affection for the dead girl, and a real sadness that this last little bit of life had now been denied to him as well.

Goodbye to the *vida loca*.

Hillary left the old reprobate to his real fire, his cat and his lustful memories.

And mentally crossed him off her list.

Next up — Red Rum. After him, if she had time, Frankie A.

CHAPTER 10

Jamie Prospect, aka Red Rum, was busy fitting new, brightly shining white dental caps on to a wannabe pop star, who was due to start filming a reality TV show in four weeks' time, and couldn't possibly be disturbed.

This was not quite how the dentist's receptionist phrased it, of course.

'Well, do you have any idea when he'll be free?' Hillary asked, letting her eyes wander guiltily over posters of anonymous pearly whites chomping down into hard-looking green apples.

When exactly *was* it that she'd last been to the dentist? Five years ago? Six? She only ever went when something began to hurt.

As she waited for the receptionist (a woman with teeth like tombstones) to check, she could feel a molar in her upper back jaw twinge ominously. No doubt as a result of the power of positive thinking. Or in this case, negative thinking.

'I'm afraid he's booked right through solid until five o'clock, Inspector Greene.'

'Well, if you'd tell Mr Prospect that I'll be calling around at his private residence later on, I'd appreciate it,' Hillary said. Meaning, he'd better be in. Or else.

She managed a smile that adequately conveyed the sub-text, and left, trying to pretend that she couldn't hear the sound of drilling, or smell the smell of whatever that foul pink stuff was that you rinsed your mouth out with, after a session. Whenever she visited such places, that scene from *Marathon Man*, with Dustin Hoffman and Laurence Olivier, kept running through her head. She got in the car and checked her notes. She'd missed lunch, and was still trying to pretend that that was a *good* thing. Of course, her stomach kept up a rumbling running commentary to the contrary, but she was willing to swear she could almost hear her fat cells thanking her.

Perhaps, if she passed a shop, she'd buy an apple.

Her back molar twinged.

Then again, maybe not.

* * *

Frankie A, alias Michael Bolder, lived in a converted mill house in a tiny hamlet that didn't even have a name on the map.

As she turned off down a narrow, hawthorn-lined lane, the sun came out briefly from behind a lowering grey sky and shone on a herd of cattle, grazing in the meadow. The river running through it looked dangerously swollen, and she hoped the farmer would be moving them soon. Many areas of the Cherwell Valley flooded in the winter.

She went over a viciously humped-back bridge, and felt her stomach do that curious, tickling leap on the other side. And there was the mill house.

It looked old, with a low slate roof, mellow Cotswold stone, and rows of small, mullioned windows. A stationary wooden mill wheel was still attached to the side of the house where a mill race gurgled and churned. As she got out of the car, a hedge sparrow sang its usual surprisingly sweet song from the depths of a weeping willow tree.

Hillary looked at the property with naked envy. Then the sun went back in, and everything looked bleak and grey once more.

She knocked on what looked like a genuine oak front door, noting the brass mermaid's head knocker.

Of course. 'Frankie A' was an interior decorator.

The door opened to reveal a good-looking man in his mid-forties. Thick dark hair hung well past his ears to brush his collar. He had level grey eyes under dark brows, and a strong line from nose to chin. He was wearing a plain white shirt and tight-fitting jeans.

Hillary smiled and introduced herself. He looked surprised.

'I thought you always came in twos,' he said, standing aside to let her in.

Hillary nodded. 'Usually we do.' And Mel, for one, would have a fit if he knew she was out interviewing suspects without Tommy or Janine (or even, at a pinch, Frank) along for backup. But what he didn't know wouldn't hurt him.

'It's about Eva, of course?'

Hillary nodded. The man had an accentless voice, neither arty/crafty, nor cockney/mockery.

She looked around the hall, curious to see how an interior designer decorated their own home.

All was wood — high stained-glass windows let coloured light filter down on to a sweeping banister, and a curved set of uncarpeted stairs. She was reminded of an old country church. She could even smell beeswax.

But the room was warm. Under-floor heating? Very nice.

'Come on through to the lounge,' Michael Bolder said, pushing open a door and standing aside for her to follow.

When she did, Hillary felt her breath catch.

Now *here* was the residence of an interior designer.

One whole side of the room was pure glass. One part of her mind wondered how on earth he had managed to get planning permission for that, while the other simply gibbered. For this glass wall overlooked the mill race, a well-tended garden, and an old red-brick bridge that swept over the water and into the field of grazing cattle. A line of weeping willows hung their pale, as yet leafless, twigs to the river's edge.

She found herself drawn to the vista like a magnet, then, on hearing the sudden echoing hollow tap of her heels, looked down and gulped.

She was standing on yet more glass. Moreover, a glass floor that was, she realised, actually positioned *over* the water. Underneath her, the mill race rushed on its way to the pond, which she guessed would be on the other side of the property.

It probably had swans on it. Black swans.

'It's stunning,' she said flatly. Then felt compelled to add, 'But since I live on a boat, I'm used to it.' She heard herself say this last sentence with something close to amazement.

Was she really that petty? This man had created a stunning room of pale apricot, mint-green and cream, with two amazing features. Why not simply admit it?

On the other hand, she couldn't help but feel a rush of satisfaction as the handsome interior designer perked up, giving her a second, distinctly interested gaze.

'Really? A narrowboat?'

Hillary nodded.

'I was thinking of buying one of those. You know, for a mobile holiday home.'

Hillary shrugged. It was undeniably the gesture of the sophisticated seasoned boat-dweller for the whims of a mere dabbling amateur.

Since when had she become a boatie? Usually she cursed the *Mollern* up and down, whenever she thought of it. Now here she was, actually feeling proud of the damn hunk of floating wood.

Pulling herself together, she took a seat and pulled out her notebook. She had a photocopy of Eva's journal in her bag, and as she looked at it, she saw once again the moon symbol she'd pencilled in beside her last encounter with this man.

'Do you happen to know what this moon symbol means, Mr Bolder?' she asked, being careful to fold the paper, and put her thumb over the writing still visible. 'Eva made it.'

Michael Bolder came closer, bringing with him a whiff of expensive cologne. He looked down. 'No, sorry.'

Hillary nodded. She hadn't really expected anything else. Nor could she understand why she had a niggling idea it might be relevant.

'How long had you known Eva Gerainte, Mr Bolder?' she began calmly.

Michael Bolder sat on the black leather settee facing the matching armchair Hillary had chosen. A few feet away, under the floor, the river rushed on. A genuinely old grandfather clock ticked solemnly on the wall facing her. 'We met last summer. At one of those May Day dos in Oxford. You know, idiots jumping into the river, that sort of thing.'

Hillary nodded. He was lying. He had to be. May Day in Oxford was chaotic. And strictly for the students and, occasionally, the tourists. This man was neither.

So he wasn't saying how they met. What else might he lie about?

'And how did you come to your arrangement?' she asked, with what she thought was great delicacy.

'You mean, how did I come to be paying her for sex?' Michael Bolder said, with a laugh. 'Simple. Eva came straight out and said what she was doing, and was I interested? And after a night in her company, which was vivacious, astringent and refreshing, I had no hesitation in saying yes.'

Hillary nodded. A *night* in her company? May Day festivities began early in the morning. So he *was* lying. It was always nice to have confirmation that her bullshit meter was still in good working order.

Had he met her in a bar? A jazz club? A private party? Or had one of her other regulars told him about her? But if he knew any of the other men, she couldn't see him admitting it. Not now he'd spun her *this* fairy story.

'I see. And you met regularly?'

'Yes, but not to any strict pattern,' Michael said, casually crossing his legs at the ankle. 'I wasn't down for Tuesdays and Saturdays, or whatever. I travel about a lot, for one thing. For two months last autumn I was in Scotland, for instance, helping with the conversion of an old manor house to a top-of-the-range hotel. I didn't see her at all then. When I got back, I saw her three nights running.'

Hillary smiled. Very athletic of you, I'm sure.

'And you never argued?'

'Oh yes, all the time. About art, about modern cinema, about books. And fashion. She was really passionate about fashion. That was her thing.'

He grinned in remembrance, then slowly frowned. 'I still can't believe that she's dead. She was the sort of girl you expected to live for ever. You know, the kind of game old bird who'd become a grande dame, scandalizing her grandchildren by taking a gigolo at eighty, and doing the Cresta Run.'

Hillary nodded. She knew just what he meant. 'Did she ever talk about anyone bothering her? Phone calls, anonymous flower deliveries? That kind of thing?'

'A stalker? No.'

Again Hillary nodded and looked long and hard at the man, trying to get some sort of insight. All this casual help-fulness, she was sure, was nothing more than a front. But a front for what? Nothing necessarily sinister. Most people played some sort of role for the police, even the innocent. Sometimes, *especially* the innocent. This was something she'd learned very early on.

This John was one of those with an alibi for the night Eva died, she remembered. A neighbour had dropped by with a bottle. But there was no point in bringing that up until it had been confirmed. And she felt sure it would be. Michael Bolder might be an accomplished liar, but she felt sure he wasn't stupid. Certainly not stupid enough to lie about something that could be so easily checked out.

'Did Eva have a pet name for you, Mr Bolder?' she asked curiously.

'What? Pooh Bear or something like that?' he laughed. 'Hell, no. That wasn't her style.'

'So you have no idea why she referred to you in her diary as "Frankie A"?'

If he found the idea of being described in intimate detail in his call-girl's diary as either worrying or embarrassing, he certainly hid it well.

'No. No, I can't,' he said simply.

'Your middle name isn't Frank?'

'No.'

She was beginning to find his helpful brevity annoying.

'Did you like Eva?' she asked flatly, but if she'd hoped to surprise him out of his irksome composure, she failed.

He simply thought about it, then nodded. 'Yes. I did.'

Narked, Hillary said bluntly, 'Was she really very good in bed?'

He simply thought about it, then nodded. 'Yes, she was.'

Hillary wryly acknowledged the one-upmanship, and sighed. 'We're treating this case as a murder inquiry, Mr Bolder.'

And that shook him.

You could see the shock wave hit him. Not that there were any protestations, or blusters, or even tears. But it stunned him, nonetheless.

And bang goes suspect number two, Hillary thought grimly. First Lambkin turned out to be nothing more than a charming, harmless, dirty old man. Now Frankie A didn't even realise she'd been deliberately killed.

So what had he thought? Death through natural causes? He'd surely have known her well enough to discount suicide.

'I didn't realise that,' he said instead. Then added simply, 'I didn't kill her.'

And Hillary believed him.

* * *

She left the mill house, with its perfect decor and underground heating and under-floor stream, and headed back to town.

Liberace was to be found in his office, with ne'er a candelabra in sight. There were, though, lots of lorries. Lorries coming in, lorries going out. Lorries full, lorries empty. The smell of petrol and diesel. Muddy forecourt. Muddy rear parking area.

A haulage company's Portacabin office in Abingdon was about as far from the mill house as you could get.

And Philip Cox was as far from Michael Bolder as you could get too.

He looked older than his fifty-two years. He was running to fat, and hadn't yet got around to buying his trousers a size bigger, so his gut simply hung over a belt that looked excruciatingly tight. His hair was thinning, and you could see how he'd changed its style recently in an attempt to brush it over and cover the bald patch. When his secretary ushered Hillary in, he immediately began to sweat. The skin of his face had the high pink look that pigs got if they stayed out in the sunshine too long.

He looked like a heart attack waiting to happen.

Hillary privately thought that Eva had earned her money with this one.

Then felt immediately ashamed.

'I didn't kill her,' Philip Cox squeaked, the moment Hillary sat down. He did indeed have a mincing voice, with that kind of endearing camp tone to it, which the famous pianist had made his trademark.

'What makes you think she was killed, Mr Cox?' Hillary immediately demanded.

It utterly wrong-footed him, as it was meant to.

'Well, I mean, it's been days now, and you're still asking questions. I mean, it's obvious something's up. Was it drugs?'

Hillary sighed. 'Did Eva take drugs during any of your, er, sessions, Mr Cox?'

'No!' His voice quavered somewhere up in the high C range. 'I mean, of course not. I'm not into that sort of thing. I've got a wife, and three kids. My wife is head of the WI branch here!'

No. You weren't into drugs, but you *were* into call girls. Hillary gave a mental shrug. She wasn't here to police anybody's sins. She was here to find out who killed Eva and why.

She went briskly through the same questions as she had with Michael Bolder and got the same results. When she'd finished, the man looked like a nervous wreck.

'You won't have to tell my wife about any of this, will you?' he asked, sweating so hard now that Hillary was tempted to get up and open the window and let in some cold winter air.

'We'll have to ask her to confirm your whereabouts on the night in question, Mr Cox,' she said firmly.

'Yes, but you don't have to tell her why, do you? I mean, you could say that it was just regular inquiries, like. I could tell her there'd been a break-in at the office, someone siphoning off petrol or something. That's always a problem.'

Hillary smiled wryly. If his wife was anything like the leaders of the WI that she knew from her mother's day, then Mrs Cox probably already knew everything there was to know about her husband's little ways.

She could see this man acting in panic, if Eva had threatened to tell his wife, say. He might just have lashed out with something, then panicked and run off.

But why would Eva ever threaten him, or any of her Johns, for that matter? That wouldn't have been her way. She'd have played the game, the way it was supposed to be played. Mutual benefit for all, and no bones broken.

Besides, Eva hadn't been killed in panic. Eva had been killed by someone who'd coolly gone to her room, prepared and ready.

Even though she knew in her bones that she was wasting her time, she nevertheless thoroughly grilled him, then left him sweating into his handkerchief.

His secretary smiled at her knowingly on the way out. She probably knew all about Eva as well. She looked the type.

Hell, scratch three. At this rate, she was going to cross off all of Eva's Johns from her list.

Perhaps Mike was on to the right man, after all. And that suited her just fine.

It would give them both no end of pleasure to introduce Mungo Johns to one of Her Majesty's higher-security domiciles.

* * *

When she got back to her car, her mobile started to ring. She slid in behind the wheel, wincing as an eighteen-wheeler trundled by.

'Hillary?'

For a moment, she didn't recognise the voice. It wasn't somebody from work.

'Graham here. I've contacted the solicitors working for your Animal Army friends.'

Hillary transferred the phone to her other ear and started the car. She turned the heater up.

It made no difference.

She hoisted the phone back to her favoured ear, and sighed. 'That was quick.'

Solicitors didn't usually work that quick. Unless they were doing a friend a favour and didn't expect to get paid the full whack. Then they didn't mess about. Time was money, and all that.

'Yes, it's not good news, I'm afraid. I think they're seriously serious.'

Hillary blinked. 'Can you translate that?'

'Sure. Some charities, especially the more spurious ones, are in it for a quick buck. They're willing to compromise, to cut and run, yeah?'

Hillary nodded. 'Oh yeah,' she said wearily. She knew all about those.

'Other charities are founded by the bleeding heart types. The dedicated sort. These are the kind who are on a crusade. They stick their fangs in and don't let go.'

She felt her heart sink. 'Don't tell me . . .'

'Huh-huh.' Graham sounded infuriatingly cheerful. 'According to the firm representing them, they're really out for blood. These people are hard-line animal lovers, and hold a special kind of hatred in their hearts for poachers and corrupt officials. They'd shoot the ivory poachers on sight, given the chance, as well as those who make money out of it on the other end. Well, out in the African bush, according to rumour, they very often *do* shoot the poachers. And some officials as well, if the rate of "unsolved fatal muggings" in Mombasa and so on are any indication. Over here, of course, their English branch have to stick to more legal means. And seeing as Ronnie is dead, and can't be got at, they've got their sights set on you. Or rather, on any asset in Ronnie's name. Being the cunning bugger that he was, that's only the house. And he only did *that* so you couldn't get your hands on it in the divorce.'

Hillary groaned. None of this was news to her, of course. 'You're telling me it's going to court, aren't you?' she said flatly.

'Yup. Sorry. The order to prevent you selling the house until the lawsuit is settled is already in the mail. They've also applied to the county court for a trial date. I thought I'd better give you a heads up.'

'That was quick too,' Hillary said bitterly. What was it with lawyers? You caught a murdering rapist who'd tortured an eighty-year-old woman, and they dragged their feet and tossed about delaying tactics as if they were confetti in order to keep the evil bastard from standing trial.

But a civil case that might see her home taken away from her — hell, let's get things done and dusted by the end of the week.

She swore. Long and low and with feeling.

'Isn't that a crime?' Graham's voice, still unerringly cheerful, cut across the tirade. 'You ought to watch out for that, Inspector Greene. Some little old lady overhearing you could sue you for mental and emotional stress.'

Hillary had to laugh. 'Don't say that! With the way my luck's been going lately, they just might!' And because he was her solicitor, and she wouldn't (hopefully) be paying him for his time anyway, she told him about Ronnie's pension being denied to her. And her reasons for not trying to fight against the ruling.

'You are going through the wars, aren't you?' Graham said, sounding, to be fair, a little less cheerful. 'Still, you've always got the boat, haven't you?'

Hillary felt like screaming. Well, no, in fact, she didn't have the boat. The *Mollern* still officially belonged to her uncle. He was being very sweet and patient letting her live in it, rent free, for so long.

Besides, she didn't *want* the bloody boat. She wanted her house back.

She agreed glumly that she'd like Graham to represent her in the case, and tried to beat him down to a no-win, no-fee payment scheme. She didn't succeed, of course. Friend or no friend, Graham was still of the same species as the rabid mole.

* * *

It was getting dark as she pulled into the HQ parking lot, but it wasn't yet four. Hillary had hours of paperwork stacked up, and she still had Red Rum to see before she could call it a day.

She was feeling fed up and put upon as she walked across to her desk and shrugged off her coat.

The case was going nowhere fast, she was about to be hauled into court to fight for her own damned house, Janine and Tommy weren't getting anywhere on chasing down dodgy Warfarin, by the looks of it, and Frank was back. And whining.

'What is this?' she muttered to herself, as she leaned back wearily in her chair. Was it officially 'Get Hillary Greene Week' and nobody had thought to tell her?

Had she somehow pissed off fate?

Had she lived the high life in a previous existence, and was now reaping the negative karma in this one?

Had she broken a mirror and not realised?

Surely this string of bad luck would have to bottom out soon. This was taking the mickey too far.

'Bloody hell, look who it is,' she heard Janine drawl in genuine surprise, and when she looked up and saw a familiar, blond-haired figure heading straight for her, mouth smiling, blue eyes sweeping over her from head to foot, she knew it for sure.

It was now official.

Somebody was *definitely* taking the piss.

CHAPTER 11

'Well, well, well, if it isn't the return of the Yorkie Bars,' Janine drawled, and Frank nearly broke his neck looking up and around.

A strange look crossed his face. It was as if his features didn't know whether to show alarm, caution or sheer delight.

But Hillary had no trouble gauging the reasons behind all three. Alarm because the man now approaching, beaming his Adonis smile on one and all, was none other than DI Paul Danvers, one of two officers from Yorkshire who'd been assigned to investigate Ronnie Greene's corruption case. Hence, he'd been one of the men responsible for officially labelling her nearly ex, and totally late, husband a bent copper.

Being Ronnie's best crony, and almost certainly in on his bent dealings with animal parts smugglers, Frank was not happy to see him back.

Thus the alarm.

As far as he knew, DI Danvers, and Sergeant Smith, his fellow investigating officer, had found no proof of Frank Ross's involvement. But, as with all internal investigations, your fat was never truly out of the fire. Old embers could be raked up at any time.

Hence the caution.

And the sheer delight, of course, was due to the fact that DI Danvers might just be here to make Hillary's life a living hell, all over again.

'Or should I say, just one Yorkie Bar,' Janine amended, noticing the absence of the taciturn, older sergeant who usually accompanied him.

'Sergeant Tyler, isn't it?' Paul Danvers said, nodding her way. He was a tall, blond man, good-looking in an understated way. Mid-thirties, unmarried.

Janine thought it a great pity he was the enemy.

'DI Danvers,' Hillary said dryly. Over by his computer, Tommy could feel a cramp start low down in the pit of his stomach, and surreptitiously eased himself around in his chair.

He had never doubted that Hillary had been oblivious to what her old man was up to, and he didn't doubt it now. So why had this particularly bad penny turned up again?

'New evidence in my husband's case?' Hillary demanded coldly, taking the bull by the horns, and asking the single question that everyone else had wanted to ask, but hadn't dared.

The rest of the CID room had become curiously quiet.

'Oh no. Nothing like that, DI Greene,' Paul Danvers assured her. 'Besides, I was seconded to that investigation. Once it was over, I went back to my original patch.'

Frank let out a long, slow breath of relief.

Tommy rubbed his stomach meditatively, while Janine wondered how his colleagues had felt about that. True, they probably hadn't known the officers involved down here in Thames Valley. But nobody liked to be around someone who'd investigated one of their own, even if the main target was already safely dead and buried.

'So what brings you here?' Hillary asked bluntly, and Paul Danvers, holding her gaze firmly, shrugged, smiled and said simply, 'A transfer.'

It took a second for it to register.

A transfer.

He was here permanently.

Over at his desk, Tommy felt his cramp come back with a vengeance. Janine whistled silently through her teeth, and looked at Hillary speculatively. She'd often wondered, in the past, if DI Danvers hadn't had a 'thing' for the woman he was investigating. She'd dismissed it at the time as ludicrous. The man was what, six, seven years younger? Besides, he was gorgeous, in a certain kind of way. Still, there was definitely something there. A spark. And she could feel it now. Just look at the way Danvers was watching her, for instance.

Janine looked at her boss and tried to see her objectively, as an unattached male might. She was good-looking enough, Janine supposed. Nothing to write home about, but her hair was good — naturally thick and shiny, but brown of course.

She refrained from touching her own golden locks.

And the DI had a figure, of sorts. Too curvaceous to be trendy, too much Jane Russell and not enough Kate Moss. Still, some men went for that look.

Hillary was wearing her usual suit. In this case, a dark blue skirt and jacket, with a plain white blouse. Her legs were good, even if the sensible shoes were a real turn-off.

Still, she couldn't see why a catch like Paul Danvers would transfer from Yorkshire to here just for her.

So why had he? What was in the wind?

Any police station was a hotbed of gossip and politics. Who was sleeping with who. Who had a finger in what pie. And a little inner voice was telling the blonde sergeant that something was going on.

'Is Mel in?' Danvers asked, and the familiar use of her lover's name made Janine grit her teeth. Who did this prat think he was?

'DCI Mallow is in his office, sir,' Janine said, ever so sweetly.

Hillary's lips twitched. Someone should warn the new boy that Janine and Mel were an item. He could make a serious gaffe if he didn't realise that in time.

Somebody really should tell him. It was only fair.

She firmed her own lips even tighter together, and turned to the pile of paperwork on her desk.

Watching the retreating figure, Janine sighed. 'Now what do you suppose this means?'

Hillary didn't even want to think about it. Had they got new evidence on Ronnie's hidden stash? Did they suspect she knew its whereabouts? Dammit, why hadn't she turned it in by now?

'Do you think it's got anything to do with Donleavy being booted upstairs?' her sergeant mused.

At this, Hillary looked up from her report in genuine surprise, and over in his corner, she noticed Frank's ears twitching.

'I mean, if Donleavy gets booted up, Mel might get Donleavy's spot, which'll leave us with a DCI position vacant,' Janine explained, in full flow now. 'Do you think there's been a bit of argy-bargy going on?'

Normally, of course, there was fierce competition for promotion and there were supposedly all sorts of safeguards in place to ensure fair and equitable opportunities for all. Naturally, it didn't always work out that way. Just because Hillary fancied her chances of getting a promotion to detective chief inspector didn't mean it was even on the cards. And if there'd been a deal done somewhere, she might just as well whistle in the wind.

Still, it irked her. Had Paul Danvers agreed to investigate Ronnie in return for a promotion and a transfer down south? It didn't totally make sense. Unless he'd wanted to leave Yorkshire for some time, of course.

Thames Valley might be regarded as a better area by some.

Or he might still be investigating Ronnie's case on the sly.

'Well, we'll find out soon enough,' she said glumly. For instance, if there was a raid on her boat, and her Dick Francis book was confiscated, and the money removed from Ronnie's account.

If she was even right about the book being the clue to Ronnie's stash in the first place, that is. For all she knew, she might have got it all wrong. Why hadn't she checked it out? At least then she'd know, one way or another.

But something had held her back from making that final commitment. As things stood now, she'd only *guessed* that the book was the key to Ronnie's dirty money. If she were to check it out, then that would mean that she'd actually *know*. And knowing something wasn't the same as merely speculating.

Was it?

But would she ever be able to convince anyone she'd never known about the book until long after Ronnie's death?

It seemed unlikely.

Hillary could feel an uncomfortable trickle of sweat rolling down from her temple and surreptitiously wiped it away.

'DI Regis left a message for you, guv,' Tommy said, coming to her rescue. She was looking pinch-faced and harried. He wanted to rant and rail about Danvers' return, but had enough sense not to.

The last thing he wanted was for anyone to know how he felt about DI Greene. Especially that squat-faced bastard, Frank Ross. So he'd settle for distracting her instead. 'He seems to think he might be on to something.'

Janine perked up at that, and Hillary spent the next few minutes bringing them up to speed about Mungo Johns.

When she'd finished, Danvers was just coming out of Mel's cubbyhole. He didn't look her way again, but Hillary was pretty sure he knew she was watching him.

Did he still fancy her?

Did it make any difference now that he wasn't officially investigating her?

If he wasn't.

The more she thought about it, the more unlikely this transfer seemed to be. Maybe the investigation into Ronnie wasn't over — except officially. It wouldn't be the first time a case was 'closed' in order to lull suspected culprits into a false sense of security.

And especially in cases where a lot of money was involved. Nobody (including herself) might know exactly how much Ronnie had raked in, but it had to be a fair bit. And where there was money to be had, people wanted it.

Had they really given up on recovering it?

What if Danvers appearing here now, six months after the investigation, was merely stage two? The first, official, out-in-the-open phase had found evidence of Ronnie's crime, but gotten nowhere in uncovering his dosh. So perhaps phase two had been agreed upon. A more subtle, softly-softly approach. Perhaps Paul Danvers had never fancied her at all, but had only been setting her up. Now he comes back, all hot and panting — but for Ronnie's cash, not for her.

Or maybe she was just getting a severe case of paranoia.

'Boss, what do you think?' Janine said, making her blink and look away from the door.

How long had it been since Danvers had gone through it?

'About what?' she said to Janine, who sighed heavily. No doubt she'd been talking for some time, and she didn't like being ignored. No doubt Mel hung on her every word.

Well, bully for her.

'Boss, about going undercover. It wouldn't take much to get into Mungo Johns' stable and—'

'No,' Hillary said flatly.

One of these days, Janine's ambition was going to get her into serious trouble.

Janine set her jaw. 'Boss, I'd be ideal. I've got the looks for it, and he doesn't know me. I could—'

'No,' Hillary said again, flatly. 'There's a time and place for undercover work, and this isn't it.'

She understood Janine's thinking. Collaring a notorious pimp would look good on her records. As would evidence of successful undercover work. But, contrary to public opinion, the police didn't do undercover work at the drop of a hat: it was dangerous and very often unnecessary. Besides, it needed special training, and it was expensive.

Janine nodded, but the look in her eye didn't fool Hillary for one minute. Her blood was up.

She tried to remember what it was to be young, a sergeant, and so keen you were willing to risk your neck. To her dismay, she couldn't.

Mel wandered over, and Frank sneered and muttered something under his breath as Janine rose and pulled down her skirt.

'I suppose you saw Danvers,' Mel said, looking at Hillary.

Hillary smiled wryly. 'He was rather hard to overlook,' she said. 'Is it true? Has he transferred down here?'

'Yes. He starts work next Monday.'

Hillary tried to read something into the words, get some clue from Mel's face, but there was nothing. If Danvers was still secretly investigating her, would Mel tell her? Would he even know?

'We were just discussing DI Regis's prime suspect, sir,' Janine said. 'I'd like to volunteer to go under—'

'Sergeant,' Hillary said loudly, her voice making Tommy drop the pen he was twirling around in his hand. He'd never heard her use that tone of voice before.

He was glad she hadn't used it on him. *Very* glad.

Janine flushed. She hadn't heard Hillary use that tone of voice before either.

Mel had. But only rarely. He shot Hillary a keen look. He and Hillary had known each other since uniform days, and had always worked well together. He shared Marcus Donleavy's view of her as one of their best detectives. She was also good at getting on with others — both superiors and juniors.

She had a knack of spotting the good ones and training them up. She obviously had high hopes for Tommy Lynch, for instance. And it was because she had a rep for being level-headed and even-tempered that the brass had sicked Frank Ross on to her. Nobody else could tolerate him.

Now he wondered uneasily what Janine had done to bring down such a reaction on her head.

'I was only saying,' Janine began.

'I heard what you were saying very clearly, Sergeant, and I thought I gave you an equally clear answer,' Hillary said, her voice straight from the Arctic now. 'That answer, let me refresh your memory, was no. Would you like me to repeat it?'

Janine felt her face flame. She distinctly heard Frank Ross snicker.

Mel wasn't looking at her.

'No, boss,' she muttered.

Tommy was busily typing into his computer. 'Well, I'm off,' Mel said, glancing at his watch. 'Hillary?'

'I've got another suspect to interview sir,' she said wearily. 'The dentist to the stars.'

Mel nodded, shot a quick look at Janine's mutinous shoulders, and sighed. No doubt he'd be getting his ear chewed later on.

Hillary watched him go, without sympathy. She had no doubts either that Janine would try and put her side of the story over, and get him to reverse Hillary's decision.

She was equally certain Mel would never do it. He knew undercover work was not the place for novices. He'd also know of Mungo Johns' reputation for slashing his women.

'I'm off, then,' Frank said. 'By the by, I've got a line on some male students who've been buying. So far none are even admitting to knowing the French bird. I'll keep at it, shall I?'

He was doing most of his nosing at student pubs, and wanted to keep on doing it.

Hillary nodded. She wanted him to keep on doing it too. With the Yorkie Bar now hovering like an ominous cloud on the horizon, and a showdown with her sergeant in the offing, the last thing she wanted was Frank's charming company.

Janine left with a grunt of a goodbye.

Tommy looked across from his computer. He winced at the way Hillary was slumped over her desk. She looked dog-tired.

'Guv, I'm getting nowhere fast on this Warfarin business. The drug's too old hat for any of the university labs to be bothering with. I was thinking of trying the animal labs next. You know — rat poison. It's bound to be used for testing in those, right?'

Hillary looked up, blinked, then nodded.

'Oh yeah. Yeah, right. Good thinking. Speaking of animal labs, how's the investigation going into the dead security guard?'

Like most cops, she liked to keep abreast of the other big cases going on around her.

'Not sure, guv. There's talk of a raid of some animal lib gang, but I don't know if that's just rumour. There's been a little bit of panic from the public — a burst of old biddies reporting stray cats, for instance, scared they'll give the Asian flu to their own Tiddles, and that kind of thing.'

Hillary laughed, just as Tommy had hoped she would. 'Right.'

She wondered if the raid would turn out to be on the same outfit as her own barmy army of animal libbers, but didn't think she could get that lucky.

'I'd better get off and see the demon driller of old Woodstock town then,' she said, and reached for her bag.

'Need company, guv?' Tommy heard himself say, and Hillary, looking up at him in surprise, smiled.

'Why not?' she said.

Not that Tommy needed to be taught how to handle an interview.

'Have you thought of putting in for your sergeant's exam yet, Tommy?' she asked quietly as they left, side by side, as the next shift began to filter in.

'Not yet, guv. I haven't been in CID that long.'

Hillary nodded. He was probably right. 'Well, start studying for it now at least. The higher you ace an exam, the better it looks on your sheet.'

Tommy nodded. 'Right, guv,' he said, genuinely grateful for the advice.

He'd start tonight.

* * *

Red Rum lived in a large detached house overlooking the estates of Blenheim Palace.

It was very nice.

Tommy, who lived with his mum in a small semi in Headington, wondered if it was too late to start learning dentistry.

'Ah, yes, Inspector Greene. My receptionist told me you'd be coming. Please, come in.'

Jamie Prospect did indeed have a head of very red hair, and the usual pale skin and freckles to go with it. He also had eyes the colour of red sherry. Very unusual. This didn't surprise her. She was beginning to get a feel for Eva's Johns now.

First there was old Marcus Gagingwell, a spent force, a charming dirty old man. He would be the grandfather figure, naughty but nice. A real lambkin.

Then there was Philip Cox, whom Hillary was beginning to suspect had spent the most on her. Or was charged the most by her. The real money-maker. She couldn't see Eva finding anything genuinely appealing about the haulage entrepreneur except his large wallet.

Frankie A, alias Michael Bolder, was obviously the kindred spirit, the handsome lover, the one the French student had probably thought of as the jewel in her crown. Funny that she still couldn't see how the interior designer had come by his nickname. Her pet names for all the others were so obvious.

Now, here was Red Rum. The unusual one. The one who'd been tossed into the pot for sheer variety?

'Would you like a drink?' The dentist was surprisingly young, and there was no obvious sign of there being a woman of the house. 'Or something hot? Tea, coffee?'

Hillary and Tommy settled themselves down on a sofa in front of a real fireplace. Logs roared and spat and crackled behind an intricately carved, brass fire screen.

'Nothing, thanks,' Hillary said. After the hellish day she'd been having, she wanted nothing more than to get back to the boat and open a bottle.

If her memory served her right, this was one of the Johns with no alibi at all. Alone all night. Hadn't Janine said something about getting the impression that he might have been entertaining a married lady?

She could understand why her sergeant might have thought that. Jamie Prospect had that young-man-on-the-make feel.

He would have challenged Eva's sense of professionalism. She'd have had to be good with this one. Keep him hooked. She didn't doubt the French girl had succeeded.

'You were home alone the night that Eva Gerainte died, Mr Prospect?' she said, careful to keep the word 'murdered' out of the sentence.

'That's right.'

'You often spend the evenings alone?'

Jamie Prospect smiled. It was a charming smile. He was wearing cream slacks and an old cricketing jersey. She had no doubt the jersey was real. He had the look of a cricketer. He was one of those loose-limbed, amiable young Englishmen that Evelyn Waugh would instantly have recognised.

'I've been thinking about that,' Jamie Prospect said, and Hillary could already feel her heart start to sink. 'When your very pretty sergeant first approached me with the news, I was rather taken aback. Poor Eva. And then when she asked me about what I was doing when Eva was dying, well . . . I rather lost my head a bit. I told a fib.'

Hillary managed not to smile.

A fib?

Yes, she supposed that in Jamie Prospect's rarefied world, telling lies to the police constituted fibbing.

She believed Janine was about to be proved right, and so wasn't surprised at the confession that followed.

Jamie Prospect had indeed been entertaining a married lady. He'd had a chance to talk to her since, and although she was naturally not best pleased, she was willing to speak to the police and confirm his alibi.

'But you will approach her at work, won't you, DI Greene?' Jamie begged her with his spaniel-dog eyes. 'That way her husband need know nothing about this.'

Hillary sighed heavily and nodded to Tommy, who took down the details. She didn't need to tell him out loud to check it out tomorrow.

Tommy merely nodded.

She went through the routine, but it was just like with all the others. Jamie had no idea who might want to kill Eva or why. He was sure she could take care of herself, and would be very surprised if any of her other lovers (his word) should turn out to be violent.

'She wasn't that sort of girl, Inspector.'

'What? The kind who wouldn't attract it, or the kind who wouldn't put up with it?' Hillary asked curiously.

Jamie Prospect grinned. 'Both, I should say.'

Hillary nodded. So, yet another John eliminated. At this rate, she'd have none left.

Then she got out her photocopies of the diary. Again she folded it and held it so that none of the words were visible.

'This moon symbol, sir. It appears sometimes by your name. Do you know what it means?'

The dentist leaned forward and studied it. He frowned. 'Can you tell me what other dates were marked?'

Hillary felt a brief lift of her spirits and rifled through the pages until she found another one. She read the dates off.

The redhead frowned, and looked annoyed. At himself, Hillary guessed, more than at the direction of the questioning.

'You know, there's something . . .' He suddenly nodded. 'Yes, got it. Those are the nights she stayed over.'

Hillary blinked. Huh?

'Those nights, she came to me. Here. And stayed the night. I didn't go to her place out in Botley for a few hours as usual. Sometimes I felt like all-night company. I'm pretty sure those are the times that she stayed over.'

Hillary nodded. Of course. A moon. The symbol of the night.

She'd stayed all night.

Now that she knew the answer to that little puzzle, she realised it didn't mean a damn thing.

Oh, it could now stop niggling at her (just as the puzzle of Frankie A's nickname was still niggling at her) but it sure as hell didn't get her any closer to solving the puzzle as to who'd killed the French girl, or why.

But there, had she but known it, she was wrong.

Dead wrong.

CHAPTER 12

The next morning, Hillary was glad to see clear skies and a frost-free verge. She emerged from the boat, wincing as it made its usual scraping sound against the metal siding. Charmingly, she found herself surrounded by a family of long-tailed tits. Their high-pitched calls as they flew from bare willow to dried and winter-blackened bulrushes made her smile.

Sparrows argued in the hedges, and somewhere a robin sang. Soon it would be spring — the wild yellow flags would be out on the opposite bank, and fluffy black moorhen chicks would appear from nowhere.

Perhaps there was something — just a little something — to be said for living on the canal.

* * *

Mike Regis was sitting behind her desk when she got in. He looked up — balding, lean, middle-aged — and she wondered, yet again, why he made her toenails tingle.

And wondered, yet again, if he was divorced.

That he was, or had been married, she took for granted. She didn't think he was a widower — she would have heard. Then she wondered, a little glumly, if she'd seriously make a play for him, even if he happened to be free. Since the debacle with Ronnie, a serial womanizer as well as an all-round loser, she'd felt almost incapable of taking on a man.

She didn't trust her judgement anymore. Not in that field, anyway.

She forced a wide smile as she approached him, and noticed Tommy Lynch turn and look at her blankly, then away again.

'Hello, thought I might catch you before you started interviewing your last two Johns,' Regis said, as chipper as a spaniel. 'About our reporter friend, the one who fancies himself as a photographer,' he prompted, and Hillary was immediately with him.

Eva's 'Clark Kent,' according to Janine's preliminary interview, was a hotshot freelance journalist, and into photography. 'You were going to ask around, see if he had a rep for porn,' she said, nodding.

Mike beamed. 'Hey, not even nine o'clock in the morning and the lady's on the ball. I'm impressed.'

Hillary grinned, much more genuinely this time. Lying sod. She'd bet DI Mike Regis didn't suffer fools any more gladly than she did, and found nothing at all impressive about a fellow police officer being up to his standard.

Still, it was nice to start the day off with a compliment. There'd been precious few of those lately.

'Yeah, yeah,' she said, slinging her bag over the back of the chair and wiggling the back of it in a silent order for him to get off.

She was territorial about her desk. Obligingly, he slipped off, and perched one buttock on the corner of the table.

'Apparently, our Mr Ryan Culver is something of an artist. He does very chic black and white shots of cityscapes that regularly get included in coffee-table books and earn him obscure photographic awards that nobody's ever heard of. Not a glimpse of naked flesh in sight.'

Hillary sighed philosophically. 'Well, it was always only a shot in the dark. Anything else I need to know?'

'Boss.' Janine, who'd come in unseen behind her, and had been watching the scene between the two DIs with much interest, reached for her notebook.

She rattled off the address, added that Culver was divorced with two kids, and due to leave to cover some athletics event in France at the end of the week.

That news did not fill Hillary with sweetness and light. Not that she'd ever be able to get a warrant preventing him from leaving the country.

The press had caught on to the student death at St Anselm's being more than another druggie overdose, and she was going to have to be far more discreet than she'd have liked.

'Right. How's the great rat poison search coming on?' she asked, and Janine grimaced.

'Nothing doing. I can't find a trace of any grad or undergrad doing chemical or biological experiments with the stuff.'

'I've had some success with some animal labs, guv,' Tommy said, wondering why the Vice copper was still here. 'Several labs testing fertilizers, weed killers and vermin control have admitted to ongoing work on Warfarin. I've had our boffins contact their boffins to see if we can come up with an exact match with our own path sample. But they say it'll be a few days.'

Hillary sighed. What else? Everything about this case seemed to be bogging her down and dragging its feet. 'You did tell them this was a murder inquiry?' she asked sharply.

Tommy looked offended and nodded. 'Yes, guv. But they say some tests take a certain amount of time, and you can't rush it.'

Hillary shrugged. 'Sorry, Tommy. It's just that I feel as if we've come to a standstill with this damned case, and I don't like it.'

Tommy flushed. 'S'all right, guv,' he mumbled.

'Cases go like that sometimes,' Mike Regis said. 'Trouble is, they either stay like it, or they suddenly shoot off like a bloody rocket.'

Hillary nodded. She already knew that, but didn't say so. If Mike Regis wanted to hang around, making idle conversation, she wasn't about to throw him out on his ear. Off her chair, yes, but not out on his ear.

'Morning, everyone,' Mel Mallow said, the polite words instantly alerting Hillary to serious rumblings. Janine glanced at him coolly, then away again.

'I've just spoken to Superintendent Donleavy. He's worried about the interest the press are starting to take. Hill, I'll be dealing with them, but I want a tight lid on this investigation. Is that clear?' He looked at Tommy, at Frank's empty spot, then at Janine, who flushed and looked ready to hit him.

Mel looked away, and his glance collided with Mike's. 'Any updates?' he asked amiably. So amiably that Hillary winced. If he got any more polite his buttons would pop.

He and Janine must have had a right old ding-dong last night about Hillary's refusal to let Janine go undercover.

Unless her radar was seriously off-base, she thought the uncomfortable romance between her sergeant and her boss might be coming to a sticky end.

'Well, Clark Kent won't interview himself,' she said dryly. She caught Tommy's yearning eye and nodded. 'Coming, DC Lynch?'

Tommy was already on his feet by the time she'd reached around for her bag. Mike watched him thoughtfully. Janine watched Mel and Mike Regis go across to his office, then looked back at Hillary.

'Instructions, boss?' she asked flatly.

Uh-oh, so I'm in the dog-house too, Hillary thought wryly. 'I want you to check out how many female, good-looking students are taught by Molly Fairbanks, then check around and see if any of them have a rep for spending money they're not supposed to have.'

Janine blinked. 'Yes, boss,' she said.

Another one being uncharacteristically polite, Hillary thought, trying to fight the urge to laugh. At other times, Janine would have made it very plain how much of a waste of time she considered that particular order.

As she and Tommy left for their interviews with Eva Gerainte's remaining two Johns, she wondered how bad the argument had been between Janine and Mel. With a bit of luck, it would have been bad enough to mark the beginning of the end.

Mel needed an office romance with a junior sergeant about as much as a hedgehog needed a vacuum cleaner. And Janine needed to earn herself the rep of a woman prepared to lay her way to the top just as much. At least DC Tommy Lynch wasn't likely to cause her any grief.

As they got in the car, Tommy, slipping lightly behind the wheel, began to hum softly under his breath. Another few hours with Hillary. And she'd turfed that cocky git Mike Regis off her chair. All he needed now was the guts to—

'Right, Hampton Poyle it is. I hope the place isn't flooded,' Hillary said pensively. Hampton Poyle, a hamlet not far from Kidlington, was a low-lying village that often got its feet wet in winter.

Tommy quickly jerked his thoughts back to the matter in hand.

* * *

Ryan Culver was definitely no Superman, but with his pair of large glasses and blackish slicked-back hair, Hillary could see why Eva had nicknamed him Clark Kent.

He was not, however, particularly mild-mannered.

His house, overlooking the small, weeping-willow-lined stream that ran through the hamlet, was small but very nice. Framed black and white photographs lined the walls. A deserted inner-city children's playground, looking forlorn and lonely. A single bare-limbed tree, set against a factory's brick wall. A tower block, set against a stark, bare sky.

She shuddered.

Give her long-tailed tits any day.

'We're investigating the death of Eva Gerainte, Mr Culver. You knew her, of course.' She opened the interview without much finesse. Something told her it would be wasted on this man.

They were all sitting around a small marble coffee table in the main lounge, and Ryan Culver eyed her with an annoyingly knowing air.

'As you say. I've already gone over this ground with a younger blonde woman.'

'Sergeant Tyler,' Hillary said, for some reason smarting over that 'younger' crack. Surely she wasn't looking all that decrepit just yet?

'Since then there have been developments, sir. This is now officially a murder inquiry.'

She had the pleasure of watching Ryan Culver sit up a bit straighter. But he didn't look particularly alarmed, or guilty. Instead he looked like a reporter scenting a story.

As well he might.

Mindful of Marcus Donleavy's misgivings about the press, she wished Eva hadn't picked a John like this one.

'Where were you the night Eva Gerainte died, Mr Culver?'

'As I told the sergeant, I was in my dark-room, developing film. No alibi. Sorry.' He didn't sound it. 'How was she killed?'

Hillary smiled. 'Had you known her long?'

'About six months or so. Do you have a suspect?'

'Apart from yourself, Mr Culver? Did you resent having to pay for her company?'

'If I had, I wouldn't have done it, would I? The fact is, Inspector Greene, I don't have much time to socialise. If I'm not travelling, I'm writing. If I'm not writing, I'm out looking for photographic shots. I can't be bothered to do the parties, the bar scene, the singles dating racket and all that. It's far easier, more convenient and practical, to find someone like Eva. And she was something special. She had brains as well as looks. And the French . . . well, they'll always be more sophisticated than most, won't they?'

Hillary looked at him, poker-faced. 'So you have no idea who might have wanted her dead?'

'Well, one of her other customers, I suppose. That is what you're thinking, isn't it?'

Hillary held on to her temper. 'Mr Culver, you seem to have the impression that I'm here to be interviewed by you for an article. Let me make things perfectly clear. You will not be told any information concerning Eva Gerainte's murder. You will not be given any information concerning the investigation. You will, however, answer any questions I have, or else you can do so back at the station. I hope I'm making myself clear?'

Ryan Culver smiled thinly. 'As the proverbial crystal. But you're barking up the wrong tree with me, Inspector. I can see you don't like me, but the simple fact is, I had no reason to kill Eva, and I didn't.'

Hillary didn't like him.

She could also see no reason why he might be the killer either. So he had no alibi. Big deal.

She would have liked to have asked him if he'd done any exposés lately on animal labs, but knew that if she did, she'd only point him in the direction of the unusual Warfarin. And the last thing she wanted was to get that titbit plastered all over the papers.

Damn all reporters to Hades.

* * *

Janine was surprised. She was surprised because she'd very quickly got on to the trail of two female students of Dr Molly Fairbanks, who were looking extremely interesting.

It annoyed her. It annoyed her considerably. She didn't want to give Hillary Greene any brownie points today, but she was going to have to anyway.

It was nearly lunchtime, and after getting a list of Dr Fairbanks' students from a reluctant college secretary, she'd camped out in the JCR and gone fishing.

Now she hastily scribbled up her notes in the front of the car, hoping her memory wouldn't let her down. She hadn't wanted to take things down at the time because nothing dried up gossiping witnesses faster than the sight of a police sergeant writing in a notebook.

But a pretty girl, almost young enough to be their contemporary, drinking coke in the JCR and talking about the juiciest thing to happen to staid old St Anselm's in its long and boring history, was another matter altogether.

So she scribbled quickly, recalling, where possible, exact quotes.

First there was Shirley Forbes, the Hon. of a titled but impoverished father.

The eager group of Hooray Henriettas she'd spent the morning entertaining had been more than delighted to dish the dirt. Vicious, some of them. Amid the miasma of Chanel perfume and horsey accents, there lurked the instincts of real predators.

Janine supposed it was a good thing for her that none of them seemed to know what loyalty to a friend was. None of them had spared Shirley Forbes, that was for sure.

She wrote out the comment that one of the Givenchy-clad vultures had made, about how the Forbes family had only managed to squeeze Shirley into St Anselm's because her mother was best buddies with the wife of someone impressive on the Milk Marketing Board, who the principal was anxious to cultivate. They wouldn't be surprised, the gang had told her in all seriousness, to find several male members of St Anselm's going on to glorious high-paying careers in milk.

Janine couldn't help but giggle as she wrote that down. Then she remembered how cheesed off she was with Mel and Hillary both, and scowled.

She'd be stuck as a DS for years unless she could get her break, damn them both.

According to one of the vulture gang, a particularly venomous South American beauty here to learn English and croquet (a direct quote), Shirley Forbes had started to wear some very expensive gear recently. And make-up. And perfume. And the usual.

Janine took the latter to mean the latest in designer drugs, but didn't push it.

Shirley, apparently, was a great musician, but nobody knew what instrument she played.

Janine wasn't sure that any of that bright-eyed bunch had failed to see that she was really angling after anyone who was particularly pally with the music teacher, but Hillary Greene hadn't said anything about being discreet. And this lack of discretion had helped Janine to land her second catch of the day, when she'd asked if any other girl was particularly musical. One Cathy Byrd, apparently, was.

Now Cathy Byrd was no aristocrat, but the daughter of a man in rubbish.

That was how the poisonous South American had put it. It had confused Janine until one of the others had told her that Cathy Byrd's father owned several huge recycling plants, refuse disposal companies, and so on.

He was worth mucho millions.

But, and here the whole gang had fallen about in mirth, this father, a self-made man who still remembered growing up in a council house in Leeds, had wanted his daughter to understand the true meaning of money, and only paid her a pittance in allowance.

Janine, at this point, had wondered what passed for a pittance with this posse of poisonous poodles. But it transpired that Mr Byrd really did give his daughter only enough to keep her in pens and paper.

However, she was assured, this Cathy Byrd, like the unfortunate Shirley Forbes, seemed to be living high off the hog.

Everyone had assumed a rich boyfriend in both cases. For all their heartless, worldly ways, she didn't think that any of the girls she'd spoken to that morning had any idea what Cathy and Shirley might really have been up to.

Although, by now, they'd be wondering about Dr Molly Fairbanks. Who might, shortly, be finding herself in the ranks of the unemployed, once college scuttlebutt got underway . . .

Feeling as if she'd done a good morning's work, Janine headed back to base. She wanted to have another go at Mel about going undercover.

* * *

Lewis Fenn opened the door to his north Oxford mansion wearing what looked like a genuine 1920s striped boating jacket. He also had on cream slacks. At least he lacked a straw hat. The jacket was in alternating cream and maroon.

Hillary saw at once what Tommy had meant when he'd written in his report that he doubted the man's given age of thirty-four.

Close up, she could make out the tell-tale nip-and-tuck lines left by a plastic surgeon, especially around the side of his face under the ears. The hair was definitely dyed too. The man was too thin. He probably exercised till he dropped every day. 'Mr Fenn?' She showed him her ID and he nodded, obviously recognising Tommy from his previous visit. 'May we come in?'

The house was probably 150 years old, with the gracious lines and high ceilings you'd expect, and looked out on manicured grounds.

It was a typical north Oxford des res. She gulped when she thought how much such a place would go for nowadays. The music business must pay very well.

He showed them through to a lovely room with bare walls, well-polished floorboards, and a grand piano. A charming kiss-me seat — a genuine antique — looked out over an expanse of lawn and standard fuchsias, which were bare now but would no doubt be glorious in the summer.

That reminded her. She'd meant to get a wooden barrel to go on top of the boat, and fill it with polyanthus. She'd look around the garden centre on her day off. It was nice when the *Mollern* looked good.

'I can't tell you how sad I was to hear about Eva,' Lewis Fenn said. 'There's so little real beauty or worth left in the world. It makes you want to cry when you hear about one more lovely thing being destroyed, doesn't it?'

Hillary nodded. So this was Eva's final punter. A sensitive soul. No doubt she found him very flattering and easy on the psyche. She had no real doubt that Mr Fenn's rather florid personality was anything other than genuine.

Tommy had told her on the drive over that he'd checked out Fenn's alibi of having 'the boys' over, and it had been watertight. So, another one scratched off the list.

'Now that you've had time to reflect, Mr Fenn,' Hillary said, unconsciously matching her language to his, 'have you recalled anything that might be of use to us? Did Eva ever mention someone — a man, for instance — who was bothering her?'

She hadn't.

'Had she behaved at all oddly on the last occasion you had reason to visit her?'

She hadn't.

'Had she mentioned a fellow student at all, someone doing chemistry, or medical research, that she was seeing?'

She hadn't.

It was all so dead-end. Hillary felt like screaming with frustration.

She had one dead student-cum-high-end call girl, and nobody wanted her dead. Nobody saw her visitor that night. Nobody had anything to link them with the dodgy rat poison. Nobody, nothing, nil, nada.

In her career she'd only ever been on four or five investigations which had finally been shunted into the 'remains open' file.

She didn't like failure.

She hadn't liked giving up on any of those cases (none of which had been murder cases, incidentally) and she sure as hell wasn't going to like it if she had to give up on this one, and consign Eva Gerainte to official limbo.

Not when she'd finally made it to SIO on her first big murder case. She couldn't let it end in failure. She just couldn't. Not after all the other crap that she'd had thrown at her recently. She might lose the house. She might have the Yorkie Bar from hell breathing down her neck, looking for Ronnie's loot. She might be stuck with the *Mollern* for ever.

But she was a damned good cop.

Besides, she owed it to Eva. She owed it to Eva's parents, who were still awaiting permission to take their daughter home for burial.

She wasn't going to be defeated, dammit!

* * *

Outside, Tommy sensed her misery. 'Doesn't look good for any of the Johns, does it, guv,' he said. 'Perhaps this pimp of DI Regis's will come up trumps.'

Although he hated to think of the Vice man coming up with the goods, it was better than seeing her slumped shoulders and the shadow of dull misery in her dark brown eyes.

He wanted to reach across the narrow width of the car and put a hand on her shoulder.

Of course, he didn't.

'No, I don't fancy any of Eva's men,' Hillary said honestly. But if not them, then who? Was it possible that her death had nothing to do with her way of earning money? It didn't seem feasible.

The French police had come up with no reason why anyone from her past should come gunning for her. And they'd unearthed no enemies at the college.

She sighed. Perhaps Janine had come up with something. She still hadn't finished with Dr Molly Fairbanks.

'I'll drop you off at St Anselm's. I want you to find out, if you can, what Eva did last May Day.'

Tommy glanced across at her.

'Guv?'

'When I interviewed him, our Frankie A said he met Eva during the May Day celebrations. I don't believe him. It's probably nothing, but when you're clutching at straws . . .'

And what the hell did his nickname stand for anyway? Frankie. Francis. What famous Francises did she know?

'Right, guv,' Tommy said, wondering why she was shaking her head like that. She was frowning, like she always frowned, when she was deep in thought.

He reluctantly got out of the car at Summertown and watched the old Volkswagen drive away. Then he turned towards the college and stopped, caught by the sight of a jewellery store display.

He walked to the window and looked down at all the usual suspects. Watches, all the battery-operated kind. Silver and gold bracelets, necklaces, brooches.

And rings. A small selection of engagement rings. Gold with tiny diamonds. Affordable rings. Just the kind he knew that Jean was expecting him to offer her sometime soon. The kind his mother was expecting him to offer Jean sometime soon. The kind he expected he *would* offer her sometime soon.

He and Jean had been going steady for over two years now, and although his mother, a good Baptist, didn't know it, they'd been lovers for nearly two of those years. Jean, also a good Baptist, fully expected that her 'fallen woman' status would one day be redeemed by just such a ring as one of these.

His bank account could just about stand it.

Tommy shifted on his big feet and stared at the tray of rings.

It made sense.

He and Jean, with their combined salaries, could get a mortgage on something small in Kidlington. He wanted a family. At least three kids.

He'd never have kids with Hillary Greene.

He and Jean matched. They rarely fought, and he never found himself looking at other women much. Oh sure, he looked when a bouncing pair of breasts went by, or long, long legs in the summertime-short skirts. Or a pretty face. But he'd never done more than look, nor had he much wanted to.

He had complete faith that Jean might also look but wouldn't touch other men.

The next logical step was a marriage proposal. Why wait? What was there to wait for? He knew he would never, ever, get up the courage to ask Hillary Greene if . . .

If what? What was there he could even ask her? Hey, guv, want to go out for a drink? Come back to my place, guv? My mum should be asleep by now.

Give us a kiss, guv.

Get real!

But his feet refused to go into the shop. Instead, when he finally pulled himself away from his self-induced misery, his feet took him firmly towards St Anselm's.

He might not be able to ask Hillary Greene for anything, but he could lay gifts at her feet.

Such as proof of what Eva Gerainte had been doing on May Day last year, for instance.

* * *

Unaware of her sergeant's pain, Hillary drove to HQ and found Janine waiting. She looked alternately pissed off and impressed.

And smug. Hillary felt her heart lift.

Yes. She knew she'd been right about that music teacher. She was not losing her touch after all.

CHAPTER 13

Molly Fairbanks was playing the piano, and playing it well. But they didn't hear her until the moment they opened the door of the music room, proof of the excellent sound-proofing St Anselm's had had installed. A perfect place to commit a murder, Hillary thought, with a grimace. In St Anselm's music room, nobody can hear you scream. *Alien* had nothing on this place.

Janine didn't recognise the music, except to note that it was classical. Hillary did know it, and walked slowly, enjoying the glorious sound for as long as she could. But then Molly Fairbanks spotted them, and silence came with the stillness of her hands.

Hillary sighed. If only she could afford a decent hi-fi system for the boat. If only it didn't run the batteries down so quickly.

Hell, she had to get off that boat and back into her house.

'Dr Fairbanks,' she greeted the older woman politely.

'Detective Inspector Greene,' Molly responded drily.

The musician was wearing slate-grey blue, a shapeless frock with a single long row of oversized fake pearls. She should have looked ridiculous, but didn't.

Hillary, wedded to her two-piece business suits, sighed again.

'We have some more questions, Dr Fairbanks, and this time I would appreciate some honesty. We now know for a fact that Eva was murdered.'

It was uncompromising, unequivocal and stark, and she was not surprised when the music tutor winced and something in her face became saggy.

'I see,' she said heavily.

'Eva was earning money as a high-priced call girl. She had only six regular Johns, and worked out of a small flat in Botley. But you know all this, right?' Hillary said, seeing Janine, out of the corner of her eyes, shoot her a quick, amazed look.

As far as the sergeant was concerned, laying out all your facts for a potentially hostile witness was crazy. It certainly wasn't in the police manual.

But she'd learn, Hillary mused, just as Hillary herself had learned. With practice, she too would be able to read people, to know when to push, when to draw back, when to lie, and when, like now, to realise that you'd already won the game. You just needed to patiently rake in the rewards.

Dr Molly Fairbanks nodded glumly. She seemed to sag over the piano, and Hillary wished, suddenly and quite viciously, that she'd never interrupted her playing.

'You think one of them killed her?' the older woman asked, pushing back a strand of grey hair that had escaped her usual, untidy chignon.

There was agony in that voice, and Hillary understood it at once.

'No, I don't think so,' she said flatly, further stunning her sergeant, who felt as if she'd just stumbled down a rabbit hole.

What the hell was going on? This was no way to interview a witness. And yet Janine began to feel excited. This was what the job was all about.

Hillary moved closer to lean against the piano. It was an amazing instrument. Not old, not prestigious, but it looked like what it was. An instrument to make music.

Not many things nowadays were as honest as this.

'You introduced her to them, didn't you, Dr Fairbanks?' Hillary said quietly, watching the old woman staring down at her hands. They were treacherous-looking hands. Knotted with ever-worsening arthritis.

Wordlessly, Molly Fairbanks folded them away into her lap and looked up at the police inspector. Her eyes were flat and calm.

'Yes. I was in a position to, you see. I know a lot of men. Had a lot of men. I get invited to the places where rich, middle-aged men, looking for adventure, congregate. I knew them. They were safe.'

Hillary nodded. It was all very much as she thought.

'And when you and Eva got talking, and you realised how much she needed money, and how little sex meant to her as a means of achieving it, it made sense to put the two of them together. Those safe men, and Eva.'

Dr Fairbanks smiled wryly, then nodded. 'Simple, when you think about it. It made me wonder why I hadn't done it before.'

'Did you take a cut? Of her earnings?' Hillary asked bluntly, although she was pretty sure she already knew the answer.

'Of course not!' Molly Fairbanks said, but there was no outrage in her voice. Exasperation, perhaps, at Hillary's perceived lack of understanding. 'I didn't need money. I've got more than I'll ever spend now. Not that I earn a fortune; it's just that my needs are so few.'

Hillary nodded and glanced at Janine. She could see that she was still half-perplexed, but beginning to understand.

'My sergeant found other girls that you've helped in this way. Tell me their names.'

Molly Fairbanks stiffened. 'If that's correct, you already know their names.'

Hillary nodded. 'I do. But I want you to tell me what they are.'

They locked eyes, and Hillary waited. This confrontation served two purposes. First, it put her firmly in the driving seat — and with such a strong personality as the musician, she needed to be in control. And secondly, she hadn't mentioned how many girls Janine had discovered, and she wanted to know if Molly Fairbanks' names matched.

If they didn't, there might be more girls to be interviewed.

Molly's lips twitched. 'I see,' she said again, and Hillary thought that she probably did.

'Their names, Inspector, are the Honourable Shirley Forbes, and Cathy Byrd.'

Hillary nodded.

'And you did the same for them?'

'Yes. Gave them the names and addresses of men I thought would suit them.'

Hillary blinked, then grinned. She couldn't help it. Molly Fairbanks had not only provided her girls with 'safe' men, she'd provided them with 'matches.'

She thought back briefly over Eva's six Johns and could see how each of them would have suited the French girl and served different needs.

'I take it the Hon. went to snobs and the aristocratically star-struck kind?'

'Predominantly, yes. But not exclusively.'

'And Cathy Byrd?' Hillary asked, genuinely fascinated.

Molly Fairbanks sighed. 'Cathy is the sort of girl everyone likes. She's fun. She doesn't judge. She's comfortable and pretty.'

And there'd be plenty of men who liked feeling comforted by a favourite 'niece.'

'I can see how it works,' Hillary said. Then added curtly, 'Or should I say, how it *worked*. Because, of course, it'll stop now.'

Hillary wasn't making an idle threat. She wasn't, in fact, making any kind of threat at all. It was a simple statement of fact. After Janine had interviewed the other girls, they'd be too scared to carry on with the arrangements. And Molly Fairbanks' days as a don at St Anselm's were already numbered. So the scam ended here and now. Simple.

Dr Fairbanks sighed. 'So what happened to Eva? Do you know?'

Hillary straightened up from the piano. 'Is there anything else you feel you can tell me, Dr Fairbanks?'

Janine felt her back go cold. Something in Hillary Greene's voice had made her take a mental step back. Something had changed, totally unexpectedly. Things had been all friendly and us-girls-together, almost amusing, in a way, and then suddenly — wham.

Janine herself felt totally floored, so how the hell the witness felt, she couldn't say.

Dammit, how did DI Greene *do* that? And would she herself ever have that kind of power? Then Janine frowned over her notebook. More importantly, *why* had Hillary done that?

She looked up in time to see a battle being fought in Molly Fairbanks' eyes.

She's on to something, Janine thought, with that familiar tug of excitement, followed by envy. You had to hand it to Hillary Greene — she was damned good. She made everything seem effortless.

'What kind of thing do you mean, Inspector?' Dr Fairbanks said, so obviously stalling for time that Janine waited for Hillary to really put the boot in.

It was what you did, when you had a suspect on the hop. You gave that little nudge that put them flat on their arse, and in a mood to talk.

Hillary shrugged. 'I've told you Eva Gerainte was murdered. I've told you I don't believe that any of the men you introduced her to did it. The French police have no

164

reason to believe she had enemies who followed her over here from France. We've found no evidence of a stalker, and no evidence that she made enemies here at the college.'

Molly Fairbanks listened keenly. Janine tried to figure out what the hell was going on. Hillary merely waited.

'You . . . What is it that you think I can say?' Molly Fairbanks asked, and for the first time, she sounded unsure of herself.

Again Hillary shrugged. 'I'm asking you, Dr Fairbanks, if you have any idea who could have killed your student.'

The older woman opened her mouth, then slowly closed it again.

'I'll have to think about it,' she said shortly.

Hillary nodded. All trace of friendliness had gone now. 'Yes,' she said, equally shortly. 'You do that, Dr Fairbanks. But don't spend too long thinking. Or the Honourable Shirley Forbes and the pretty, cheerful Cathy Byrd might be next.'

But although the shot went home, it didn't draw blood. Molly Fairbanks lowered her head.

Hillary sighed, turned and left, an utterly bewildered Sergeant Tyler following silently.

Outside, it was overcast and dreary. Janine put her notebook away, determined not to ask. 'She's obviously holding something back, boss,' she said instead.

Hillary nodded. 'But we could question her from now till next Sunday and she won't speak. She's got to do something first.'

Janine scowled. She didn't like it when suspects, or witnesses, or whatever-the-hell Dr Fairbanks was, got the upper hand. It upset her feeling for the natural order of things. She'd joined the police to be the one with the power. Not to await other people's pleasure.

'Boss, do you know what it is? Do you know what she's up to?'

Hillary frowned. 'Maybe,' she said at last. But what if she was wrong?

But if she was right . . . The clock might be ticking on Shirley Forbes and Cathy Byrd.

Shit. She'd have to do something.

'Janine, rout out the other two girls and find out who their Johns are. Tell them Eva was murdered. Put a scare into them. They need to be kept on the straight and narrow, for their own safety. Make that perfectly clear to them. And if you can persuade them to leave college and go home, all the better. OK?'

Janine nodded. 'Right, boss.' Although she doubted that either of the two girls would be able to shed any light on the killing, at least she'd be doing something that would help keep them safe.

That was another reason she'd joined the force. She rather liked it when she could protect someone. Even if it was only a couple of pros.

Hillary watched her go, then glanced up at the façade of St Anselm's. Somewhere else, near the Sheldonian Theatre by the sound of it, a college clock chimed the hour. That was Oxford. Always with the bells. On the Isis, swans drifted and cadged bread from out-of-season tourists, while in the lecture halls and dons' studies, obscure texts and unimaginable philosophy were discussed.

She loved this city.

She just didn't like it much.

* * *

Back at HQ, the canteen was only a quarter full. The lunch hour had come and gone, but police work was as irregular as a hypochondriac's bowels, and there'd always be someone starving.

Hillary took a tray, trying to pretend she couldn't smell chips frying, and reached for a salmon salad plate and ordered a cup of tea.

The salmon was pink and juicy and probably farmed. Wasn't the latest food scare over something to do with farmed salmon? Hillary shrugged and tucked in, liberally dosing her wilted lettuce leaves with salad cream. No bread and butter. She could always go back for a roll. Wasn't wholemeal supposed to be good for you?

She glanced up as Paul Danvers approached, his tray containing a vegetable curry and brown rice.

'Mind if I join you?'

Hillary did, rather. 'I thought you didn't start work until next week.'

'I don't, officially. I'm just getting a feel for the place.'

Hillary speared a cherry tomato. If she squinted at it, could it be made to look like a nice piece of rare beefsteak?

'You got a place down here?' she asked curiously.

'Yeah. One of those neat semis overlooking the back end of a field. Out by the railway tracks.'

She wasn't sure where he meant — in Kidlington they were always building housing estates in fields. Semis that sold for mind-boggling prices, mostly.

'The mortgage must be a killer,' she said.

'Ebola ain't got nothing on it,' he admitted.

And Hillary grinned. She wasn't paying a penny for the *Mollern*. Well, mooring fees, and all that. But no crippling, frightening mortgage — that modern-day Grendel that had to be kept fed in order to keep the wolf from the door. Or the Beowulf.

If she managed to snatch her house back from the maws of the animal rights people, she'd be stuck with the mortgage on it, of course. And without a partner to help her pay it off. Years and years of debt.

'You live on a boat, right?' Paul said, forking some dubious-looking peppers and rice into his mouth. He was dressed in a smart charcoal grey suit that did a lot for his fair colouring. His chin was slightly square, with just the hint of a cleft.

He was, no two ways about it, good-looking.

'Right. The *Mollern*. She's moored up in the next village down.' She nodded her head vaguely to the north.

'It sounds idyllic,' Paul said. 'I envy you.'

Hillary said nothing. Would he still envy her on a cold Christmas Eve morning, emptying out her loo tank?

She didn't think so.

'I was wondering if you might like to go out for a drink one of these nights,' Paul said, very casually.

Hillary speared a piece of suspect salmon. According to the latest scare, exactly what was this supposed to do to her? Give her breast cancer? Make her earlobes fall off? It amazed her how her parents' generation had managed to survive at all, with all the things they had happily chowed down on. Caffeine, fat, sugar, salt.

'I didn't mean tonight, necessarily,' Paul added, seeing her eyes glaze over blankly. 'I know you've got a big case on. But when it's over?'

Hillary shrugged grimly. 'That might be never.'

What was this? Could he really be interested in her, or was it just a way of getting a foot in the door? To have a nose around her boat, see if he could get a handle on Ronnie's stash? Or was she getting utterly paranoid about that damned money? The investigation *had* been over nearly six months ago.

But say he was still working on the case on the Q.T., wasn't it better to keep an eye on him? Keep your friends close, but your enemies closer and all that jazz?

'Ask me again sometime,' she heard herself say. 'Sometime soon.'

Paul nodded. He looked genuinely pleased. 'All right, I will.'

Hillary wondered if she should tell him he was wasting his boyish charms on her.

But then again, why give the sucker an even break?

* * *

Either he knew to quit when he was ahead, or else he had other things to do, but Danvers left as soon as he'd finished his meal.

Hillary knew she couldn't linger much longer, but ordered a second cup of tea anyway. If nothing else, she'd have to find out where Frank had been hiding himself, much as she'd rather let the poison cherub stay hidden.

It was as she was returning to her table with her tea that a gaggle of coppers came in, most in uniform, but some plain clothes, and it was obvious they were excited.

She recognised Sam Waterstone, the sergeant who was working on the animal lab raid case, the one where the guard had died just recently. The group congregated at the table next to hers, and from their chatter, she surmised that a raid and arrests were expected any time now. From what she could make out, they'd had a particularly militant group of animal lovers under close surveillance for some time, and confidence was running high that they'd got the right gang.

Hillary, sick and tired of the inertia of her own case, wished that she was going with them. A raid, with batons and riot shields, was an adrenaline rush she could do with right about now. The camaraderie, the satisfaction of achievement, the sensation of action.

Sometimes, just sometimes, she missed her days in uniform. She'd quite liked being young and stupid. It beat middle-aged and fairly intelligent. Sometimes.

'Here, there's that Vice guy,' she heard one of the younger uniforms mutter sotto voce to his companion and felt, ridiculously, her heart lurch. Distinctly lurch.

She refused to look up from her cup of tea, but she knew, just knew, Mike Regis would be heading her way. Now if *he* asked her out for a drink there'd be no uncertainty as to what it meant.

'Not much to look at, is he?' a female voice said in response. 'I thought all those Vice guys were supposed to be lookers.'

'Nah, that's only on the telly,' said someone else scornfully.

'Besides, he's married, so some poor cow must find him tasty.'

'Yeah? You mean there's actually a copper in this nick who isn't divorced?' another voice, sounding mock-scandalized, shot back.

'So I hear. He's got a seventeen-year-old daughter, so he must be coming up for having twenty years in. Can you imagine it? Shackled to the same woman for twenty years? You don't get that for murder these days.'

Hillary put down her cup and grabbed her bag. She didn't look across at the tables and she didn't look behind her, towards the entrance — and exit — of the canteen.

Instead she made her way through the tables to the ladies'.

Inside, it was empty and quiet.

She walked to the sink and rinsed her hands, then looked at her reflection.

She remembered, once, during her first week on the job, being called out to a distraught old-age pensioner. It was bonfire night, and some thug had tied a rocket to the tail of her pet cat and set it alight. The cat had died, eventually, after crawling her way (minus a back leg) to her home. The old-age pensioner had been perfectly willing to commit murder, if only she'd known which of her neighbours' children had done the deed.

Hillary frowned at her reflection, wondering why she'd thought of that now.

And then she realised.

At the time, she'd felt this curious, tickling sensation in the back of her throat, while she'd been talking and calming the tearful old lady down.

The dead cat lay in a box at their feet. It had been a white and ginger cat, she remembered. A pretty thing. Or the front end of it had been, anyway.

Tears.

That was what had been clogging her throat that night.

Tears.

Hillary seldom cried. Even as a child, she'd not been much of a weeper. During the course of her job, she'd seldom cried over road traffic accident victims, suicides, old men and women left for months, undiscovered, in their homes because nobody visited.

But she had cried, of course, sometimes. She'd cried when her dad had died, for instance. And she'd almost cried when someone had killed an old lady's cat, just for the fun of it.

And bugger me, she thought, genuinely amazed, if I don't feel like crying now.

She shook her head and swallowed, and her throat worked just like normal again. Again she shook her head and smiled at her reflection.

'What a wimp,' she mouthed at herself, then slung her bag over her shoulder and went back to the canteen.

DI Mike Regis wasn't there.

She went outside, got in her car and drove into the centre of Oxford.

There she found the last of the internet cafes and sat down in front of a terminal with an over-priced cappuccino and a fiddly mouse.

Finally she got on to the website she wanted.

Cayman Island banks.

There were lots of them. Lots and lots of them. She might know Ronnie's account number, and she might know his password. She sure as hell didn't know the name of his bank.

She sipped the coffee and scrolled down the bank websites.

All offered discretion, financial services up the wazoo, sky-high interest rates, promises, promises, promises.

If she was Ronnie, which bank would she choose? Now there was a question to tantalize the academics of

Oxford. She'd have needed a psychiatrist, a philosopher, a sociology major, an MD and who knew what the hell else, just to get past those first few words. If she was Ronnie. *If she was Ronnie.*

How the hell could she possibly think like Ronnie?

She wouldn't even—

Her eyes stopped moving. She blinked. It took her a second to realise that the words she was staring at weren't even in English.

She registered *Blanc.* White. The French word for white. And then *Cheval.* Horse. The White Horse Bank. Or the *Banque* of the White Horse, if you wanted to mix your languages.

Of course, the English translation was right there underneath, for anyone not even vaguely multilingual, to read. So Ronnie would have had no trouble with it.

He'd put his numbers down in a Dick Francis novel, to remind himself of them. He might have used 'Stud' for his password.

And now here was a bank called White Horse.

For a long while Hillary sat and stared at the screen. All she needed to do was click on with the mouse and . . . and answer the questions, feed in the numbers, see if anything happened.

What if it didn't? Easy. Nothing would happen. Ronnie hadn't chosen this bank, or she might have got the password wrong.

If she had all day, she could scroll through all the banks, and type in any number of horsey-related passwords. Stallion. Yeah, Ronnie probably thought of himself as a stallion. All men did, right? The twenty-years-married Mike Regis with a seventeen-year-old daughter must be self-satisfied in the knowledge that he'd sired the next generation.

The blond and good-looking Paul Danvers, who'd no doubt kill to be sitting right where she was now, was a prime example of prize-winning male flesh.

Hillary shook her head.

She was being stupid. She shouldn't be here. If she pressed that mouse and got into the system and found out that this was Ronnie's bank and got the right password and . . .

Damn. She didn't have the book with her. And she hadn't memorized the numbers. *Deliberately* hadn't memorized the numbers, for one very good reason. Once she knew for sure where Ronnie had hidden his dirty money, she'd be an accessory after the fact if she didn't then turn it in immediately.

She'd be a criminal.

Suddenly, Hillary heard the world around her again. A seven-year-old boy whooped as he played some sort of space invaders game. A group of teenage girls were giggling over some dating agency website.

The woman serving coffee behind the counter was chewing gum and popping it.

And Detective Inspector Hillary Greene was sitting in a muck sweat in front of a computer screen, contemplating the greatest idiocy of her life, just because some man she barely knew had been happily married for twenty-odd years.

Talk about getting a wake-up call.

She got up on stiff legs, messily pressed the keys to get the screen back on to the main menu, and stepped outside.

She took deep, gulping breaths.

Get a damn grip!

She might not have a cat relying on her to keep it in on bonfire night, or a man who wanted her in his life, as well as in his bed.

But she had a murder inquiry that needed her.

So what the hell was she doing here playing silly buggers?

CHAPTER 14

'Janine, bring in Molly Fairbanks.'

Sergeant Janine Tyler's head snapped up from the desk, and she was frowning already at the tone of her boss's voice. It was nearly clocking-off time, and besides, they'd only interviewed the music tutor that morning. When, unless her ears had deceived her, Detective Inspector Hillary Greene had said it would be pointless sweating her any more.

So what had changed?

She opened her mouth to object, then saw the look in Hillary's eye. A frisson of excitement climbed up her spine. Hillary looked grim. Almost angry.

Over at his desk, Tommy Lynch was also gaping at her. He too had caught the unusual amount of tension in her voice.

'Boss,' Janine said, and grabbed her coat. There was obviously going to be some action, which was a much more interesting prospect than going home and having another barney with Mel. Especially since she was beginning to think that the bastard was never going to relent and let her go undercover.

DCI Mel Mallow was turning out to be a big disappointment.

'What if she objects? Calls in a brief?' she asked Hillary over her shoulder.

'Bring her in,' Hillary snapped back. She was tired of sitting around and doing nothing and getting nowhere.

She was already reaching for the phone. She jabbed in DI Mike Regis's mobile number.

'Regis.'

'It's me, Hillary. Can you round up Mungo Johns and bring him in? I've got an experiment I want to try out on him.'

She was obviously firing on all four cylinders because, even over the phone, Mike Regis could tell instantly that she meant business. It was as plain as the nose on Frank Ross's face.

Which was pretty plain.

'He'll be there in an hour,' Regis said curtly. 'Where do you want him?'

'The same interview room as before. Give me a bell when you're outside. I don't want him running into another suspect I'm pulling in now. At least, I don't want them face to face until I'm ready for it.'

By his computer terminal, Tommy Lynch let out a silent whistle. That was playing it close to the wind. Official procedure would frown on manipulation like that.

Unless it got a result the Crown Prosecution Service was happy taking to court.

He could feel the electricity in the air. He'd never seen his superior so wired. What had bitten her? He wished, more than anything, that he'd been there to see it.

'OK, I get it,' Regis said into Hillary's ear. He hesitated, wondering if he should ask her why she'd ignored him in the cafeteria, then quickly decided now was not the time.

She was too obviously buzzing.

But he was convinced she'd known he was behind her, there at the cafeteria, and her quickstep to the ladies' loo was as good as a two-fingered salute.

He just couldn't figure out what he'd done to piss her off. And it annoyed him that it was annoying him so much. So she'd got the hump. So the hell what?

'We caught a break?' he asked instead.

Hillary grimaced. Had they? Or was she just suffering yet more backlash from looking up the name of that bloody bank?

'I'm not sure,' she said at last. 'We'll have to wait and see.'

She was pretty confident in her own mind that they could winkle out of Molly Fairbanks whatever it was she was holding back. She just wasn't sure it was going to be of any help in finding Eva's killer.

Already four days into the investigation and she didn't have a sodding clue. The Keystone Cops had better luck than she was having at the moment.

She hung up, glanced at Mel's closed door, then shrugged. Sod him. She didn't need a shoulder to cry on.

'Guv, I found out Eva Gerainte spent May Day in London. She was attending some sort of fashion show. Left the college for the Oxford Tube at 7:30 a.m. Didn't get back until the last bus home,' Tommy said quietly.

Hillary nodded. 'Good work,' she replied vaguely. She didn't bother to tell him that his inquiries had been made null and void by Molly Fairbanks' earlier confession. She now knew that Frankie A, and all the others, had been introduced to Eva by the musician.

All Tommy had proved was that Frankie A was a liar. In a way, a gentleman. He'd obviously lied to protect Molly.

Well, give the man a peanut.

Hillary sat down at her desk and leant back against her chair. Absently she swivelled back and forth. There was nothing to do now but wait. And calm down.

At least things couldn't get any worse.

And with that thought, Frank Ross came swaggering through the door.

Hillary mentally groaned.

So did everyone else.

'Guv, I've got something,' Frank said smugly.

And Hillary groaned out loud.

Frank beamed. 'I've got a nark downstairs. I pulled him in last night. A snorter. One of Luke Fletcher's runners.'

Hillary immediately tensed. Luke Fletcher was the local bad boy and a big thorn in the Thames Valley's side, a major drugs runner and extortionist. He and Mungo Johns had the prostitution racket divided up equally, with an east/west divide.

'Playing with fire, Frank,' Hillary murmured wryly. But then, what did Frank care? If the fact that the snitch had been pulled in ever got back to Fletcher's ears it wouldn't be Frank Ross who took the beating.

Or worse.

'Yeah, well, he's just about climbing the walls for his fix,' Frank went on, making Tommy shudder.

The DC looked at the older sergeant with an odd mixture of disgust and interest.

Didn't Ross know there were rules about things like this?

'And?' Hillary asked, curious now in spite of herself. She was interested to see just where Frank was going with this.

'And he and me have been having a chat. And guess what?'

Hillary rolled her eyes. This was typical of Frank. Making her ask for every little thing. The poison cherub was nothing if not a power junkie.

'Just report, Frank,' she snapped, losing patience.

Frank sniffed. 'It seems our Mungo Johns has been a bad boy.'

His eyes narrowed as Tommy Lynch jerked in his seat.

Tommy bit back a wide grin. It was just as he thought. Hillary was on to something. Why else had she asked Vice to pull in the pimp? The fact that it proved she was already streets ahead of Frank Ross he just took for granted.

'How's he been a bad boy, Frank?' Hillary asked, with exaggerated patience.

'It seems yesterday evening, Johns and a mate of his, a gorilla called Brian Mayhew, paid a visit at the college.'

Hillary blinked. 'At St Anselm's?'

'No. Bloody Balliol. Of course St Anselm's,' Frank said. He didn't like the way this was turning out. Here he was, bringing in a nice juicy bone, and everyone was acting as if it was nothing.

'Does this snitch of yours know why?' Hillary demanded, ignoring the rudeness. She could report him, but what the hell good would that do? It would only piss Mel off, having to deal with the paperwork involved when a senior officer wanted a junior officially reprimanded. And it was not as if Mel was ever going to reassign Frank.

Nobody else would have him.

'Yeah. According to the snitch, Mungo wanted to put the frighteners on someone.'

'A student?'

'Nah,' Frank said and grinned. 'A don.' He waited for the applause, but there was none. 'Come on,' he said again. 'A don. Think about it. It's a lead.'

Hillary nodded. 'I've already got Janine bringing in Dr Fairbanks,' Hillary said. 'Vice are bringing in Mungo. We're going to arrange for a little accidental meeting in the corridor and see what happens. Should be interesting.'

Frank flushed. Shit. He'd been working his guts out, slogging away in the local pubs, and when he finally found a lead, the bitch from Thrupp had beat him to it.

'Nobody tell me nothing, will you?' he snarled, and slung himself behind his desk, where he caught Tommy Lynch grinning at him.

Frank instantly shot him the finger.

Hillary jerked forward as the phone rang. 'It's Regis. We're bringing in Johns now. He called for his brief, who'll be thundering in like one of the four horsemen of the apocalypse any minute now. So you'd better be quick.'

'Right,' Hillary said, slamming down the phone, then rang Janine's mobile.

'Where are you?'

'In the car, boss, just past the roundabout. Be with you any minute.'

'When you get here, bring her to interview room four.' She hung up and looked at Tommy. 'Meet them in the foyer. Give my mobile a buzz. One ring, then ring off. We'll be moving Mungo to a different interview room on your mark.'

'Right, guv,' Tommy said, moving quickly to the door.

'Does he bark and roll over too?' Frank said snidely, and Tommy felt the back of his neck burn.

Damn! Had his eagerness to please been so obvious? He didn't dare risk a look around, but he was pretty sure that Hillary Greene wouldn't have paid any attention to Frank.

She never did.

In that he was right. Hillary barely registered Frank's bile. Now things were happening, she was getting slightly cold feet. She went to Mel's office and knocked.

She opened the door before waiting for a summons, then drew up short.

Shit.

'Sir,' she said abruptly, as Superintendent Marcus Donleavy turned around in his chair and gazed at her, with that unsettling blank look for which he was famous.

'Hillary,' Mel said, looking more amused than annoyed. 'Is there a fire?'

'No, sir,' Hillary said. She'd been about to tell him what she was up to, but she sure as hell wasn't going to do so with the super there. 'Just thought I'd let you know,

Vice and ourselves are bringing in a suspect on the Eva Gerainte case.'

Donleavy, wearing his trademark black tie, nodded. He'd obviously been following it. 'How's it going?'

'Slowly, sir, but we might have caught a break at last.'

Donleavy nodded dismissively. 'Good.'

Hillary didn't need telling twice, and quickly withdrew.

Marcus Donleavy turned back to his old friend and sighed. He'd been putting this moment off, but there was no way out of it now.

Still, he prevaricated.

'How's Hillary doing? This is her first big murder inquiry as SIO, right?'

Mel nodded. 'After her success with the Dave Pitman affair I thought it was time she went solo. Mind you, the case is turning out to be a bit more complicated than I originally thought. But she's keeping on top of it.'

Donleavy had no doubts about that. When it came to detective work, he would put Hillary Greene at the top of the pile. Pity about her husband dragging her down like he had.

'Talking of Hillary, do you know we've got one of the Yorkie Bars down here permanently now?' Mel said, obviously fishing, and Donleavy sighed. 'Paul Danvers. Yes. A good man. When he's not investigating his own.'

'Nothing going on there, is there, Marcus?' Mel asked cautiously. 'I mean, the case against Ronnie is all done and dusted and closed?'

'Oh yes. Oh, I see what you mean. No, Danvers isn't working on the sly.' Then he frowned. At least, he didn't think so. Or if he was, nobody had told him.

But he knew as well as the next man that internal investigations could be a law unto themselves. Still, he had eyes and ears in high places. If Danvers was a plant, he'd have been told.

'Good,' Mel said flatly. And wondered why the super was still here. He and Donleavy had been friends for years, but they didn't have cosy chats.

'I thought I'd better tell you,' Donleavy said heavily. 'I've been promoted. Starting next month, I'm a CS.'

Mel felt his stomach clench. So it had come at last.

'Congratulations. You're holding a party, of course?' he asked rhetorically, already grinning at the thought of a booze-up.

Marcus smiled. 'Sure. But that's not why I'm here, Mel. The thing is . . . they're bringing in another super to replace me. From outside Thames Valley.'

Mel felt his smile freeze on his face, and then forced a shrug. 'Yeah? Well, it's not always a good policy to promote from within,' he heard himself comment. He was rather pleased with his offhand tone.

Marcus grunted. 'Don't try and kid a kidder, Mel. I know you thought you were in line for the job.'

Mel shrugged again. His throat felt dry. He swallowed, then reached for a packet of lozenges. 'Reckon I'm coming down with something,' he lied, but reaching for the sweet and unwrapping it, then popping it into his mouth, gave him time to think.

He decided on cautious honesty.

'Yeah, OK, I fancied my chances. But not this time, eh?'

Donleavy sighed again. 'Mel, the thing is . . . the brass don't like the way you've been acting lately.'

Mel blinked. The liquorice taste in his mouth turned rancid. He wanted to spit the lozenge out, but couldn't.

'Come again?' he said, struggling to keep his voice on the level. 'In what way have I been acting?'

Donleavy spread his hands. 'Let's face it, Mel, shacking up with a sergeant in your team hasn't been the greatest move, has it?'

Mel flushed. Shit. He knew it!

'First off, Marcus, we're not shacked up. Janine Tyler lives out in bedsit-land,' he said, already cursing the way he'd been forced on to the defensive.

'But she spends the night regularly at your place, right?'

'What the hell's that got to do with it? I wasn't aware my private life was anybody else's business but my own,' Mel said, then realised he sounded like a rebellious teenager, and took a deep, calming breath.

Donleavy grunted unsympathetically. 'Then you're a bloody idiot. You used to know how to play this game, Mel. You've got two divorces behind you, which is one too many for some. You know the promotion committee have little boxes they like to put neat little ticks into. Read the right newspaper. Go to the right church — or seem to. Speak the politico babble. And keep a ship-shape and tidy personal life. Nothing the tabloids can cotton on to. You know how they think.'

Mel did. And he'd forgotten.

No, not forgotten. Just hadn't made himself remember.

For all that Janine could be an ambitious pain in the arse sometimes, she was still like a breath of spring. He'd gone stale, and hadn't even known it, until Janine had taken him on.

'Hell, what am I supposed to do? Live like a monk just to make the promotion board happy?' He wasn't even trying to hide his resentment now.

Marcus looked at his old friend without pity.

'No,' he said flatly. 'Just don't shack up with pretty blonde sergeants half your age. Look, to be fair, Mel, I think they were looking to promote outside anyway. This new man they're bringing in — and don't ask me who it is, I don't know yet — is something of a high flyer they've poached from the Met. So they were already looking for a good reason to pass you over. But you didn't have to give them one on a silver platter.'

He got to his feet. 'I'm sorry, Mel, but that's how it is.'

Mel also rose to his feet. He hoped he didn't look as shattered as he felt.

'Thanks for the heads up,' he said shortly. After all, shooting the messenger was pointless. Besides, with his promotion, Marcus was a good friend to keep sweet.

Donleavy nodded. He turned, then, with his hand on the door handle, looked back at his old friend. 'Dump the blonde, Mel,' he said softly.

Mel watched the door shut behind his superior and slowly sank back down on to his chair.

If he hadn't been so shell-shocked, he might have realised that Hillary Greene didn't report routine stuff to her boss. He might have wondered what it was she'd wanted to see him about. He might have gone out and asked her.

But he didn't.

So Hillary was free to play with fire.

* * *

And she was so good at it. Right on time, her mobile rang, just the once. She walked rapidly into the interview room and saw Mike Regis and his silent sergeant, Colin Tanner, glance up at her.

The pimp, dressed in a silver-grey suit that probably cost more than her month's salary, gave her a curious look. 'I'm sorry, Mr Johns, but we have to move you to another interview room, I'm afraid. We have a problem with the heating in this one.'

Mungo Johns laughed. 'What's the matter, officer? Not been paying your electric bills?'

He got up and smirked anew as Colin Tanner and Mike Regis moved to either side of him.

Regis, who still didn't know what was going on, glanced across the room, but Hillary was already holding the heavy door open.

'Don't know if I should co-operate, officer,' Mungo laughed. 'This could be construed as harassment.'

'It's just next door, Mungo,' she said dryly. 'It's not as if I'm asking you to trek fifty miles across a desert.'

Johns stepped outside, just as Janine and Tommy went past, a coldly disapproving Molly Fairbanks between them.

It was a classic.

Johns stopped jeering, and Molly Fairbanks went from ice maiden to flounder in the blink of an eye.

'What . . . ?' Dr Fairbanks began to say, at the same time as Mungo lifted his arm.

'Shut it!' he yelled, stretching past Hillary with his arm, as if to poke the older woman in the chest. 'Just . . . Aaggh!' he yelped as Hillary, grabbing his extended arm, forced it up and back. Behind him, Colin Tanner neatly took over the arm lock.

'Settle down, Johns,' he said smoothly. 'It's not smart to instigate an attack in a police station now, is it? What would your brief say?'

Regis, remembering the Scottish harridan, rolled his eyes. 'She really wouldn't be pleased,' he put in with a genuine laugh.

Dr Fairbanks looked from the pimp to Hillary. A resigned look crossed her face. 'I think you and I need to talk, Dr Fairbanks,' Hillary said firmly. Then she turned and glanced at Mike. 'Take Mungo here next door. I think, after Dr Fairbanks and I are through, we'll be charging him.'

'Yeah? In a pig's eye,' Johns snapped, and lapsed into threats so lurid they made even Colin Tanner's eyes widen in appreciation.

Molly Fairbanks flinched, but then turned and watched as Regis and Tanner frog-marched Mungo Johns away.

As they dragged him through the door, still swearing and cursing and threatening, their eyes met. And it wasn't Molly Fairbanks who looked away first.

Regis had no idea what Hillary was on to, but he smiled in triumph. He knew a break when it fell into his lap.

Hillary smiled grimly back. She, at least, was not half so confident.

Well, she'd got some action, that was for sure. The thing was, where was it going to take her?

* * *

Molly Fairbanks collapsed into a chair as Janine and Tommy set up the interview tape, went through the introductions, stated the time, and once again informed Molly Fairbanks of her rights. Not strictly necessary, since they were not about to charge her, but you couldn't be too careful. Besides, it sounded impressive. And with the likes of the plucky music teacher, Hillary needed all the psychological advantages she could get.

Hillary sat down and rubbed her eyes tiredly. 'We know from independent witnesses, Dr Fairbanks, that Mr Mungo Johns—'

'Is that his name?'

'Yes. Mungo Johns. We know that he visited you at the college last night, along with another man called Brian Mayhew. Did they threaten you?'

Molly Fairbanks nodded.

'Please speak your answers, Dr Fairbanks. The interview tapes don't pick up head movements,' she said quietly.

Molly Fairbanks nodded, then said clearly, 'Yes, he did.'

'What did he say, exactly, Dr Fairbanks?'

Molly looked pale but staunch. 'He said that he knew I had been procuring girls, students at the college, for men. He told me in no uncertain terms that I was trespassing on his turf. All the prostitutes in Oxford worked for him. He told me that unless I gave him a list of the girls' names, and their regular Johns, that . . . that, something unpleasant would happen to us.'

She saw Janine clench her fists in victory.

Too soon, she thought helplessly. Too easy. But she said nothing, and, catching Tommy's eye, shook her head in silent warning.

'Can you be more specific, Dr Fairbanks?' she said calmly.

'No, not really. He wasn't specific himself. He just said that very unpleasant things could happen to call girls. Even high-class ones. He said just look what had happened to Eva Gerainte.'

Again, Janine's fists clenched in silent jubilation, but Tommy was still looking uncertainly at Hillary.

'Did he actually say that he'd had Eva Gerainte killed?' Hillary asked, still in that calm, flat voice.

Molly shook her head. 'No, Inspector, he didn't. And I believe he had nothing to do with the killing.'

Janine scowled. She opened her mouth to tell the witness to stick to the facts, then looked up, caught Hillary's repressive eye, and subsided.

'Why do you think that, Dr Fairbanks?' Hillary asked mildly.

'Because I don't think Mr Johns knew anything about our . . . our arrangement until long after Eva was dead.'

Molly Fairbanks didn't sound as if she was making an accusation, but Hillary could nevertheless feel herself cringe inside. Because she knew, for a fact, what the musician had only guessed: that it had been she herself who had put Mungo Johns on to his rivals, during that first interview.

Mungo Johns hadn't had any idea about this select, small-time operation until he'd left this nick and nosed around some.

Mea culpa, Hillary thought with a small mental shrug. Well, apologising would do no good.

'Dr Fairbanks, did you give him the name of the two other girls you . . . er . . . help?' she asked, in no mood for beating herself up. There was a whole long queue of people already waiting and willing to do that for her.

'No,' Molly Fairbanks said flatly.

'Did Mr Johns try and coerce you into telling him their names?'

'He did.'

'And what did you do?'

'I threatened him back.'

Hillary grinned. She'd just bet she had.

'I told him that I was perfectly capable of hiring people to look after both myself and my girls. I told him he didn't understand people like myself, or the power we had. I told him he was a gutter rat, and that I had friends in high places who knew how to stamp out vermin.' Molly Fairbanks smiled grimly at the memory. 'It seemed to surprise him. I suppose he thought that that hulking brute he had with him should have been enough to cow me. I made him see otherwise. And since we were on my home turf at the time — and all I had to do was scream to bring the police running — he backed off. But he made it clear that this wasn't the end of things.' She paused for breath, then looked Hillary long and hard in the eye. 'I also recorded this conversation.'

Janine nearly fell off her chair.

'In the music room, we often use recordings to chart a musician's progress. I have them all over the place. I simply turned one on when Mr Johns wasn't looking. I have no idea whether that's legal, but I have the recording in a locked drawer in my desk, back at college.'

Hillary nodded. 'It's perfectly legal to tape yourself, Dr Fairbanks.'

Whether it would stand up in court was another matter. Mungo Johns had been taped secretly, without his knowledge or consent. Any solicitor would immediately start yelling entrapment.

Still, it was leverage. Very nice leverage.

'What happened after you told Mr Johns this?' Hillary asked. She glanced at Tommy, who nodded back that he'd retrieve the recording the moment the interview was terminated.

'I needed time to see the other girls and find out if they'd been approached. And I wanted to talk to their . . . lovers . . . and make sure they would keep quiet also, if approached.'

Hillary nodded. So that was what the music teacher had wanted to do before co-operating more fully. Warn the others. Very altruistic.

Another one who deserved a peanut.

'Sergeant Tyler, would you please take over.' She leaned across to Janine and whispered that she wanted her to get anything and everything they could on Johns. She wanted to hold on to him this time.

Then she signed herself off for the recording and stepped outside.

She got out her mobile and dialled upstairs. When Frank finally answered, she was stunned that he hadn't slunk off early. She ordered him to find and bring in Brian Mayhew.

Then she walked the few paces to Mungo Johns' cell, glanced inside the small, wire-enmeshed window and saw that the rabid mole was already in residence.

She sighed, and beckoned Mike Regis out.

There she quickly brought him up to date.

For a second, when she'd finished, they were both quiet.

'So, how do you want to play it?' Regis said at last.

Hillary frowned. 'He doesn't know what Fairbanks is saying,' she mused out loud. 'Right now he thinks he's looking at nothing but a whole bunch of petty ante stuff. Intimidation. Threatening behaviour. He admitted to living off immoral earnings, though he thinks he can deny all this. He doesn't know about Fairbanks' hidden recorders.

Besides, all this petty ante stuff is mere grist for the rabid mole's mill, and she'll almost certainly fight it tooth and claw.'

'The rabid mole?' Regis grinned. Then thought that that was probably the best nickname for a lawyer he'd ever come across.

'So, if we can persuade him that Fairbanks is willing, and able, to finger him for Eva Gerainte's killing . . .' she said, and glanced inside.

'Even though she's said nothing of the kind . . .' Regis nodded, following her thinking flawlessly.

And they both looked thoughtfully into the interview room.

Mungo Johns did not look happy.

The rabid mole did not look happy.

Sergeant Colin Tanner, however, looked very happy indeed. And Hillary couldn't wait to make him look even happier still.

'It could backfire,' Regis warned, but he didn't sound exactly reluctant. 'Ah, sod it, let's go and mess with Mungo's head,' she said, pushing open the door.

She was feeling rather happy herself.

CHAPTER 15

'Also present are Detective Inspector Hillary Greene, and Sergeant Colin Tanner.' Mike Regis finished the introduction for the tape, stated the time, and smiled across at Ms Burns.

The rabid mole didn't smile back, which surprised no one.

'Mr Johns, for the record, would you please tell us what you were doing on the night of the twelfth of January, when Eva Gerainte was murdered.'

'Are you charging my client with murder, Inspector Regis?' the rabid mole jumped in, before Mungo Johns could even open his mouth.

'Not yet,' Regis said, with exaggerated patience and yet another redundant smile.

'You don't have to answer that question,' Ms Burns said to Mungo Johns, who, surprise surprise, didn't answer the question.

The pimp was looking good in Armani. He eyed Hillary's breasts with a connoisseur's thoughtfulness.

'We have a witness who says that you threatened her the night before last, Mr Johns. She is also prepared to testify that you admitted to running a string of prostit—'

'Oh please, Inspector Regis,' the rabid mole butted in yet again. It was a common enough tactic with solicitors, Hillary had quickly learned. It prevented a questioning officer from getting into their flow, sapped their patience and wrecked their line of thought. Unless, of course, the questioning officer was as old a pro as the solicitor, in which case it was just generally annoying.

'I thought we'd been over this old ground before,' Ms Burns huffed.

'Now we have new evidence, from a very reliable, very respectable witness, Ms Burns. And on these charges, we *will* most definitely be arresting Mr Johns.' Regis's smile was, this time, pure pleasure.

'The old bitch has got nothing on me,' Mungo said, inspecting his nails. They looked manicured to Hillary. She tried to remember the last time she'd had her nails done, and couldn't.

It was a funny old world all right.

'Mungo, shusssh,' the rabid mole said.

Hillary blinked. Shusssh?

'I take it you still refuse to say what you were doing the night Eva Gerainte was murdered?' Regis said aggressively to Mungo, who merely shrugged.

'I've already advised my client not to answer that, Inspector,' Ms Burns reminded him nastily, rolling her eyes behind her thick-lensed glasses, and making the older man's lips twitch as he recalled Hillary's nickname for her. If she started twitching her nose, he didn't think he'd be able to stop himself from rolling about.

He turned his attention to the pimp, who, he was pleased to note, was sweating slightly, in spite of his conspicuous nonchalance.

'I don't think that's a very wise course of action, Mungo,' Regis warned chidingly, as if talking to a naughty small boy. (Ms Burns was not the only one who could be generally annoying.) 'We've already got one witness who's prepared to testify that you threatened her and several other students of St Anselm's College with actual bodily harm. Now you're refusing to say where you were when a student from that same college was brutally murdered. I—'

'Like I said, that old bitch can say what she likes,' Mungo jeered.

'Ah yes,' Hillary finally spoke. 'And so can Brian.'

The pimp flinched. Hillary studied her own unmanicured nails. 'We're bringing in Mr Mayhew now. We'll be putting him in a line-up. It will be interesting to see what our Oxford don makes of him.'

This time, it was the rabid mole who looked unhappy. Having an Oxford don as a witness against your client wasn't so good. People like judges and juries tended to believe in Oxford dons.

Having known quite a few herself, Hillary was not sure why.

'And of course, Mr Mayhew may not be prepared to stand up alone on a charge as serious as that,' Hillary continued musingly.

The rabid mole snorted. 'What, on charges of threatening behaviour? Really, Inspector Greene, that's hardly even a misdemeanour.'

Hillary smiled lazily at Mungo. 'Ah, but the charge I was talking about was murder. Aiding and abetting. That sort of thing.'

This, of course, wasn't about to go unchallenged by the thistle of Scotland, but it didn't matter. By now, Mungo Johns was really sweating.

Regis leaned slightly forward in his chair, like a wolf scenting blood.

The rabid mole finally wound down, and scowled. 'Surely all this is rather premature,' she began firmly, this time pretending to take a more reasonable line, but even she was beginning to look less sanguine. 'I suggest you have no evidence at all linking my client—'

'We have plenty of evidence linking him to a large-scale prostitution racket,' Hillary put in. 'We have an impeccable witness, and once Brian Mayhew—'

'Brian'll say nothing,' Mungo snarled automatically. But he didn't look all that convinced.

'That's the trouble with thugs nowadays,' Hillary said, nodding sympathetically. 'Good help is so hard to find. Used to be, in the old days, rent-a-thug would go to jail rather than rat out his boss. But let's face it, Mungo, you're no Luke Fletcher, are you?' she taunted. 'Brian won't do time for you. Not when he realises who's behind the glass mirror in the line-up room, he won't. Did you tell him beforehand that you were heading out to put the frighteners on someone like Dr Fairbanks? No, didn't think so. Brian knows that toffs have their own rules. People like her always have friends on high looking out for them. He's sure to sweat buckets, and will soon be itching to get out from under.'

'Screw you,' Mungo snarled.

Hillary smiled. 'No thanks, Mungo. With the business you're in, you might charge me, and I doubt you'd be worth it.'

'Inspector Greene!' The rabid mole was almost bouncing up and down in her seat now.

'Where were you on the night of the twelfth?' Hillary all but snarled. 'If you've got an alibi, now's not the time to sit on it, believe me,' she carried on, dropping her voice and leaning slightly over the table. 'I'm this far—' She held up her thumb and index finger, a scant centimetre apart '—from arresting you for murder.'

'Bollocks,' Mungo snarled again, but she had him on the run. She could feel it. Mike, feeling it too, just grinned.

'Fine,' Hillary said. 'Mungo Johns, I'm arresting you . . .' She was about to let rip with a string of minor offences, prepared for a long softening-up process, when suddenly Johns folded.

It happened like that sometimes. The ones you assumed were real hard cases, under pressure, turned out to be made of jelly. And cowed little hen-pecked husbands turned out to have wills of iron.

As the Yanks would say — go figure.

'All right, all right, I was in London when that girl got topped,' Mungo Johns muttered ungraciously.

Regis raised an eyebrow. 'That it?' he laughed. 'Come on, Johns. You were in London where, doing what, and with whom?'

'Mungo,' the rabid mole warned, her Scottish accent so thick you could feed it haggis.

'We were hitting the clubs, all right? Brian, a bloke called John Dixon and myself.'

Hillary glanced across at Regis. She was now in a bit of a cleft stick. Having got him on the run, she needed to keep him moving. But she couldn't tell Johns that Dr Molly Fairbanks had taped their conversation, because then he'd know that it was on record exactly what he'd said and hadn't said. And he'd know that he had made no out-and-out confession about killing Eva. He'd made, at best, an oblique reference to the dead girl, but nothing that would stand up in court.

So they had to be very careful how they played it now.

On the other hand, this alibi had to be broken.

'What clubs?' Regis said, reaching for his notebook.

Mungo shrugged. 'Can't remember now. It was ages ago. We got blotto. Got off with some girls. You know how it is.'

'No,' Regis said shortly. 'But I dare say our friend Brian knows. And can be made to say.'

Mungo paled.

Hillary smiled and shook her head. 'Mungo, Mungo, Mungo,' she said sadly. 'What is it that you're trying to hide from us?'

'That's enough of that!' the rabid mole shot out. 'I'll be filing a complaint about your behaviour — both of you — as

194

regards my client. This is nothing short of verbal abuse. You will treat my client with respect!'

Regis burst out laughing. He couldn't help it. She looked so much like an outraged, rabid mole that he just couldn't help it. That, plus the fact that he was being asked to treat a second-rate pimp with respect, was just too much.

Ms Burns fumed.

'Mungo,' Hillary said softly, and again held up her hand, her thumb and index finger so far apart.

'For the tape,' the rabid mole screeched, 'Inspector Greene is making graphic hand-signals to my client . . .'

And at this, Hillary had to laugh too. 'Really, Ms Burns, anyone would think, hearing that, that I'd been giving Mr Johns the finger. As if I'd be so disrespectful.'

Mungo wasn't finding any of this at all funny. The interview was getting out of control. He had no idea what that music teacher bitch was saying, and although he thought Brian was a stand-up guy, what if he wasn't? If the cops were bandying about accessory to murder charges, would he keep his lip zipped?

On the other hand, no way was he going to tell these plods what he'd really been doing down in London.

The door opened and Frank Ross stuck his unlovely head through the door.

'We've got Mayhew, guv,' he said with undisguised glee. Giving scum like these guys aggro was the best part of the job as far as he was concerned. And Hillary — as reluctant as he was to give her her due — at least understood that he was very good at it, and let him have his head. Well, more often than not.

'Thank you, DS Ross,' Hillary said dryly. Discretion never had been one of Frank's virtues. Still, she couldn't grumble in this instance. The timing had been perfect. 'Excuse me a moment.' As she got up, she saw Mungo Johns' eyes narrow on Frank.

Interesting. Perhaps the pimp had heard of Frank Ross's reputation. It sometimes went before him. Rather like his body odour.

Outside, she closed the door and stood leaning against it, gathering her thoughts for a moment. Then she mentally nodded.

'Right, Frank, here's what I want you to do. Lead Mayhew on. Charge him with anything and everything you can, regarding his "chat" with Dr Fairbanks. Then start talking about murder. How St Anselm's was where that girl was killed. About how she was working the game without giving Johns his due cut. Make it clear we've got Johns in on a murder rap. And since Mayhew was his muscle when it came to threatening the girls, maybe he helped pop this one? Make like the sergeant keen for promotion by banging up an accomplice killer.'

'Right, guv,' Frank grinned. He was liking the sound of this more and more.

'Then start harping on about the night Eva was killed. Say that Mungo is giving us a supposedly airtight alibi — he was playing poker with friends in Headington. But make it clear that Mayhew isn't being named as being one of the group.'

Frank nodded. 'Got it. You want me to give Mayhew the idea that Mungo's setting him up as the hired help.'

'Right. If Mayhew thinks we've got him in our sights as a hired killer, it should loosen his tongue nicely. I've got a sneaking suspicion our friend Mungo was up to no good that night. I want Mayhew to spill it.'

Frank nodded and trotted off, a very happy bunny.

Hillary sighed and re-joined the fray. As she opened the door, the high, outraged, Scottish accent of the rabid mole made her wince.

She shut the door behind her and reintroduced herself on the tape.

To Mungo she said softly, 'I'm sure Sergeant Ross and Mr Mayhew will get on famously. Frank's so good with people.'

* * *

Upstairs, in the main office, Tommy Lynch chased up the Warfarin lab people, who faithfully promised a result tomorrow. He saw Mel Mallow leave, grabbing his coat and stalking to the door. He didn't look so very mellow just now.

Janine also watched the boss go, a small frown tugging down her eyebrows.

'Know what the super wanted?' he asked, for word had got around about Donleavy's appearance, but Janine shook her head. She was busy typing up her notes from the Dr Fairbanks interview. She wasn't sure what Hillary wanted done about the music teacher, so she was still waiting downstairs in the interview room.

The old girl was nothing but a madam, even if she didn't take an actual cut of the money. As far as Janine was concerned, she could sit and stew.

Tommy knew he could go home. It was clocking-off time, and Jean and his mother were planning on cooking something Caribbean and a bit special, but he wanted to stay and hear how the interview with Johns had gone.

'I saw Frank downstairs just now,' Janine said. 'He looked pleased about something.'

Tommy shuddered.

* * *

'Mayhew's coughed it,' Frank said, two hours later. Mungo and the rabid mole were deep in conference downstairs in the interview room, while Hillary and Mike Regis were taking a break in the cafe. Indicating the jubilant sergeant to sit down, Hillary leaned forward.

'Keep your voice down,' she said quietly. 'What's he coughed to, exactly? Did he and Johns kill the girl?'

'Nah, guv,' Frank said easily, and Hillary felt her heart sink. 'But he and that gang of pimps of his were in London all right, like Mungo said. Only they weren't doing no clubbing. They were buying some girls. Bosnians, or Serbs, or whatever.'

Mike Regis let out a long, slow, hissing breath. Hillary rubbed a hand tiredly across her forehead.

Since the wars, there had been no shortage of young women, desperate to start over in a new country. Their homes, families, livelihoods were all gone. They were the wrong religion, or spoke the wrong language, and might just 'disappear' one night, if they stayed put.

A circumstance that the Mungo Johns of the world had been quick to exploit. Pimps from all over congregated in the trouble spots, offering to 'sell' passports to these girls at inflated prices. Of course, they couldn't afford it, so the men offered a 'work' scheme instead, whereby they'd come to the UK, get jobs, and pay off the cost of the passport. Except the 'work' turned out to be the kind done flat on your back, and the girls were herded into brothels, where they were guarded and beaten into submission.

Sometimes, like with Johns, gangs 'sold on' their wares to other pimps. It was white slavery, pure and simple.

'The bastard,' she said softly. 'Mayhew copped to it?'

'Yeah. Time, date, place. He even knew a few of the first names of the sellers.'

Regis abruptly got up. 'I've got to report in. Get the Met involved. If we can turn Mayhew, we can set up a sting.' Hillary nodded. Regis was fizzing. And well he might. Taking down a major slaving ring was a feather in anyone's cap.

But it did her case no damned good at all.

Another dead end.

Her prime suspect, out of the loop.

Shit.

* * *

Hillary went back to her desk, surprised to find Tommy still there. 'Janine's clocked-off, guv,' he said. 'Dr Fairbanks is still downstairs. Shall I turn her loose?'

Hillary nodded glumly. 'She picked Mayhew out of the line-up OK?'

'No problems, guv.' He reached for the phone and passed on the information to the desk sergeant, who'd send someone to tell Molly Fairbanks she was free to leave.

When he hung up, Hillary put him in the picture, then reached for the case file and began rereading glumly. There was a lot of paper. Forensics, interview reports. Pathology. Somewhere, she must have missed something.

If Eva's killer was neither a pimp nor a John, then who did that leave?

She couldn't see either of the other two student call girls being jealous or wanting to knock her off in a fit of rivalry. Still, she'd need to check for certain.

'Tommy, tomorrow I want you to get on to the other two girls in Fairbanks' stable. They might even have left Oxford by now. I need to know where they were and what they were doing the night Eva died.'

Tommy nodded. He understood her thinking, but like his superior, didn't really think they were serious contenders.

Somewhere, *somewhere* amongst all this paper, there had to be a clue. A lead. Something that could be followed up. Give them a fresh angle. She was missing something. She had to be.

This case simply didn't have any of the hallmarks of a random killing. It didn't reek of mindless violence. Eva Gerainte had been in her room at college. She hadn't just been in the wrong place at the wrong time, when some nutter decided it might be a good day to kill.

Someone had gone to her room, prepared and ready to kill. To kill only Eva Gerainte. And for some specific reason. It shouldn't be beyond her capabilities to find out who and why, damn it.

She pulled out a notebook and started from scratch. Forced herself to become calm, and empty her mind of frustrations and questions. Simply to look for something that felt 'off.' To feel what niggled. To sense, with mental fingertips, something, anything, out of place.

When she'd finished, her notebook was still almost bare.

Glumly, she looked at the list.

(1) Frankie A?

For some reason, the fact that she wasn't able to pinpoint the reason for Michael Bolder's nickname was still rankling.

(2) Full moon symbol by his name.

Eva's last time with Bolder had been an all-nighter. So she'd stayed at his place. It must have been very romantic, the mill at night. The moon out, the sound of the mill race. But hardly significant?

(3) The date.

For some reason, 5 January was still ringing a bell in the back of her mind. Why? As far as she could see, nothing about that day had been significant for their victim. Besides, Eva had died on the twelfth.

There'd been no evidence of an argument, no sign of a stalker. Nothing to link the two dates.

(4) Warfarin!

Such an unusual murder weapon. By all accounts, they should be concentrating on that. Tommy had already told her that the animal lab sample should be ready by tomorrow. So if they matched, they would at least know where the killer could have got the stuff.

But it was pointless to go swooping on the animal lab staff like a storm of Nazi troopers until, or unless, the match was confirmed. Perhaps there was a seventh John they didn't know about?

'Molly Fairbanks confirmed all six Johns as her introductions, right?' she said out loud, and Tommy nodded. 'She didn't mention any others?'

'No, guv. She reckoned an even half-dozen was all Eva wanted.'

Hillary nodded. Still, she could have picked up a seventh guy on her own. Someone who worked at the lab maybe?

She heaved a massive sigh.

'Guv,' Tommy said.

Hillary shook her head. 'I'm going to see Michael Bolder again,' she said, unaware of what she'd been thinking until she heard herself say the words out loud.

She got up, and so did Tommy. She grinned.

'You can drive.' After a day like today, she was more than willing to let a big strong police constable take the strain.

Tommy grinned back. 'Guv,' he said happily.

* * *

Michael Bolder didn't seem to be in. It was the perfect ending to the perfect day.

The drive out into the sticks had been relaxing, though, with the winter countryside going some way towards washing off the stench of Mungo Johns and the claustrophobia of the interview room.

'Perhaps we should try round the back,' Tommy said, as reluctant as Hillary to call it quits. It was getting dark, and somewhere a single blackbird was singing.

It sounded unbearably lovely.

Hillary shrugged and followed Tommy wearily around the side of the house. The sound of racing water was clearly audible now, and out the back, sure enough, a series of lights shone brightly.

What had once been stables, attached to the back of the mill, had been converted into a studio. Inside, through the big panes of glass that would normally let the natural light flood in, Hillary could see Michael Bolder leaning over a sloping desk.

She walked over and glanced through. On the large sheet of paper he was working on was a pastel-coloured drawing of a bedroom interior.

White and blue, with touches of old gold. Very chic.

She tapped on the window and saw him jump. He peered through the glass, having some difficulty in making out who it was, then indicated the door.

She didn't bother knocking.

'Mr Bolder. Sorry to interrupt you at work,' she said, rather less than truthfully. She walked in, glancing curiously around. The conversion had been well done. All the original oak beams were exposed, the thick stone walls covered with an unfussy whitewash, the floorboards stained a dark mahogany colour. Large lights, recessed into the plaster of the ceiling, had been turned on, now that the daylight was fading.

There was a single piece of artwork on the walls, and Hillary, with her copper's eye, noticed at once that it was wired and alarmed.

She drew closer, genuinely curious to see what an interior designer would hang on his wall.

It was old.

Very old.

Nothing big, bold, modern and full of colour, as she might have expected.

It wasn't big, but . . . it was pre-Renaissance!

Not one of the famous old masters but surely a respected student, or a minor name in his own right. Florentine, maybe.

She'd had the opportunity to study art as a second major, but hadn't taken it. Now she wished she had.

'This is stunning,' she said simply.

Michael Bolder nodded, and mentioned a name. Italian. It meant nothing to her, but she had a definite idea that it should.

'No wonder you have it wired,' she said instead. 'It must have cost a fortune.' A good bet, surely?

Michael Bolder laughed. 'I wouldn't have been able to buy it. It was left to me by my uncle. He was a collector.'

The painting was of one of the saints. A vaguely Mona Lisa-like background of mountains and streams thrust into prominence a middle-aged man climbing a high, rocky path, with an injured deer tucked under one arm, a rabbit and a goat following at his heels.

Hillary blinked.

If she'd been a character in a cartoon, she knew a light bulb would just have appeared over her head.

'It's St Francis of Assisi, isn't it?' she said. Frankie A. Of course!

'Yes.'

'I'll bet Eva loved it,' Hillary said softly.

'Yes,' Michael Bolder said again, this time more softly. 'It's the only proper work of art I possess, she used to say. And she teased me about it.'

Hillary nodded.

'Lucky to have an uncle like that,' she said enviously. Then realised, even if she had a painting like this, where the hell on a narrowboat could she even hang it? It would probably get mildewed anyway.

Michael Bolder nodded. 'Uncle Simon knew I loved animals, you see. Even as a boy, I was always rescuing sparrows from cats, and cats from dogs, and dogs from car wheels. So he said it was appropriate I should have it.'

Hillary nodded. Well, that was one more niggling little thing to cross off the list. And just as she'd expected, it put her no farther forward.

'Can you tell me again about the last time you saw Eva? She stayed overnight here, didn't she? On the fifth?'

Michael nodded. 'That's right, she did.' He shrugged. 'What can I tell you? We spent the night, I gave her break-fast, I dropped her off at college, and she said she'd call me. And she did. About two or three days later. We met for lunch, then went back to her place in Botley for an hour or so. That would have been . . . what . . . the ninth? Somewhere round then.'

Something Eva hadn't put down in her diary.

'Did you pay her?' Hillary asked bluntly. 'For the time in Botley?' she elucidated.

Michael smiled sadly. 'Not then and there. I didn't have any cash on me. But I would have got round to it.'

Hillary nodded. But wondered. How many freebies did she give out to her favourite John?

And what the hell did it matter? Michael Bolder had an alibi for her death.

'Well, thank you Mr Bolder,' she said, trying not to sound as defeated as she felt.

'Can I ask . . . ?' he said swiftly, and when she turned back, he shrugged helplessly. 'Are you, you know, any closer to finding out who killed her?'

He sounded genuinely upset. Here, at least, was somebody besides her parents who mourned her passing.

She nodded firmly. 'Oh, we're following up several leads, sir,' she said positively.

But back in the car, she felt like a fraud.

And as close as she'd ever come to despair.

CHAPTER 16

Hillary woke up with a start when her bed started to tilt to the right. Her eyes shot open, and she grabbed the edge of her mattress in sheer panic, although she wasn't in any real danger of falling out. Even as her confused mind realised what was happening, her bed began to gently tilt the other way. She lay, swaying, staring up at the ceiling so close above her head.

And roundly cursed passing craft. Despite a British Waterways noticeboard standing on the side of the towpath, clearly and visibly asking craft to slow down past moored boats, nobody ever did.

She could hear the engine of a small river cruiser going by.

'Bastards,' she muttered, sitting up and rubbing the hair out of her eyes. She drew back the pocket-handkerchief-sized curtain from the small round porthole in her bedroom and looked outside.

And blinked.

Snow.

It was bloody snowing.

Instantly, she wondered if the car would start. Then she wondered if the gas for the radiators had run low in the night. But hadn't she put full ones in at the weekend? She put a tentative toe out of bed, relieved to find that it didn't immediately frost up.

Muttering, she padded two steps to the minuscule bathroom, keeping her elbows tucked in from sheer habit now, as she set about cleaning her teeth and washing.

The water pressure from the taps was ominously sluggish.

She glanced outside at minute, icy-looking particles being swished past by a strengthening wind. It howled against the boat, like something out of a Hammer Horror movie.

Her days just kept getting better and better.

She dressed in yesterday's suit, which she'd hung over the bathroom radiator to de-crease (it hadn't worked), and went into the galley. She put the kettle on the gas stove and looked up as the postman knocked on her roof.

It was another letter from her solicitor.

She didn't open it. She didn't want to know.

Turning the dial, she listened to Radio Oxford as she bent down to the tiny fridge and brought out two beef and pork sausages. She swilled them under the tap then put them in a small glass casserole dish. Next, she opened a jar of sausage casserole goop and poured it over the meat, then put it in the oven and set the timer. She checked the contents of her cupboard, and came out with a small tin of new potatoes and one of processed peas. Five minutes to heat the vegetables up, and she'd have a dinner within a quarter of an hour of getting home.

She thought, fleetingly, of the women in posh magazines. Their lifestyles seemed to consist of one-minute Chinese cookery in a wok big enough to house a third-world family. *They* washed down the lemongrass with a thirty quid bottle of wine, all the while sitting opposite a boyfriend who looked like Keanu Reeves and discussing their day running their own small advertising firm in the latest wharf makeover.

Oh yes, and wondering where to go for their winter vacation.

She glanced at the cooker to make sure it hadn't come on yet by mistake (the timer was a bit unreliable) and was relieved to see that it hadn't.

She supposed there were women in the world who lived like that, but she was bloody relieved not to know any of them.

She glanced up as a thud came from the back of the boat and the floor beneath her juddered. Instantly her hackles went up. Then she heard a hard knock, and a vaguely familiar male voice.

'Hello in there. Can I come in?'

Not a burglar or mad rapist then. Well, unless he was a polite mad rapist. Hillary moved forward and cautiously opened the door.

She looked, dumbstruck, at Paul Danvers.

'Hello. I thought this was yours. The woman next door confirmed it. She was dressed in this see-through pink thing. She must have been freezing.'

Hillary grinned. 'Nancy doesn't feel the cold.'

Paul smiled back. 'I got that impression.'

'You'd better come in,' Hillary said grudgingly. 'I'd offer you a cup of coffee, but my water tank's low.'

She moved back to the tiny kitchen, which had a hatchway looking out into the main living area. Through it, she saw him looking around.

She did the same, trying to see the boat as others did. Her uncle had always been handy with wood, as well as basic DIY, and the cabin was cosy and well-fitted. He'd gone for creams and pale greens with touches of aquamarine for highlights, and since she was naturally a tidy person, the boat looked good.

'Nice,' Danvers said, looking genuinely impressed.

Hillary supposed the old *Mollern* wasn't a bad boat. When speeding bastards passing by weren't trying to toss her out of her bed, that is.

He'd moved to the bookcase and was looking at the titles. She knew what he'd see.

'You read English lit. at college, right?' Paul said, peering nervously at the poetry section. He had no idea who John Donne was. Shelley and Byron and Keats he recognised. But Leigh Hunt?

'I can do you toast,' Hillary said. She wasn't short of bread. 'Oxford marmalade?'

'Sure. Thanks. I came, really, to offer you a lift.'

Hillary grunted in disbelief. What? He'd forgotten she already had a car? Then she wondered how Puff the Tragic Wagon (as she sometimes called it) would feel about starting in the snow and decided not to look a gift horse in the mouth.

'Do you like your toast well d . . . done, or light?' she asked, turning around and seeing him standing there with the Dick Francis book in his hand.

She felt suddenly sick. Very sick. A cold and hot hand each grabbed a part of the back of her neck, and she felt just how you feel when you've got a stomach bug and need to either get to the loo in a hurry or throw up.

She took a deep breath.

'Hmmm. Oh, how it comes,' Paul said, putting the paperback back on to the shelf and moving on to study a selection of decorative plates. Her uncle's choice, all of old-time barges being pulled by heavy horses. A bit twee for her taste, but she was hardly in a position to redecorate. Officially, she was still a guest on the boat.

Hillary forced herself to make the toast.

She knew the paperback was out of place amongst the Brontës and the Hardys. Had he noticed? Then she gave herself a mental shake. Don't be daft. He was a cop. Of course he'd noticed.

Perhaps he'd read the inscription and assumed she'd kept it for sentimental reasons?

Except everyone knew she and Ronnie had finished up hating each other's guts.

Perhaps he'd known all along about the account numbers inside it. Had he been rifling through the pages? She hadn't heard the sound of paper. But if he did know . . .

The toast popped up, nearly making her jump out of her skin. She almost laughed out loud. Face it, Hill, you'd make a pretty lousy crook. You just don't have the nerves for it.

She spread the marmalade and took the plate through. She sat in the one and only armchair, and watched Danvers sit on the communal sofa that pulled out into a bed.

He didn't look as if he was about to arrest her.

'So, how's your case going? A dead student, wasn't it?'

Hillary grunted. 'It isn't.'

Danvers nodded. 'I know that kind,' he said dryly. He looked good. His hair was probably newly washed that morning, and it sat boyishly across his brow. His dark blue suit suited his eyes as well as his lean build.

She couldn't believe he really fancied her. Why would he?

But if he suspected the clue lay in Ronnie's book, why the hell didn't he confiscate it right now and give her a formal warning?

Damn it, why didn't she just turn the bloody book over to Mel and have done with it? She wouldn't be in this fix then.

But she was human. And had a human nature. The kind that couldn't just hand over a fortune without at least putting up a damned good fight about it.

Paul Danvers took a big bite out of his toast and looked across at her. Her suit, a dark chestnut colour, looked sexily rumpled, and brought out the deep chestnut-coloured highlights in her hair. Leaning back in the chair, her white blouse stretched taut across her ample breasts.

He wished her husband hadn't put her off men. It was going to be hard work breaking down her barriers.

'It seems I'll be working closely with Sergeant Cropley. Bob, is it?' he asked casually.

'Ben,' Hillary corrected. 'You'll like him. What you see is what you get with Ben.'

Paul nodded, then took another bite out of his toast. If he'd picked up a tinge of innuendo in her last comment, he wasn't letting on.

Hillary wasn't going to put up with this. 'So what really brings you here?' she demanded.

Paul, wishing he didn't have a mouthful of toast, hastily chewed and swallowed.

'I told you.'

'Nobody "just passes" through Thrupp. Apart from anything else, it's on a no-through road. It says so on the road sign. So this "just offering you a lift" routine sucks.'

Paul grimaced. 'OK, OK. I was curious. I wanted to see the boat.'

Hillary lifted an eyebrow. He flushed. 'And you. OK, so shoot me. Look . . .' He shifted uncomfortably on the sofa, his plate and half-eaten piece of toast held awkwardly out in front of him. 'I wanted to clear the air between us. You know, about the investigation last year. Your husband was as bent as a three-pound note, I think that was always taken for granted. But they had to be sure you were in the clear. I was glad to prove that you were. Now, I know nobody likes to be under investigation—' He stopped as Hillary snorted again. 'But if it hadn't been me, it would have been some other poor sod who had to do it. So can we just, you know, forget about it? Put it behind us? I'm just a regular copper, now, just like everyone else. Besides, I only did the investigation because I had a promotion board coming up.'

'Did it work?' she asked bluntly.

Danvers shrugged. 'Nope.'

Hillary laughed. 'You expect me to sympathise?'

Danvers grinned. He looked really good when he grinned. 'Nope.'

Hillary kept her eyes firmly from straying to the Dick Francis. 'OK. Fine. Let's just forget about it,' she said.

In a pig's eye.

* * *

At the station (Puff the Tragic Wagon had started first go, after all), she found Sergeant Sam Waterstone was the man of the hour.

She'd gone straight to the canteen for illicit bacon and eggs, and found a celebratory uproar centred around the middle tables.

Sam spotted her going by and grinned. 'Hey, we got that animal lib gang that did for that night-watchman,' he said, although she'd already guessed as much. 'Did a dawn raid at this place out by Adderbury. Found all the missing animals, plus an ocelot nobody seems to know about. You should have seen Shifty Smith dodging the rats. He squealed like a baby.' Hillary blinked, then deciphered. 'Shifty' Steven Smith was a fifty-something DC, who'd never wanted to rise in rank (which was just as well) and who was famous for his extreme hypochondria. No doubt his comrades had told him the rescued lab rats were carriers of bubonic plague, the Black Death, and everything from galloping gut rot to scurvy and all known diseases in between.

'He's gone home to take his temperature,' another of the gang laughed.

'Did anyone cop to doing the guard?' she asked, and Sam shook his head. But he was grinning.

'Nah. But someone else copped him for us. Apparently going down for some honourable cause is one thing, but being thought of as an OAP basher just isn't on. Mummy and Daddy wouldn't like it.'

Hillary nodded. People.

'Well, congratulations. And let's hope Shifty doesn't come down with Ebola.'

'He'd be in seventh heaven if he did,' a WPC said. 'Just think, a real corker, after all those years of imaginary Asian flu!'

Everybody laughed.

Hillary was still smiling as she sat down. The group was noisy and buoyant, but nobody begrudged them their party atmosphere. Well, apart from a miserable DCI with marital problems, and a solitary WPC who was known to be having foot problems. And nobody was about to pull *her* up over it.

Bunions were a bugger.

'Yeah, I reckon we'll get a pat on the back for this one,' Sam Waterstone was saying. 'From start to finish, a result in less than two weeks.'

'Not even two weeks, guv,' someone said. 'The raid was on the fifth, and today's only the sixteenth.'

Hillary paused with a piece of bacon halfway to her mouth. The fifth.

She could have groaned out loud. So *that's* why the date had been niggling at her all this time.

She remembered, now, coming into the canteen just before she'd been told of Eva Gerainte's suspicious death. Sam had been in then and told her the guard had died. Of course, the whole station knew the animal libbers had raided the lab on the fifth — it was one of those cases where everybody had an opinion. But because it wasn't her case, she'd half-forgotten it. Yet her subconscious had remembered, and when she'd noticed that one of Eva's dates with a John had been on the fifth, it had sent up memory signals.

She dunked her bacon into the egg and took a bite. It was lovely. Salty and full of grease. She couldn't remember the last time she'd allowed herself a fry-up.

It was funny, now she thought about it, how her life suddenly seemed to revolve around animals.

First the barmy army of animal lovers trying to get their hands on her house.

Then the station following the drama of Sam Waterstone's case.

The coincidences of the dates matching and . . .

Hillary stopped chewing.

Frankie A, being Francis of Assisi. A known animal lover.

Eva having an all-nighter at Frankie's house the night of the animal raid.

The guard dying . . .

'Shit!' Hillary dropped her knife and fork, and swung around. 'Sam!' she said sharply, the tone of her voice surprising the others, who all fell suddenly silent. 'Your guard. When did he die exactly?'

Sam frowned.

'The eleventh, guv,' one of the uniforms said. 'About four thirty in the afternoon.'

Hillary felt her heart-rate accelerate and tried to calm herself down.

'Did it go out in the local evening newspapers or over the radio?' she asked, her voice calmer now, but Sam Waterstone was looking like a pointer that had just seen a pheasant fall.

He was a very old hand at this, and he knew when a colleague was wired.

'Yeah, it did. The old guy's family was with him at the time, at the hospital bedside, so we didn't need to delay the announcement before contacting next of kin,' he confirmed.

'So your lad would have known the watchman was dead almost straight away?'

'Yeah,' Sam said slowly.

Now everyone at the table was looking at Hillary hard.

She took a deep breath. She might be about to make the most stupid ass of herself, but . . .

'During your investigation, has the name Michael Bolder come up?'

'Bolder?'

'Guv,' the same uniform who'd supplied the date (and who was obviously the team's walking computer) piped up again. When Sam looked at him and nodded, he turned to Hillary. He was a young, curly-haired lad, and would probably go far. If his backbone was strong enough. 'Bolder's a known animal lib sympathiser, but not a doer. He donates heavily, and is part of a string of bleeding hearts who help re-home greyhounds and smuggle out stolen beagles and the like. But he's not hardcore. He doesn't go on raids or participate in anything he can get nabbed for.'

'That's right,' Sam said now, nodding slowly. 'I remember. He was never interviewed, although he was "known" for his allegiances, because we knew this wasn't his bag. And we were right — he wasn't on the raid. We've got that all sewn up,' he added a shade defensively. 'We got a clean sweep.'

Hillary nodded quickly. 'Yeah, yeah, I'm sure you did.' She wasn't trying to rain on Sam's parade, and wanted him to know it. 'Besides, your Mr Michael Bolder has an alibi for the night of the raid. He was with my vic.'

There was dead silence then.

Sam's eyes gleamed.

Hillary took a slow, steady breath. 'The lad you've got for the killing . . .'

'Walt Townsend.'

Hillary frowned. 'Walt? Is he an old guy?'

'Nah, about late twenties. His ma just liked old-fashioned names. Her other kids are Fred and Winnifred. Twin girl and boy.'

Hillary nodded, not really listening now. She felt on fire. 'Was Walt a particular friend of Michael Bolder?'

Sam looked around, but there were blank looks, even from the walking database. 'Not sure,' Sam said. 'You want me to find out?'

'Yes,' Hillary said firmly. 'Oh, and Sam, did your gang raid another lab late last year . . . Hold on.'

She ran to the canteen counter wall and grabbed the phone. She phoned Tommy Lynch's desk, cursing under her breath.

'You'd better be in, Tommy. Or I'll have your gu . . . Tommy! The name of the lab you're chasing over that Warfarin sample.'

'They haven't rung back yet, guv,' Tommy said instantly, but didn't get the chance to say any more.

'I don't care about that. Just give me the name.' Dammit, she should have remembered it. What she wouldn't give for a teenager's memory.

She hung up without another word and rushed back to Sam. 'Grenfell and Corbett Labs. Last October they were raided by some animal rights group. Usual vandalism and graffiti, stolen animals, and in their case, some valuable research and samples were stolen. Amongst them rat poison. A batch of experimental Warfarin. Can you find out if your mob did that raid too? And if so, was Townsend present that night.'

'Sure. I dare say one of them will be lily-livered enough to cop to a whole load of jaunts for a shorter sentence. Something?'

Hillary nodded. 'My vic was killed by a very dodgy, very experimental dose of rat poison.'

Sam whistled between his teeth. Already the walking computer was scribbling ferociously in his notebook.

'We need to liaise,' Sam said simply.

Hillary nodded. 'Yeah,' she said flatly.

They did.

* * *

Tommy glanced up as Hillary walked into the room, bringing an electrical storm with her. Janine, newly in, also looked up.

'Tommy, I want you to go and find a chap called Sam Waterstone.'

'The sergeant in charge of that night-guard killing?'

'That's him. They're on a high at the moment — they've just made a clean sweep.' Briefly and succinctly, she told them what she had in mind.

'It all fits,' Janine said when she'd finished, almost glowing with the scent of success. Like it or not, working with Hillary Greene had its advantages. She'd done it again.

'Maybe,' Hillary said warningly. '*If* Walt Townsend knew our Frankie A. *If* his gang was the same gang that robbed the Warfarin lab. *If* the Warfarin samples match. That's a lot of ifs. Tommy, you need to keep Sam up to speed. Concentrate on the lab and the Warfarin angle. Janine, get Frankie A in here. I want another word with him.'

Janine didn't need telling twice.

She grabbed her bag and all but ran. She was wearing a tight-fitting black trouser-suit and had her hair down. As she ran past his door, Mel looked up and saw her flying blonde hair.

He wondered where the fire was.

And what the hell he was going to do about her.

He looked up as Hillary tapped on the door. 'Come in.' Hillary came and sat and laid it all out for him.

'So, in summary,' she finished, 'I'm hoping it'll play out like this. Eva spent the night with Michael Bolder. Her diary confirms this, and Bolder himself hasn't denied it. On that same night, the animal libbers raid the lab, and Walt Townsend bashes the guard over the head. They grab the animals, smash the place up and run. But Townsend's upset. Maybe he suspects he hit the old guy a bit too hard. Maybe the others in the group have rounded on him. From what Sam Waterstone was saying, they sound like the usual mixed bunch. Hardliners, but also housewives, and bleeding-heart teenagers. Some of those might still have enough respect for the homo sapien species of animal for them to be anti-hitting-them-over-the-head too. Whatever the reason, Walt feels a bit in need of comfort, and goes to his old and best friend, Michael Bolder.'

'If he is,' Mel put in, but he was beginning to get infected with her enthusiasm.

'Right. If he is. But say he is,' Hillary ploughed on. 'He goes to the mill. He gets Michael out of bed, leaving Eva behind in it. He confesses, or at least talks about the raid, and things going wrong. Perhaps Eva, miffed at being deserted in the middle of the night, goes looking for

Frankie A. Or maybe she just sneezes, or snores. Whatever. It's enough for Walt Townsend to realise they're not alone, and that he might have been overheard.'

'All circumstantial,' Mel pointed out.

Hillary nodded. 'Don't I know it. We'll need Frankie A to fill in the gaps. But just go with me a moment. Michael Bolder calms Walt down, and Townsend goes off, but he's still not altogether happy. But next day, there's no cops at the door, or the day after, and after a week or so he begins to feel safe. But then, whammo. The guard dies. He's now wanted for murder. He's fairly sure that none of the gang will shop him now, as they'll all be facing accessory charges. And the hardliners usually keep a tight grip on the more wishy-washy element. Michael Bolder's a pal so he won't dob him in it. But . . .'

'But the girlfriend's a risk.' Mel nodded. 'Could be.'

'He'd be even more worried about her if he knew Michael's penchant for high-price call girls. What's to stop a pro turning him in? Or what if the animal lab offers a reward? Pros are known to be money-grabbers, right?'

Mel nodded. 'OK. I agree it's a bit of a coincidence that Eva is murdered the same day the guard dies.'

'Damn right it is! He couldn't afford to wait. At any minute, Eva might hear about the guard dying and decide to go to the cops.'

'Fair enough. What else have we got on him?'

'Well, if the Warfarin matches, we know Townsend had access to the murder weapon. He's a youngish guy, probably dresses like an eco-warrior. He could easily walk about St Anselm's without anyone raising an eyebrow. And if Eva had heard or seen him that night he went to Michael's, she'd have recognised him as a pal of his, and would have let him into her room without too much fuss.'

'Well, as a working theory it fits. But we'll have to wait to see whether or not those loose ends pan out.'

Hillary knew it. She was having trouble sitting still. What was keeping Waterstone? And how long did it take to analyse rat poison, for Pete's sake.

'Go and get a coffee,' Mel said, recognising the symptoms and sympathising. 'A caffeine shot will do you the world of good.'

Hillary laughed. 'Thanks, you're all heart.'

But she went straight back to her desk and stared morosely at the phone. Ring, you bastard, ring, she thought.

But she didn't really have any doubts. The Warfarin *would* fit. The gang that had killed the old night-watchman *would* be the same gang as raided the Warfarin lab. And Townsend and Bolder *would* be buddies.

She just knew it.

Because it all fit. It explained why someone wanted Eva dead. It would explain the unusual method of the killing. Most of all, it would explain why the case had seemed deadlocked — because, quite simply, they'd never been looking in the right places. And never would have, if it hadn't been for Sam Waterstone.

Sometimes cases got solved like this. Hours and days of plodding, getting nowhere, and then suddenly, like manna from heaven, the solution came. It wasn't very Agatha Christie, but Hillary didn't care how her cases got solved, so long as they did.

The phone rang.

She pounced. It was Tommy.

The Warfarin was a match.

Yes!

She saw Mel watching through the glass in his door and gave a cheerful, clenched-fist salute of triumph.

One loose end tied in, just two more to go.

We're nearly there, Eva, she thought jubilantly. We're nearly there.

CHAPTER 17

Things began happening very fast. From a dead slow start, they'd now gone to an all-out pelt for the finishing line before Hillary really got a chance to get her breath back.

Not that she was complaining. So long as her case got closed, she didn't care if it was pretty.

Hillary paced downstairs, her blood fizzing. Eventually Sam Waterstone came down to the interview rooms with Walt Townsend and some more good news. It was definitely Walt and his team who'd raided the Warfarin lab.

'I think we'll find someone in the bunch who'll admit to taking the lab samples,' Sam told her gleefully, once Townsend, a lean, spotty individual who didn't have enough sense to be scared yet, was safely ensconced with his brief inside interview room three. 'We've got an environmental studies student from Bristol in the gang, and he's just dying to be a martyr for the cause. I think, with the right handling, he'll be boasting about it before long. You know, taking rat poison from the imperialist fascist dogs, thus making the world safe for rats everywhere.'

Hillary grinned.

'So, your lot are bringing in Michael Bolder?' Sam asked, and Hillary nodded, once more glancing at her watch. 'Yeah. I thought you and my sergeant, Janine Tyler, could interview Townsend. I want to take Bolder.'

Sam nodded. 'How much interview technique has DS Tyler got?'

It was a fair question. This was probably going to be one of the biggest busts of Sam Waterstone's career, and he didn't want some gung-ho junior officer messing it up.

'She's good, but she needs practice,' Hillary said, after some thought.

Sam grunted. 'Don't we all.' But although he clearly didn't like it, he didn't object either. He knew as well as Hillary that everybody had to start swimming with the sharks sometime. And the only way you got to learn how was to get wet.

'She can get ahead of herself, so make sure you make it clear you're leading,' Hillary advised. 'But she's well up on our case, so whenever talk comes around to Eva Gerainte, try and follow her lead. She'll be fine,' she said flatly.

And hoped she was right.

* * *

Michael Bolder looked alarmed. As she watched Tommy Lynch, Frankie A and Janine Tyler approach, Hillary felt her stomach tighten. This was it.

'DS Tyler, you're with DS Waterstone, interview room three.'

Janine's eyes immediately lit up. 'Yes, boss,' she said, and slipped past her, all but running to interview room three. She wasn't about to give Hillary time to change her mind. It was her first time interviewing a two-time stone-cold killer.

Tommy also smiled at this arrangement. It meant he got to be with Hillary.

'Mr Bolder, thank you for coming in,' Hillary said, careful to lead him into interview room one. The last thing she wanted at this stage was for Bolder to know that they'd already got his mate Townsend tucked away.

'I wasn't left with the impression that I had much choice,' the interior designer said, with just an edge in his voice, and a swift, non-too-friendly glance at Tommy Lynch.

Yes, he was definitely edgy, Hillary mused.

Good.

She set up the tape, and asked Michael Bolder if he wanted a brief. She literally held her breath while he thought about it.

'Am I under arrest?' he asked eventually.

'No, sir. We're merely asking for your co-operation. We're about to make an arrest for the murder of Eva Gerainte, though.'

Michael Bolder tensed. He was wearing a dove-grey pair of slacks, and a hand-knitted, chunky Arran sweater in deep cream. He looked affluent, elegant and unhappy.

'I see. Well, that's good news,' he finally said.

Hillary smiled and nodded. She glanced across at Tommy, who was managing to sit quite still but look massively intimidating at the same time.

'Yes, sir. Now, if we could just clear up a few matters.' She pulled her briefcase towards her and took out the copies of Eva's diary.

'On the night of the fifth of January, Eva Gerainte spent the night at your residence, is that correct?'

'Yes.'

'Yes. She drew a sign next to that date, a sign we've since learned meant that she stayed with her . . . er . . . boyfriend overnight.'

Michael Bolder shifted on his seat. 'But . . .'

'Did you have any visitors that night, sir?' she asked calmly.

And under the harsh lighting, she could see a fine sheen of sweat appear on his forehead.

'Inspector, I fail to see what that night has to do with anything. Eva wasn't murdered until a week later. In her room, at college.'

'Yes, sir. But the seeds for that murder could have been sown anywhere, anytime previously to that. We now believe that they were sown in your house on the night of the fifth. So, let me ask you again. Apart from Miss Gerainte, did you have any visitors that night?'

Michael Bolder licked his lips nervously. 'I may have done. I can't really recall.'

'But you were enjoying a long romantic interlude with Miss Gerainte. Surely you'd have been annoyed to be interrupted.' She let exasperation leak steadily into her voice. 'You'd remember that, surely?'

Michael Bolder shot a look at Tommy, who stared impassively back. He scratched his head, and tried to fold his arms over his chest. Not liking that position, he sat up a little straighter in his chair.

Hillary understood his dilemma. He didn't want to lie to the police. On the other hand, he didn't want to tell them the truth either, or drop his friend in it.

Decisions, decisions.

She leaned forward, willing to take a risk. The last thing she wanted to do was get him so rattled that he started shouting for his brief.

'Let's do this another way, sir, shall we?' She smiled gently. 'We have reason to believe that a friend of yours, a Mr Walter Townsend, dropped in briefly to see you. You do know Mr Townsend, sir?' she prompted.

See how reasonable this was? How harmless? She smiled gently again.

'Walt? Of course. We both belong to the RSPCA and RSPB. We often go to all-night badger watches together.'

Hillary nodded. Nice and easy does it. Let him get comfortable. 'Yes. Of course, I remember your Francis of Assisi picture. You're an animal lover, right? And so is Mr Townsend.' Now for the quick punch to the gut. 'In fact,

Mr Townsend was arrested today for taking part in the animal liberation raid of a laboratory that took place on the night of the fifth.'

Michael shrugged. Looked sheepish. 'What can I say?' He spread his hands helplessly. 'Walt feels deeply about the injustices perpetrated on animals in the name of science and economics.'

'And you agree with him?'

'Yes. But not to the point where I'm willing to break the law.'

Hillary nodded. 'Very wise of you, sir. So, after your friend and his buddies raided this lab, and, incidentally, attacked an old man who was acting as a night-watchman, he came to your place.'

Michael shifted on his chair. She could almost read his mind. Did they have witnesses to that? Had Walt told them? Or were they just bluffing?

'I still don't see what this has to do with Eva,' Michael said and looked quickly around the room. There was something hunted and haunted in the way his eyes tried and failed to find something to look at.

And with a jolt, Hillary understood.

He knows, Hillary thought. Deep down inside, he's always known. But he doesn't *want* to know. He pretends he *doesn't* know.

When Eva was killed, he probably never, for a moment, thought of connecting her death to his friend, good old Walt Townsend.

Then he probably heard that the guard had died. And remembered Walt coming over that night. And Eva also being there in residence.

And slowly, bit by bit, he'd have begun to wonder. Telling himself he was imagining things. That it meant nothing. That of course Walt, good old wouldn't-hurt-a-fly Walt, would never have killed Eva. He was an animal lover, for pity's sake.

And yet, knowing. Somewhere, deep inside, knowing that he had. Because it all made sense.

But so long as he never accused Walt openly, or put any pressure on him to tell him the truth, then he could pretend everything was all right. Until Hillary and a police constable came along and made him face it all again.

No doubt, right about now, he was thoroughly hating them both.

Hillary supposed she could live with it.

'But we think it has a lot to do with Eva Gerainte, Mr Bolder,' she persisted. 'You see, when your friend Walter Townsend raided that lab on the night of the fifth, he hit an old man over the head. He didn't die right away though. He died . . . guess when, Mr Bolder?'

Frankie A was now pale. He was also beginning to shake just a little.

'I don't know when,' Bolder said, but his voice came out like a croak, and he quickly swallowed, trying to work up some spit.

'I think you do,' Hillary said softly. 'The guard died on the same day as Eva Gerainte was murdered.'

Bolder shrugged. 'Coincidences happen,' he croaked again, and coughed.

'Yes, they do. Did we ever tell you how Eva was killed, Mr Bolder?' Hillary carried on in the same soft, reasonable tone she'd used throughout.

She looked up to find Bolder staring at her like an appalled mouse that has suddenly spotted a python.

'She was injected with a lethal dose of rat poison, Mr Bolder,' she said simply.

And Frankie A began to cry.

* * *

Sam Waterstone glanced across at the pretty blonde girl who'd just taken over the questioning. Hillary Greene had better be right about her.

So far, Sam had softened Townsend up with a devastating series of blows. His flat had been raided, and evidence of his activities was piling up. His pals were turning evidence against him even as they spoke, and several had already signed statements citing Townsend as the one who'd coshed the guard over the head.

He was already reeling from one murder charge.

Now it was up to Goldilocks here to bring her own case home to him.

If she could.

'Mr Townsend, I want you to think back for a while to the night of the fifth,' Janine said, and smiled gently. 'After the raid. It had all gone terribly wrong, hadn't it?' she asked, her voice soft and caressing.

Walt Townsend looked at her hopefully. After the sneering male cop, her gentle voice was like balm.

'It's understandable that you went to see a friend,' Janine carried on. 'But he wasn't alone, was he?' she murmured, and Walt Townsend suddenly realised that the nightmare wasn't over.

Not by a long shot.

* * *

Hillary and Tommy let him cry. Tommy was even learning not to be embarrassed by the sight of male tears any more.

Hillary never even gave it a thought. During her time, she'd seen the gamut of human emotions dragged out and paraded in front of her, like the aftermath of a psychological car accident.

Entrails of guilt were nothing new to her.

'Mr Bolder, your friend stole some experimental drugs from another lab raid, prior to the fifth. A particularly potent form of Warfarin, to be exact. Do you know what it does, Mr Bolder? It makes rats bleed to death. From the inside. It does exactly the same thing to human beings. When the coroner came to examine Eva Gerainte he was amazed—'

'Stop it,' Michael Bolder snarled, looking at her. 'Are you even human?'

Hillary leaned slightly forward. 'Your friend went to you on the night of the fifth, because he was upset, wasn't he? He was scared. He wanted a shoulder to cry on, but you turned him away, didn't you?'

'No! No, I didn't. I took him into the kitchen. I made him cocoa. We talked. He was fine when he left.'

Hillary nodded. 'And Eva walked in on you? What, was Walt surprised? Scared that he'd been overheard?'

'No!' Michael Bolder shot forward in his chair, like a supplicant after redemption. 'He never even knew she was there. I swear.'

Hillary sighed. 'You're sure of that, are you, sir?'

Bolder nodded eagerly.

'She never came into the kitchen?'

Bolder shook his head.

Hillary slowly scratched her chin. 'And did Mr Townsend ever leave the kitchen himself?'

'Only to go to the . . . loo. He needed to wash.'

'Yes. Old men tend to bleed a lot when they get bashed over the head,' Hillary said brutally. Bolder winced, but made no comment. 'And this bathroom, sir. Was it upstairs? Near the room where Eva was still, presumably, sleeping?'

Michael Bolder stared at her. He opened his mouth, then closed it again, then opened it.

'But he never said anything. Walt. He never mentioned seeing her. He didn't!' he wailed.

Hillary sighed heavily. 'Tell me, sir, was Eva awake when you went back to bed?'

Michael nodded slowly. 'Yes.'

'So she might have been awake when Mr Townsend was washing up in the bathroom. She might have gone in, thinking it was you. She could have seen this strange man, washing blood from his hands and clothing. She could have done all that, couldn't she? Or maybe Walter Townsend merely thought that she had?'

'She never said!' Michael yelled. 'She never said so.'

In the years to come, Hillary Greene could see Michael Bolder saying those words to himself over and over, like a mantra. As if they could protect him. As if they would absolve him.

Hillary nodded. 'Did you never think to ask Mr Townsend about Eva, Mr Bolder? After she died.'

'No. I didn't . . . it wasn't . . . what was the point?'

Hillary nodded.

'I cared about her,' Michael Bolder said, looking at her, as if demanding that she believe him.

'I believe you,' Hillary said simply. And for a second, they simply sat and stared at each other.

Then Michael Bolder said, forlornly, 'I got her killed, didn't I?'

Hillary said nothing.

Suddenly, Michael Bolder leaned forward and was violently sick all over his shoes.

* * *

Hillary and Tommy walked into the observation room abutting interview room three, and Hillary glanced at her watch.

Michael Bolder, cleaned up and looking like a victim, was giving his statement to a WPC.

Inside interview room three, Sam Waterstone was leaning back in his chair, arms folded, looking relaxed.

Hillary let out a long, sighing breath. Things had to be going well, then.

Janine looked wound tight, but in control.

Just then, Frank Ross tapped on the door and handed a piece of paper to the uniformed constable standing just inside. He passed it on to Sam, who read it and then slowly slid it in front of Janine, without breaking her concentration or her flow of talk.

'We're interviewing Mr Bolder now, sir. I'm sure he'll be only too willing to confirm that you went to his residence on the night of the fifth . . .' she was saying.

'Find out what Frank brought in,' Hillary said to Tommy, never taking her eyes off Walt Townsend as he shrugged his sunken shoulders.

He was wearing a waterproof mac that couldn't be giving him much insulation from the cold. His nose ran, and he constantly used the cuff of his sleeve to wipe it. He had a wispy, tired-looking beard, as if his hair couldn't really be bothered to grow but liked to show willing at least, since Townsend didn't shave.

He looked distinctly unimpressive. Null and void. Not at all like a man with enough energy to kill two people.

His mum probably loved him.

She wondered if Eva's ghost was insulted by this nondescript killer, or whether the young French girl found him simply hilarious.

'Guv. The Warfarin matches,' Tommy said. 'Frank just heard from the labs.'

Hillary nodded, and inside, saw her sergeant read the note surreptitiously.

Now she had the final bit of confirmatory proof, this shouldn't take long.

* * *

It didn't.

Within half an hour, Walter Townsend confessed to the killing of Eva Gerainte. It had been just as they'd supposed. While in the bathroom, washing, he'd heard movement from next door and seen the French girl sitting up in bed. She'd seen him.

He became convinced she'd overheard the conversation in the kitchen. The doors were open, after all, and he'd been loud, sometimes shouting, because he was so upset, and the nights out in the country were especially silent.

When the guard had died, he'd panicked. He'd had to kill her before she could talk. He'd used the poison, he'd said tearfully, because he didn't like violence. He didn't want to frighten her too much. He was gentle, really. That's why animals liked and trusted him.

Janine stared at him open-mouthed at this, but Hillary was unsurprised. Self-delusion was nothing new to her. With a profound sense of anti-climax, she climbed the stairs and went to inform Mel.

'Congratulations. You and Sam must be over the moon,' Mel said, after hearing her out. But even he seemed subdued.

Hillary wondered what was biting him.

Whatever.

'Drinks at the pub tonight, my place,' Hillary said, turning around, one hand reaching out for the door knob. 'Can you tell Sam and his people?' By her place, it was understood that she meant The Boat pub in Thrupp. She couldn't fit more than five people on the *Mollern* without everyone beginning to feel like sardines.

* * *

Paul Danvers leaned against the bar and watched the pub door, unaware that Mike Regis was watching *him*. It was still early, but The Boat was already full of celebrating coppers, with Sam Waterstone and his mob well on the way to becoming rowdy.

Regis and Colin Tanner had just got back from London, having sewn up Mungo Johns and six others for the illegal slave trade deal, so it was a good result all round.

No wonder it felt like cup final night. Someone had even bought Frank Ross a drink, though nobody would own up to it.

'He looks familiar,' Regis growled across to Tanner, who followed his friend's eye line. He thought a moment, then grunted.

'One of the Yorkie Bars,' he said, and Regis suddenly twigged.

'What the hell's he doing back?'

'Transferred, guv,' Tanner said. 'Regular duties again,' he added soothingly.

Regis snorted. 'What's he doing here, though? At the party. He wasn't in on the Gerainte case, was he?'

Tanner shook his head.

The door opened and Hillary walked in.

Tommy Lynch, who was at the bar buying a drink for Jean, glanced across and hoped his girlfriend wasn't watching him.

Hillary had dressed to impress — never having much opportunity to put on the glad-rags — in a long buttery-coloured suede skirt, black boots and a beaded black top. She knew she looked good. A matching suede jacket fell to her hips, while her newly washed hair gleamed. She was made up, and wearing pretty amber drop earrings.

Regis straightened and began to move off the stool.

Tommy glanced around and saw Jean waiting for him at their table. She didn't really like pubs, but wouldn't have dreamt of saying no when Tommy had told her about their collar and asked her if she wanted to come out for the celebration.

Like his mother, Tommy knew Jean would prefer him not to be in the police. But she was loyal. Always loyal.

He smiled at her and walked back with her orange juice.

Out of the corner of his eye, though, he saw a pale blond head go by, and when he sat down, and felt Jean slip her hand into his, he looked across the room.

Paul Danvers had moved up beside Hillary at the bar. Janine was already there, with Mel, ordering drinks.

The Vice man, Mike Regis, was coming up on Hillary's other side.

He sighed heavily, and Jean, noticing where he was looking, squeezed his hand. 'You'll be promoted soon,' she said. 'I'm glad you got that man who killed the night-watchman,' she added. Tommy was looking tense tonight. Almost miserable. She didn't understand it. Tommy nodded, still watching the scene at the bar. 'That wasn't our case,' he said softly. 'We got the French girl's killer.'

'Hillary, congratulations,' Paul Danvers said. Hillary turned to him, the low-cut V-neck of her top exposing a wonderfully deep cleavage.

'Thanks,' she said briefly.

Behind him, she could see Mike Regis waiting in line at the bar.

'I was wondering if you and I could go out for a meal sometime,' Paul said. 'You told me to ask you when the case was over. Remember?'

Hillary knew Mel, Janine and probably half of the Thames Valley constabulary there tonight had heard him.

And suddenly, she knew that was just *why* he'd asked her.

And felt like laughing.

Because she'd finally worked it out.

Danvers was hanging around her, angling for a way to ask her out, not because he still suspected she might have a line on Ronnie's dirty money, or because he was so hot for her he couldn't stand it.

No. It was out of simple self-interest.

He knew that if he was to have any hope of settling down in Oxford, of getting other coppers to trust him, of making friends and starting his own network, he had to have her blessing.

Kidlington was *her* nick. *Her* stamping ground. Everyone from the commissioner to the tea-lady had stood in her corner while Ronnie was being investigated.

Now it was over, but nobody would be falling over themselves to include Paul Danvers in their coterie.

But by asking her out, and being publicly accepted, Hillary could announce to the whole world, and her colleagues in particular, that the vendetta was now well and truly over. That no grudges were being held.

She wasn't sure she liked being used in that way.

But on the other hand, it was better than constantly worrying about the contents of that Dick Francis book! Besides, she could see the back of DI Mike Regis's neck going red.

The very married, long married, DI Regis.

'Sure,' she said loudly. 'There's a pub I know in Bicester . . .'

She pretended not to notice the relief in Paul Danvers' eyes. Or the way they dropped to her cleavage.

Perhaps he did fancy her, just a bit, after all.

* * *

Outside, later, after the sounds of revelry had died away, Hillary walked along the quiet, snow-lined towpath. The moon was out, glinting on the whiteness that blanketed everything, making the night look almost magical. A full moon illuminated the icicles hanging from the tow lines.

Her own boat roof was lined with the diamante-sparkling white stuff, and from Nancy's boat came the sound of aroused male laughter.

Hillary paused beside the *Mollern* and shivered. Somewhere, a hunting tawny owl called.

She wondered if Eva's parents had buried her yet.

Something cold and fleeting touched her, and then passed on. Probably nothing more than a wintry breeze.

Hillary shivered again, and then climbed inside the boat, where it was warm and dry.

It felt curiously like home.

She reached for the kettle, but no water came out of the taps.

'Shit,' she muttered to herself. 'I really am going to have to get off this bloody boat.'

THE END

ALSO BY FAITH MARTIN

DI HILLARY GREENE SERIES
Book 1: *Murder on the Oxford Canal*
Book 2: *Murder at the University*
Book 3: *Murder of the Bride*
Book 4: *Murder in the Village*
Book 5: *Murder in the Family*
Book 6: *Murder at Home*
Book 7: *Murder in the Meadow*
Book 8: *Murder in the Mansion*
Book 9: *Murder in the Garden*
Book 10: *Murder by Fire*
Book 11: *Murder at Work*
Book 12: *Murder Never Retires*
Book 13: *Murder of a Lover*
Book 14: *Murder Never Misses*
Book 15: *Murder at Midnight*
Book 16: *Murder in Mind*
Book 17: *Hillary's Final Case*

JENNY STARLING SERIES
Book 1: *The Birthday Mystery*
Book 2: *The Winter Mystery*
Book 3: *The Riverboat Mystery*
Book 4: *The Castle Mystery*
Book 5: *The Oxford Mystery*
Book 6: *The Teatime Mystery*
Book 7: *The Country Inn Mystery*

MONICA NOBLE SERIES
Book 1: *The Vicarage Murder*
Book 2: *The Flower Show Murder*
Book 3: *The Manor House Murder*

Join our mailing list to be the first to hear about
Faith Martin's next mystery, coming soon!

www.joffebooks.com

Thank you for reading this book. If you enjoyed it please
leave feedback on Amazon or Goodreads, and if there is
anything we missed or you have a question about then
please get in touch. The author and publishing team
appreciate your feedback and time reading this book.